TO EVERY
LOVE
A SEASON

TO EVERY
LOVE
A SEASON

A ROMANCE COLLECTION

USA TODAY BESTSELLING AUTHOR
STACY HENRIE

Copyright © 2020 Stacy Henrie
Print edition
All rights reserved

No part of this book may be reproduced in any form whatsoever without prior written permission of the publisher, except in the case of brief passages embodied in critical reviews and articles. This novel is a work of fiction. The characters, names, incidents, places, and dialog are products of the author's imagination and are not to be construed as real.

Interior Design by Cora Johnson
Edited by Kelsey Down and Lisa Shepherd
Cover design by Stacy Henrie and Rachael Anderson
Cover Image Credit: Arcangel

Published by Mirror Press, LLC

ISBN: 978-1-947152-91-5

CONTENTS

Her Winter Suitor
An Unlikely Spring Courtship
A Summer for Love
Romance in Autumn
A Long Winter Kiss

"To every thing there is a season, and a time to every purpose under the heaven."

—Ecclesiastes 3:1

Her Winter Suitor

CHAPTER 1

New York City, January 1892

"CALLIE SLOAN! WHERE are you going dressed in that hideous scarf?"

Eying herself in the mirror of the marble-inlaid hall tree, Callie finished looping the multicolored scarf evenly around her neck. "It's Tuesday, Mama. I'm going to visit Grandma Emelie."

The scarf had been given to her by her father's mother two years ago. And though Callie's mother abhorred the knitted garment, she herself treasured it. The vivid colors provided something cheery to wear on cold winter days such as this one—and Callie felt a thrill each time she wore it. So much of her life, as an heiress, meant deferring to her parents' wishes and preferences. But in this one thing she allowed herself a bit of defiance.

The scarf also symbolized a labor of love from her grandmother. Once a prominent woman in society, Emelie

Sloan had taken ill several years earlier and had never fully recovered. These days she occupied most of her time indoors, reading or knitting.

"I must speak with you first, Callie." Her mother waved toward the open door of the parlor.

Callie stifled a sigh of impatience. Visiting Grandma Emelie was a regular part of her weekly routine. Every Tuesday at half past three, for the past two years, she'd been driven in the carriage to Hauser Chocolates to purchase a sweet, which she then presented to her grandmother before they enjoyed tea together.

"I've already called for the carriage," Callie said, adjusting her winter hat to achieve a precise angle over her dark-brown hair. "I don't wish to make the driver wait in this chilly weather."

From the corner of her eye, Callie caught her mother's darkening look. "You can delay your visit for a few minutes. We have something far more important to discuss."

Callie frowned at her reflection. Should she remove her scarf and coat or simply keep them on, despite knowing how overly warm the parlor would be in her current attire? A glance at the grandfather clock revealed it was already fifteen minutes after three. If she didn't wish to be any later after the conversation with her mother, she'd best remain in her outerwear.

"I'm coming." She crossed the tiled floor and followed her mother into the parlor. Sure enough, a blazing fire immediately chased away the coolness of the foyer.

Agnes Sloan sat on the settee and waited for Callie to do the same before speaking. "I received the most distressing note earlier." She glanced down at the slip of paper she clutched with all the solemnity and dread of a death notice.

A knot of anxiety tightened inside Callie's stomach. "Is something wrong with Grandma Emelie?"

"What?" Agnes shook her head. "Of course not. The note is from Belinda Browncomb."

Callie peered at the paper in confusion. "What is so distressing about a note from Mrs. Browncomb?" Belinda and her mother shared the same circle of friends.

"Learning that her daughter Beatrice is engaged to be married is quite distressing," Agnes retorted.

Pressing her lips together, Callie chose silence over asking another question. Her mother would supply a lengthy explanation sooner or later. Though she hoped it would be sooner. She didn't like the idea of being uncharacteristically late to the chocolate shop and to see her grandmother.

"Do you know what this means, Callie?" Agnes shook the note as if doing so would make the words themselves fall off. "Every one of the girls you debuted into society with last year is either married or engaged . . ."

Her mother let the sentence hang there, though Callie had no difficulty filling in the last part. Every one of those girls was married or engaged—except for her. Callie stared down at her gloved hands, her cheeks flushing from more than the heat in the room.

"Your sister was engaged two months after her debut. *Two months!* And your brother proposed to Miss Gilbert less than six after she was introduced into society."

Callie's throat tightened at her mother's incredulous tone, yet she fought the urge to unwind her scarf. Doing so would disrupt the symmetrical lines and make her even later. "I'm sorry, Mother. I've attended every dinner, ball, and event that you've wished me to."

"But you haven't attracted any suitors," Agnes lamented.

The lump in Callie's throat was growing harder to ignore. "I know . . ."

"You're a very pretty girl, Callie." The words came out

softer than her others. "All of my friends say so, but you must be more charming and vivacious if you hope to catch a husband. You do want a husband, don't you?"

Callie dipped her chin in a nod. She did wish to be married and have children of her own. Yet none of the men she'd met thus far struck her as interesting or kind, and none of them seemed the sort to show patience for her naturally quiet nature or her need for order and contemplation.

"Good," Agnes announced. "Because I have come up with the perfect incentive."

The dread inside Callie expanded. "What is it?"

"You attract the interest of at least one suitor before the Patriarch Ball at the end of February." Their invitations had recently arrived. Agnes leaned forward. Her green eyes, the same color as Callie's, shone with frightful determination. "Otherwise, you and I will head to London for a season. I know there are plenty of gentlemen there who would be eager to marry an heiress from America, no matter how reticent her personality."

London? Callie tried to draw a full breath into her tight lungs, but the hot air in the room only made her choke. "I-I don't understand," she sputtered.

The thought of living elsewhere, in a foreign country no less, with foreign routines and customs, filled her throat with a constricting lump. Lifting one hand, she pulled her scarf an inch or so away from her collar in a vain attempt to breathe.

"I thought I made myself perfectly clear."

"Of your requirement, yes, but . . ." Callie shook her head. If no one had shown interest yet, how likely was it that someone would in less than six weeks? "I suppose I can try to be more like Dina." Her sister had been the consummate debutante, long before she'd actually entered society.

Agnes rose to her feet. "Wonderful. That will surely

attract a suitor or two, and then we won't have to worry about going to England at all, will we?" She ripped the note in two, a satisfied look on her face, and tossed the pieces into the fire. When she turned back, she raised an eyebrow at Callie. "Aren't you leaving?"

"Y-yes." Callie had to force her legs to stand. As she moved to the door, a feeling of cold settled inside her—one her scarf could not warm. What if she tried to be like Dina and failed? The consequences of such a disaster would be life altering.

With her hand on the doorjamb, she paused and faced her mother once again. "Does it have to be by the Patriarch Ball?"

"It does," Agnes replied with a stiff nod. "To wait any longer would be a mistake. You are not on the shelf yet, but being unattached for another season here would only result in embarrassment to you and our family." Her eyes softened as she added with more gentleness, "It's time to embrace your future."

Callie woodenly nodded and exited the parlor. She could see her future stretching before her, and it held nothing but bleakness and dread.

Leo Hauser guided the liquid chocolate back and forth across the table. Once it was cooled to the right temperature, he would coat the waiting molds. His eyes went to the cuckoo clock on the wall of the shop's back room, and he frowned. Thirty-seven minutes after three o'clock. Where could Callie Sloan be? Every Tuesday she walked through the front door of the chocolate shop at precisely 3:27 p.m. Sun, rain, snow, wind—Callie had never missed dropping by to purchase her grandmother some chocolate in two years.

Naturally Tuesdays had become Leo's favorite day of the week, and his father knew it. Whenever Callie came into the shop, if Leo wasn't out front, his father would call for him to come assist her.

Simon Hauser had told Callie that he didn't speak English as well as Leo, though it was hardly true and likely just an excuse to allow his son time to speak with the lovely young lady. The man's prowess in the language had significantly improved since bringing his wife and three children to America twenty years ago. Leo had been three at the time.

As the youngest, he remembered the least about their Austrian homeland. His two older sisters, who were both married now, had far more memories than Leo did, but they'd been good about sharing the family stories with him.

Leo poured the chocolate into the molds, scraped off the excess, and set them aside. He threw another glance at the clock. Hopefully Callie hadn't taken sick. He didn't like the idea of some ill befalling her. And his week wasn't going to feel complete without seeing her soft smile today.

It had taken more than four months of weekly visits for Callie to do more than offer him a shy smile and a few pleasantries. Then gradually she'd started to say more. He had counted it another victory when she'd agreed to call him Leo rather than Mr. Hauser. The very next visit she'd insisted he call her by her Christian name too. Leo had been more than happy to comply.

Though certainly beautiful, Callie had other admirable qualities, not the least of which was her regard for her grandmother. She also treated Leo and his father as equals, unlike the other members of high society who occasionally came into the shop.

Leo filled the coated molds. Hopefully this newest creation of his would be appealing to their flagging number of customers. And while he disliked the typical arrogance shown by members of Callie's social class, the chocolate shop still needed more of them. If not, Hauser Chocolates would eventually be forced to close.

After going over the books after the holidays, Leo had realized they had sold far less in December than they had counted on. Hopefully Valentine's Day would bring in more business, but Leo wasn't sure it would be enough.

Every night he prayed, if possible, that things would turn around for the shop. His family had been making chocolates in this very room for more than fifteen years. And while his mother and sisters had helped, none of them loved creating the delectable sweets as much as Leo and Simon did. The last few years, as rheumatism had begun to affect his father more and more, Simon had handed over all of the chocolate making to Leo. At some point, the shop would become his. If only he could guarantee that it would still be in operation for his children and grandchildren to enjoy.

"'To every thing there is a season,'" his mother had gently reminded him through the years when things were difficult or uncertain.

He hoped this season of slowness would become a season of success for the shop, but Leo could trust that whatever happened, he had his family and the Lord on his side.

"Leo?" his father called from the other room.

Had Callie finally come? "One moment, Papa."

Leo covered the filled molds with a final layer of chocolate, then wiped his hands on his untidy apron. That was something else he'd learned about Callie—she was the epitome of tidiness. He hurried out of the back room and grinned when he saw Callie standing before the glass display case. She turned at his approach, but she didn't smile. Instead her green eyes held distress, and her normally precise scarf hung askew down the front of her coat.

"Hello, Leo." Even her voice hinted at weariness. "I'm very late today, so instead of me looking around for something new, if you'd please just select whatever you think Grandma Emelie might like."

He stopped on the other side of the case from her. Though he wanted to know her reason for being so late, he didn't think it his place to ask her straight out. "Is everything all right?" he asked instead.

Callie pressed her lips together in obvious hesitation. Then she shook her head.

Glancing at the backroom doorway, through which his father had disappeared, Leo lowered his voice. "Can I be of any help?"

"I don't see how," she admitted as she straightened the ends of her scarf.

As he waited for her to say more, Leo picked up a box and began putting various chocolates inside—ones Callie had informed him that her grandmother always enjoyed, especially his coated caramels.

"Unless you can come drum up one or two ardent suitors for me," Callie said, her gaze lowered, "I'm afraid there's nothing to be done."

Leo placed the lid on the box of chocolates. "I don't understand."

"I'm not entirely sure I do either." She released a sigh. "But the truth of the matter is if I can't attract the interest of some suitor by the Patriarch Ball next month, I will be shipped off to London."

Startled at her news, he nearly dropped the chocolates before he handed them over to her. "London? Why there?"

"Because my mother believes there must be at least one English gentleman who will overlook my quiet nature, unlike the bachelors here apparently."

The confusion and hurt in her tone twisted his heart, but it was the sheen of tears in her eyes that pained Leo the most. He didn't like the idea of her going away for a time, much less leaving New York forever if she married an Englishman.

"Is there nothing you can do to stay here?" The question sounded bold, even coming from a friend. But he had to know if there was any hope.

Callie lifted her shoulders in a shrug. "I can try to be more like my sister Dina." She ran her gloved finger over the top of the box. "But being outgoing isn't something that comes naturally to me."

Leo knew how much she spoke the truth, though he found nothing wrong with her natural quietness. If anything, it made whatever she had to say all the more anticipated and welcome.

"I'd better go. Grandma will be wondering where I am." She moved to the part of the counter where the large cash register held dominance, shifted the box to the crook of her arm, and opened her purse. "How much for the chocolates?"

"No charge today." He'd likely have some explaining to do to his father once Callie left, but right now, he couldn't bear the thought of making her pay after receiving such bad news.

Callie frowned. "Leo, I'd like to pay for the treats."

"I know, but I'd like you to consider it a gift—to you and your grandmother."

She didn't smile, though the worry in her eyes faded a little. That was compensation enough. If only he could do something else to help her.

"Thank you," she said, her sincerity evident in her grateful expression. "I'll see you next week—on time, I promise."

Leo offered what he hoped was an encouraging smile. "I'm sure you'll think of something you can do to stay in New York." He would mull it over too. There had to be a solution that didn't require her to leave the country.

She nodded. "I hope—"

"I've got it!" His smile widened as he thought through his growing idea. "I know what we can do."

Her eyebrows rose in question. "We?"

Had it been wrong of him to think she would welcome his assistance? Not that he could take back what he'd just said aloud. "I'd like to help you, Callie. As a friend," he hurried to add. "And I think I know a way to do that."

"How?" She watched him with open curiosity.

Leo leaned forward to tap the box of chocolates she still gripped within the crook of her elbow. "What if I pretend to be your secret admirer?"

"My secret admirer?" she echoed, her brow furrowing.

"Exactly. I'll send over notes and chocolates. Maybe even flowers." He nearly laughed out loud at the brilliance of the plan. "Your mother will see all the gifts and attention and will naturally assume . . ."

Callie finished for him. "That I have an interested suitor."

He dipped his chin in a nod. "What do you think?"

"I . . ." She stared down at the box of chocolates. "I suppose that might work. However, what happens after the Patriarch Ball when no suitor shows up to court me?"

Leo considered that. "She did say you only had to attract the interest of a suitor by the ball, right?"

"Yes," she said slowly. "There was no stipulation for what happened after that."

He ducked his head to look her in the eye. "Is that a yes then?"

"Why would you want to help *me*?"

His earlier unease over the possibility of not seeing her today returned. If he didn't help her, he faced the reality of never seeing her again.

"We're friends, aren't we?"

Her cheeks turned pink as she answered, "I'd like to think so."

"So would I." He offered her another full smile. "And that's why I'd like to help."

"I want to do something for you in return." When he opened his mouth to protest, Callie added, "Please, Leo. I insist."

Did that mean she was warming to his idea? "All right. I'm not sure what to have you do, though."

Leo folded his arms and glanced about the room. He needed help turning things around for the shop. But he didn't know what Callie could do to help with that. She was already a loyal patron. If only there were dozens of others like her who came here for their chocolate . . .

"The ball," he said, snapping his fingers. "Do you think you could arrange to have our shop provide favors for the Patriarch Ball? Being a part of an event like that would be a real financial boon and bring more attention to Hauser Chocolates."

Callie pursed her mouth in thought. "That's a good idea. My grandmother still has high social connections, and she loves your chocolates. I can ask her about it this afternoon."

"Then it's settled." He held out his hand. "I'll play the part of your secret admirer, and you'll help me get my chocolates into the ball."

Her lips curled up at the corners in the first real smile he'd seen today. The sight of it loosened the concern that had tightened his chest since exiting the back room earlier and finding her looking so forlorn.

"It's settled," she said with a nod as she shook his hand.

Chapter 2

"Excellent chocolates as usual," Grandma Emelie said with a satisfied smile.

She and Callie had finished their tea and sandwiches and were now sampling the sweets from the Hausers' shop. Callie murmured agreement, though the deliciousness of the treats wasn't foremost on her mind. She kept reliving the moment when she'd shaken Leo's hand.

In the two years she'd known him, they had never touched, other than the occasional brushing of their fingers when he handed her a box of chocolates. This afternoon, though, something warm and pleasant had spread through Callie as Leo's hand had enveloped her gloved one.

She'd thought him handsome, with his light-brown hair and blue eyes, from the first moment they had met. That had only increased her shyness in the beginning. But eventually Leo's friendly, cheerful manner and kind smile had won her over, easing her natural bashfulness.

"Is something wrong, my dear?" Grandma Emelie studied Callie over her spectacles.

Would she guess that the flush on Callie's face had nothing to do with the fire? "I'm fine." And she meant it. Now that Leo had agreed to play the role of her secret admirer, she felt as if a great weight had lifted off her shoulders. If all went well, she wouldn't have to leave her life here. "I do have a favor to ask, though."

"Anything."

Callie couldn't help a smile. Her grandmother didn't voice such agreement to simply anyone. Especially since both Callie's sister and brother were hoping Emelie would leave a portion of her large inheritance to each of them.

"I don't think Hauser Chocolates is doing as well as it once was." Leo hadn't said as much to Callie, but she'd noticed fewer and fewer customers during her weekly visits. "Over the holidays, it wasn't nearly as busy as I would have expected, and today I was the only customer while I was there."

Grandma Emelie sat back with a frown. "I would hate to see the shop close."

"So would I." Truth be told, it wasn't even the chocolates she would miss the most. Callie had come to think of Leo as a friend, and she'd been more than pleased to have him confirm that fact today. She would greatly miss their effortless interactions if the shop closed its doors. "Leo—I mean Mr. Hauser," she quickly corrected, "had an idea of how we might help."

"I'm listening."

Callie leaned forward. "Do you think you could use your social connections to secure them an opportunity to provide chocolate favors for the upcoming Patriarch Ball?"

Her grandmother's eyes widened in delighted surprise. "That's a wonderful idea."

"You'll ask around, then?"

Grandma Emelie feigned a pointed look. "I'll do more than ask, Callie. Give me until next week, and if I don't have their shop down to provide some of the favors, you never have to bring me another piece of chocolate."

Callie chuckled in relief. If Grandma Emelie was willing to permanently part with her favorite sweet if she failed at her task, Callie felt more than confident that the arrangements were as good as made.

"Thank you, Grandma."

"You are most welcome, my dear."

The tender smile her grandmother sent her way eased some of Callie's lingering worries over her part in the plans she and Leo had made. Now that she'd obtained her grandmother's help, the only thing left to do was to be a bit more outgoing at the next two social events she had this week. That way, Leo had explained before she'd left the shop, her mother would see that Callie was trying. It would also make the sudden arrival of gifts from an anonymous admirer much more believable.

"Any other way I may be of help?" her grandmother asked, her expression earnest.

Reaching out, Callie grasped the woman's lined hand. "I can't think of anything else right now, but I promise to let you know."

"Please do." Grandma Emelie gently squeezed Callie's fingers. "You and your visits are truly a gift in my life. And I would gladly match your selfless generosity with my own, should a need for it ever arise."

Callie gave a nod in acknowledgement, though her grandmother's acceptance served as all the generosity she could need. In Grandma Emelie's comfortable, tasteful home, she didn't feel overly quiet or odd. The only other place she felt the same way was during her time in the chocolate shop—with Leo.

Leo watched the hands of the clock inch toward three o'clock. He couldn't wait to see Callie. She might not have any news yet about the shop doing the chocolate favors for the ball, but she would have received the first two gifts from her "secret admirer." He'd sent her a short note the day after she'd supposedly attended the theater. The following evening she had gone to a dance, so a box of chocolates had arrived at her home the next morning.

Knowing Callie would visit this afternoon, Leo had been plagued all day by restless energy. He'd accidently ruined a batch of chocolate that he had to throw out, and he had nearly put nuts into his cream mixture before catching his mistake. After that, he'd made up excuses for lingering in the front of the shop. Finally, Simon had relented his position behind the display case before disappearing into the back room and chuckling to himself.

The bells on the door tinkled. Leo lifted his head in anticipation. But the woman entering the shop, with a small boy in hand, was not Callie. Belatedly, he remembered to smile and ask, "May I help you, ma'am?"

She glanced down at her son. "Do you want a treat, Willie?"

The boy nodded, his eyes wide.

"Which one?" his mother prompted.

"That one." He pressed a finger to the display case.

Leo moved to retrieve the chocolate. Except the boy shook his head and indicated another sweet. "No, I want that one."

"Are you sure, sweetie?" The mother pulled him toward the other end of the case. "These look good."

Fighting a groan, Leo looked up as the bells signaled another customer. Callie entered the shop, stirring a leap of emotion inside Leo's chest. He studied her face, but he couldn't read in her green eyes if she had more bad news or good this time.

"I believe we're ready," the boy's mother said. "We'll take two of the mint chocolates."

Leo tore his gaze away from Callie. "Wonderful." The sooner he finished with them, the sooner he could learn how things had gone this first week of his and Callie's plan.

Just as he pulled out the selected chocolates, the boy changed his mind again. "No, Mama. I want the one next to it."

"Why not try them all? Today's special is four chocolates for the price of two."

Leo grabbed a box and quickly added two of each chocolate to the box before the child decided something else fit his fancy.

The woman's face brightened. "Oh, wonderful." She paid for the chocolates, then popped one into her son's mouth before the pair exited the shop.

Callie approached the counter, a smile twitching at her lips. "Was that actually today's special?"

"No," he answered with a shake of his head. "But that was the fastest way to get them moving along before that little rascal changed his mind a fourth time."

She laughed. The happy sound pleased him. Had he heard her laugh with such ease before? Leo felt sure he would have remembered. He hoped her laughter was a good sign.

"Did you get the gifts I sent you?"

A faint blush colored her cheeks, but she didn't look away as she nodded. "I did, thank you."

Leo folded his arms and eyed her pointedly. "Well? Are you going to keep me in suspense?"

"It is a bit fun," she admitted.

He sniffed. "Then the day's special has just changed. One

piece of chocolate for one piece of information. Which means, no information, no chocolate."

"Very well."

He could tell her sigh held no sincerity—she was merely teasing him back. And he found he rather liked it, a lot. Had he known jesting with Callie would be this enjoyable, he would have attempted it much sooner.

"Your two gifts certainly piqued my mother's interest." Her fingers strayed to the ends of her scarf.

Leo rested his forearms on the top of the display case. "Did you smile and speak up more during your social events?"

Callie dipped her chin. "Not a great deal, though enough for my mother to see me trying. She is, of course, convinced that doing so is what precipitated the gifts."

"I knew that would help," he said with a smile.

"You were right." She glanced away as she added, "And I can't thank you enough for being willing to help me, Leo. It's the nicest thing anyone, except maybe my grandmother, has ever done for me."

Happiness wound through him at her words. "You're welcome, Callie." He straightened away from the case. "Speaking of your grandmother, were you able to talk to her?"

"I was . . ." She clasped her hands together, her expression giving nothing away.

Had her grandmother been unable to help? "And?" he prodded when she paused.

"She sent me a note yesterday." Callie withdrew a slip of paper from her pocket and smoothed the note's wrinkles against her skirt.

Leo held his breath. He'd thought of little else the past week, other than Callie and his hope for providing chocolate favors for the Patriarch Ball. So much hinged on her grandmother's answer.

"*Please inform Hauser Chocolates,*" Callie read in a solemn voice, "*that they will need to provide enough chocolate favors to accommodate three hundred and fifty guests. One of the patriarchs will be in contact soon regarding payment.*"

Had he heard her right? "We're providing the favors?"

"You're providing the favors." The full smile she sent his way was nothing short of dazzling, and it drew him forward.

Coming around the counter, Leo swept her up in an embrace and twirled her around. "We're doing the favors!" He set her down, though with his arms still around her, Callie remained standing close.

"I'm so happy for you, Leo."

He'd never done more than touch her hand, though he didn't regret embracing her. Not when it gave him a chance to study her features up close. From this vantage point, he noticed the faint freckles dotting her upper cheeks and nose. And her mouth bowed perfectly, its shade as pink as her cheeks at this moment.

Reluctantly, he let her go and stepped back. "Thank you, Callie. To you and your grandmother. You can't know what this means for the shop. It may prevent us from having to close the place altogether."

"Are things really that bad?" she asked with a slight frown.

He shrugged and forced himself to return to his proper place behind the counter. "They could be better."

"I wondered." When he raised his eyebrow in silent inquiry, she continued. "There aren't nearly as many customers when I come on Tuesdays as there used to be."

"That's putting it kindly," he said, chuckling.

Callie straightened her coat and scarf. "But all that can change now that you're doing the favors for the ball. Do you know what type of chocolate you'll make?"

"Not yet." He picked up a box and began to fill it with the chocolate caramels her grandmother loved the best. "I've thought of some ideas, but I want something truly memorable."

Once Callie had paid for the sweets, they discussed her upcoming social functions, so Leo would know when to send another round of secret gifts. "I'll try to think of something besides chocolate."

"I don't mind, truly." Callie lifted the box as if to prove her point. "Is there anything else I can do to help you? For the ball, I mean? After all, I only had to do one thing for you. You have far more to do to help me."

"I could use your expertise in tasting," he said, thinking aloud. But they would need more than fifteen to twenty minutes on a Tuesday.

As if she'd come to the same conclusion, Callie suggested, "Perhaps I could come to the shop on another day, besides Tuesday." Her lips pulled to the side in contemplation. "My mother takes tea with her friends every Thursday afternoon. I could come then."

He couldn't help a grin at the thought of seeing Callie twice a week, at least for the next while. And this time, he'd only have to wait two days rather than six. "I'd welcome the help."

She offered him her soft smile as she took a step backward. "Then I will see you Thursday."

"Thursday," he echoed.

Leo couldn't wait.

Callie followed her parents into the opera house. Normally the crowd of patrons, all talking in animated tones, filled her with trembles of dread. But not tonight.

Tonight she didn't need to remind herself to smile more. Her mouth curved naturally each time she thought of her interaction with Leo yesterday—and the anticipation of seeing him again tomorrow. His enthusiastic embrace had taken her by surprise, though it hadn't been unwelcome. Far from it. For those brief moments, standing within his arms, she'd felt safe and appreciated for simply being herself.

At the coatroom, she waited for her mother and father to check their outer garments with the attending clerk. "Very good, Callie," Agnes murmured as she turned to face her daughter. "More smiles like that, and you're sure to enamor more than one secret admirer."

Callie had to force her lips to stay tilted upward. Her and Leo's plan had worked so far, but there were still several weeks to go before the Patriarch Ball. Would her mother see through their ruse? She swallowed hard as the ever-present threat of leaving her home for England loomed large in her mind once again.

I don't want to live away from here and from my grandmother, Lord, Callie silently prayed as she removed her coat and scarf. She'd voiced a similar prayer every day since hearing her mother's edict last week. *But, as Grandma always says, if I trust in Thee, I'll be led to where I'm supposed to be and do.* She only hoped that place would remain New York.

Callie handed her things over to the clerk and gave him her name.

"Did you say Callie Sloan?" he repeated.

Blushing, she offered a nod, unsure of the reason behind his interested tone.

"I have something to give you," the clerk announced with a smile. From behind the counter, he produced a small bouquet of flowers, which he handed to her. "These were left for you earlier this evening."

Callie brought the flowers to her nose and breathed in their sweet scent. Not only had Leo given her another gift, but he'd cleverly arranged for its delivery at the opera house too.

"Who are they from?" Her mother glanced at Callie, then at the clerk.

The young man shrugged. "I'm afraid there is no note, ma'am. A delivery boy simply dropped them off, with instructions to give them to a Miss Callie Sloan, who would be attending tonight's opera."

"I see." Agnes took her husband's arm, and the three of them headed for the grand staircase. "I wonder if it's from your first admirer," she mused aloud, "or someone new."

Callie didn't comment as she trailed them up the stairs, one hand holding her bouquet and the other the train of her gown. As she smelled the nosegay again, her earlier smile returned.

Even knowing the bunch of flowers had come from Leo didn't erase her genuine pleasure at receiving them. And just when she'd needed a spot of hope.

She may have felt initially unsure that they could pull off their plan. But now ... There was something to be said for thoughtful gifts brightening one's outlook. If she could only relegate her mother's ultimatum to the back of her mind, Callie believed she might actually enjoy the next four weeks with her "secret admirer."

Chapter 3

Leo enthusiastically rubbed his hands together, in spite of the flicker of unusual shyness he also felt. No one, save him and his family, had ever been inside the shop's back room. Yet now Callie Sloan stood here with her coat draped over her arm, observing the clutter around her with large green eyes.

"I made several chocolates for you to try," Leo explained as he grabbed a chair and positioned it before the clean worktable. "I can take your coat and scarf."

Callie handed over her outerwear, which Leo hung on a peg beside the work aprons. She took a seat. "Thank you for the flowers. It was a lovely surprise to have them waiting at the opera for me."

"You're welcome," he said, smiling with satisfaction that his gift had been delivered as planned. "Was your mother surprised?"

It was Callie's turn to smile. "She is definitely intrigued and can't decide if they came from the same admirer or a different one." They exchanged a knowing glance. Resting her hands in her lap, Callie glanced around the room expectantly. "So this is where you make all of your chocolate?"

He nodded with pride. "Some of my favorite memories were also created here." *Fifteen years' worth of them,* he thought. Each one filled with plenty of love, laughter, and the ever-present aroma of chocolate.

"That's a lovely sentiment." She gave him a wistful smile. "It's how I feel about my grandmother's home."

"I can't thank you enough, Callie, for enlisting her help."

He'd shared the good news with his father first, but the rest of the family had been equally overjoyed when Leo had told them about doing chocolate favors for the upcoming ball. Simon had also delighted in sharing that it was Leo's weekly visitor, as the others had come to call Callie, who had helped make such a thing possible.

After several minutes of teasing, Leo had decided against revealing the other part of their plan. He had no doubt there'd be more merriment at his expense if his family learned he was pretending to be anyone's secret admirer, but especially Callie's.

Callie shook her head at his thanks. "It was no trouble. Grandma Emelie wanted to help just as much as I do." She rested her gloved hands in her lap and gave him a curious look. "Which chocolates you would like me to try?"

Leo slid the small plate he'd prepared across the table toward her. "Try this rectangular one first."

She picked up the chocolate and placed it in her mouth, drawing his attention to her rosy lips. He watched carefully for her reaction as she chewed. Swallowing, Callie offered a nod of satisfaction.

"It's good, Leo."

He raised an eyebrow, unsure whether she meant it or not.

"Truly," she said with a laugh. "It as good as anything else of yours I've tried over the last two years. And I have certainly tried and enjoyed a great deal."

Leo indicated the next chocolate. "What about this one?"

She sampled the sweet, then another and another, each followed by a murmured compliment. Leo recognized her sincerity, but he couldn't help a flash of disappointment that none of the chocolates had produced the amazed expression he'd been hoping for. The kind of reaction demanded by a chocolate worthy of the Patriarch Ball.

Would the final chocolate, one filled with white chocolate cinnamon ganache, receive the same level of praise? Callie popped it into her mouth. Her eyes widened slightly as she chewed.

"Well?" he prompted with mounting hope.

This time she didn't wait to swallow. Callie covered her mouth with her hand and spoke from behind her fingers. "It's delicious." A blush flooded her cheeks at her breach in manners, but her smile also conveyed true pleasure at the chocolate morsel.

Leo grinned and leaned his hip against the table. "Delicious is better than good, right?"

She blushed even more. "The others were delicious too . . ."

"Not to worry." He shook his head. "I don't feel like you hate the others."

"What sort of chocolates are those?" Callie pointed to a nearby tray.

"Those are my hand-dipped almond clusters."

She nodded. "I remember trying one before, but it's been ages." Her grandmother preferred the creams and caramels to nut-filled chocolates. "May I sample one?"

Shrugging, he pushed the tray toward her. He'd

dismissed these earlier as being too simple for a fancy ball. But there was no harm in letting her try what was one of his favorite chocolates to make.

Callie bit into the chocolate. This time her eyelids fell shut, and she released a happy sigh. Once she'd swallowed, she leaned forward. "Leo, these are amazing. I'd forgotten how much I love them."

"Really?" He glanced between her and the tray.

"I mean it." Her countenance glowed with interest. "I think they should be the favors for the ball."

Leo folded his arms as he considered the idea. "Aren't they too simple and untidy?" While slightly uniform in shape, the chocolates weren't neatly molded like the others.

"The taste is as important as the look, and these are more than delicious." She seemed to search for the right word. "They're scrumptious."

"Scrumptious?" he repeated with a laugh. "That's not something to take lightly. Though I'm still not sure it's the right one."

Callie cocked her head in thought. "Then what if you offered more than one type of chocolate as a favor? You could have the cinnamon ones and the almond clusters." She rose to her feet, her gloves clasped in one hand. "Maybe you could give out Grandma's favorite chocolate caramels too."

"So offer more than one chocolate . . ." he mused out loud.

He'd planned on using only one type to wow the ball patrons and bring more customers into the shop. But maybe giving away several chocolates would secure more interest and appeal to more varied tastes.

"What if you put them inside small boxes?" she suggested. "With the shop name printed on the top?"

It was a good idea but an expensive one. "I'm not sure we

could afford it, especially if I make twice as many chocolates as planned."

She pulled her gloves on. "I can take care of the boxes."

"Callie, you've already done enough."

"As I said, my grandmother made the arrangements for the ball favors. I'd like to cover the cost for the boxes." Her face colored again as she added, "Perhaps I could help you make the chocolates too. That is, if you wouldn't mind teaching me what to do first."

She wanted him to teach her how to make chocolate? Leo couldn't fully imagine Callie working with her hands that way and wearing a soiled apron—not with her evident love of tidiness. On the other hand, if she was willing, he couldn't think of a nicer way to spend an afternoon than helping Callie learn to do something he loved.

"I'd be happy to teach you." Leo scooped up her hand in his.

His heart leapt when Callie's soft smile made another appearance. "Would next Thursday work?"

"Yes. You'll still come by for your regular visit on Tuesday, though?" he asked as he willed himself to release his grip on her fingers. He could accept seeing her just one day a week, but if she was able to come by twice again . . .

She gave him a nod. "Of course. Grandma Emelie would be disappointed if I missed it."

Something in her gaze, though, told him that her grandmother wouldn't be the only one who would be sad if she didn't come. Callie would be too. And that realization filled him with as much delight—and a bizarre sense of hope—as figuring out what chocolate to make for the ball.

Before her regular visit to the shop the following

Tuesday, Callie had received several more gifts from Leo. She'd liked all of them, but her favorite had been the small bag of almonds and its accompanying note of longer length than his first one had been.

Her mother had insisted on reading the message inscribed on the folded piece of paper. Though reluctant, Callie had handed over the note, knowing her mother would never identify the sender. Leo had remained general enough in his compliments to not implicate himself, but she still sensed the sincerity behind his words. And that secretly made them more special.

"What has you smiling to yourself today?" Grandma Emelie asked, her eyes full of curiosity and amusement.

Her grandmother wasn't the first one to notice the ease with which Callie smiled these days. At a dinner party she and her parents had attended over the weekend, the gentleman seated beside her had remarked on her smile. Callie had been thinking of Leo's note—again—and it had naturally drawn her mouth upward.

"You should smile more often, Miss Sloan," her dinner partner had said. "It lights your entire face and hints at some secret delight."

She'd blushed with self-awareness at his compliment, but she also hadn't felt as out of place the rest of the evening as she normally did.

"I'm simply feeling happy," Callie said in answer to her grandmother's inquiry.

"Because?" She should've known Grandma Emelie wouldn't be satisfied with anything less than the details.

Callie shrugged with nonchalance and sipped her tea.

"Would this have to do with the anonymous gifts you've been receiving the past two weeks?"

The tea caught in her throat as Callie gasped in surprise.

Sputtering, she gaped at her grandmother. "H-how did you hear about that?"

"You are not my only visitor, my dear."

"Papa."

Grandma Emelie nodded. "My son said Agnes is quite thrilled at the prospect of your secret admirer."

"Indeed," Callie murmured before sampling her tea again.

The truth of her secret pressed against her lips. Did she dare tell anyone? She couldn't afford her mother finding out before the ball. Yet she trusted her grandmother explicitly.

"The gifts and notes are actually from Leo Hauser."

Her grandmother lowered her teacup at the same time her eyebrows shot upward. "As in Hauser Chocolates?"

"He's the son of the owner."

Grandma Emelie openly studied her. "You know for certain that he is your secret admirer?" At Callie's nod, she continued. "And he has developed an affection for you?"

Callie hurried to shake her head, her cheeks flushing with heat. "No, it's part of our plan."

"Plan?"

"To keep me from having to go to England after the Patriarch Ball." Callie hurried to explain her mother's ultimatum and how Leo had offered to help her by acting as her secret admirer. "That's why I wanted your assistance in ensuring his shop provide chocolate favors for the ball. It was something I could do for him. I'm also overseeing the purchase of small boxes for the favors to go inside, and Leo is going to teach me how to make the chocolates so he doesn't have to do all that work by himself."

Her grandmother eyed her over the brim of her cup. "That's rather generous on both sides."

Why did her tone convey caution? "It's going well so far."

"I'm glad to hear it," Grandma Emelie said, her voice gentling. "Just remember that sometimes fantasy can encroach upon and complicate our reality."

Callie frowned. "Leo and I are friends, Grandma. That's all." Should she ever wish to find something deeper with him, her parents would never allow it.

"Having a friend who's willing to help you in such a way is a precious gift in and of itself." Her grandmother reached out to touch Callie's knee. "And if he's the one who has helped put the happiness on my granddaughter's face, then I am also indebted to him."

Her approval brought Callie some relief. Yet as they continued to chat and eat their chocolates, she couldn't rid her mind completely of her grandmother's cautionary words.

She thoroughly enjoyed her time with Leo, especially the last few weeks. After the ball, though, her visits would probably have to go back to Tuesdays only. That thought drew Callie's lips downward again and filled her with the same measure of sadness she knew she'd experience when she could no longer see Leo Hauser more than once a week.

Chapter 4

Though Callie had never worked with chocolate before, Leo was impressed with how quickly she'd caught on during her first lesson as she learned to make filled chocolates using a mold. He'd decided to extend their lessons over two Thursday afternoons rather than one, though his motive wasn't just an excuse for Callie to come back. He didn't want to overwhelm her either.

Callie had seemed to enjoy their lesson. True to character, she'd tackled her first attempts at chocolate making with precision. She had made certain to evenly scrape the excess liquid from the molds and had wiped her hands on the towel he'd provided for her rather than on her apron. However, by the time they'd finished making a batch of the cinnamon cream chocolates, Leo had noticed that her apron sported a number of large smudges that hadn't been there in the beginning.

Between their two Thursday lessons, he'd sent Callie several more gifts. His anonymous notes grew a little longer each week, especially after the time they'd spent together making chocolate. Leo made certain to keep the details vague, since he suspected her mother might read the notes, but every sentiment he penned was sincere.

Callie was intelligent, caring, and beautiful. And when she smiled—really and truly smiled—her entire countenance lit with a soft glow of pleasure that made him wish to inspire such a response over and over again. How she remained unattached, he didn't understand. Were the men of her social circles all blind, or were they foolish enough to think that taking the time to get to know Callie Sloan wouldn't be worth it?

For his part, he enjoyed every minute with her. He'd seen, too, that the more time they spent together, the more her normally quiet demeanor slipped away. It was like a special chocolate that revealed itself with each slow, savoring bite. And while Callie would never be the outgoing sort, as his sisters were inclined to be, Leo thoroughly liked talking with her. Her questions and interest about his work and his family never felt feigned or forced. She'd even confided to him that she was much closer to her grandmother than anyone else because her Grandma Emelie treated her with compassion and respect. Leo had been more than a little relieved to hear that someone else recognized Callie's intrinsic value.

Already he was half dreading the arrival of the Patriarch Ball. He felt confident the event would help the shop, but it would also signal the end of his extra time with Callie.

Pushing the sad thought aside, he set out everything they needed for making the almond clusters. He wasn't sure how Callie would feel about dipping them by hand, but he hoped today's lesson would turn out as well as the first one had.

"To make these sweets," he explained once she'd arrived, "you'll need to mold the chocolate around the nuts by hand."

He watched Callie's expression for any sign of concern, but she simply nodded. "I'll demonstrate, and then you can try."

He intentionally kept his movements slow so that she could see what he was doing. After placing a cluster of nuts in the chocolate, he swirled the mixture together until it was entirely coated. Then he placed the creation to the side of the table.

"Now it's your turn." Leo offered her a reassuring smile.

Callie's green eyes narrowed with determination. "All right." She picked up the nuts and set them in the chocolate. Using the tips of her fingers, she attempted to make the same swirling motion he had. But the nuts were barely covered when she released them.

"That looks nothing like yours," she said with a frown.

"Believe me, I didn't get it on my first time either." He nodded with encouragement toward the chocolate. "Try again."

She did so, though the end result was much the same. "What am I doing wrong?" Callie blew out a breath, ruffling the dark-brown strand of her hair resting near her cheek.

"It might work better to use more than just your fingertips."

Her eyebrow rose in confusion. "I'm not sure what you mean."

He lifted his hand to show her how the chocolate covered more than his fingers—it spotted the top of his palm too. She didn't look any less perplexed, though, which gave him an idea. "What if I show you how to use your more of your hand to coat the nuts?"

"But you already did." Callie laughed lightly.

Leo shook his head as he cleaned his hand on the towel. "If I stand behind you, I can put my hand on yours and guide you through the motion."

"Oh . . ."

The pink in her cheeks grew suddenly more distinct. Had he overstepped their friendship with his suggestion? It definitely meant standing much closer to Callie. And though he wouldn't mind, he knew she might not feel the same.

"I can try to talk you through it," he started to say.

"No, I'd like the help." When he threw her a skeptical glance, she dipped her chin in a firm nod. "Please."

Despite the leaping rhythm of his heartbeat, Leo managed a smile in reply as he moved to stand behind her. He reached his arm forward and covered Callie's hand with his own. Her skin felt warm and smooth against his palm, though he felt tension in her fingers as well.

"Now what?" she half whispered, casting him a look over her shoulder.

He moved his head near hers. The scent of crisp, clean soap wafted off her hair and mingled pleasantly with the smell of chocolate. "Relax your hand a little." As she did so, their hands seemed to meld into one. "Now," he said in a quiet voice that belied the drumming feeling in his chest, "we'll try it together."

Callie couldn't draw a full breath—not with Leo standing so close that she could feel the warmth of him on her back as his hand gently embraced her own. Never mind the chocolate covering her fingers and palm. Could Leo hear the thundering of her pulse? She willed the tension from her limbs as she allowed him to guide her hand. Of course, she still had to be the one to grip the almonds and swirl them through the chocolate. But with slight pressure here and there on the back of her palm, Leo directed her movements.

"Look at that," he murmured near her ear, causing a pleasant shiver down Callie's back.

She trained her concentration on the table rather than on the wonderful man behind her. Leo lifted her hand, and there beneath it sat a nut-covered chocolate nearly as perfect as his. They'd done it; she'd done it!

Spinning around to face him, she couldn't help a grin. "It looks like yours."

"You're a natural." His gaze locked with hers.

Callie found she could not look away, nor did she want to. "I have an excellent teacher," she said, her voice betraying some of her breathlessness.

"Do you want to try another?"

She nodded, though neither of them moved. Up close, she could see turquoise flecks in his eyes and the hint of stubble on his handsome face. An irrational urge to run her palm down his jaw nearly overtook her.

"Thank you for your help, Callie. All of it." The words came out little more than a whisper. "You can't know what it means to the shop and . . . to me."

The sincerity in his gaze melted her inside as thoroughly as the chocolate they'd been working with just now. But when he glanced at her lips, she felt grateful that at least one of her hands grasped the table behind her for support.

What would it be like to be kissed? She hadn't given much thought to kissing a gentleman, unsure whether she would like it or not. In the past, her grandmother had tried to assure Callie that with the right man, sharing a kiss was a lovely experience.

Was that what it would be like to kiss Leo? She couldn't think of anyone whose kiss she wanted more. And judging from his intent expression, he felt something similar.

Leo leaned closer, robbing her of breath all over again. As if some unseen thread had tugged her forward, Callie drew nearer too. His mouth drifted within a few inches of her own.

"Leo?"

Mr. Hauser's voice washed over Callie like cold water. She jerked back, but the table thwarted a full retreat. A blush burned her cheeks at being caught standing so close to the man's son.

A flicker of what appeared to be disappointment filled Leo's eyes before he stepped away from the table and turned to face his father. "Yes, Papa?"

"Someone is asking if we have more of the vanilla creams."

Leo glanced around the back room as if he couldn't remember. Perhaps he was feeling as muddled in his head as Callie did. "No, I don't think so."

His father held his hands out in an imploring gesture. "Maybe you could suggest something else then."

"Yes, of course." He threw Callie an apologetic look. "I'll be right back. You can try another if you'd like."

"All right."

As Leo left the back room, his father smiled at her. "You have been a great help, Miss Sloan. And now you make chocolates too. We are all grateful."

"It's my pleasure," she managed to say before he followed after his son.

Only in the throbbing silence did Callie realize Mr. Hauser had spoken near-perfect English. Why would he have pretended to the contrary these past two years? Was it so his son could wait on her with some degree of privacy?

Though flattered by the prospect and the man's gratitude, Callie felt a surge of her earlier confusion. This time it wasn't about making chocolate—it was about her wonderful chocolatier.

She'd sensed her connection and friendship with Leo deepening these past few weeks. Yet she didn't know if he felt the same. His notes and thoughtful gifts certainly hinted at regard, perhaps even growing affection. But as she'd observed with his chocolate making, Leo put his whole heart into whatever task lay before him. That likely included being her secret admirer until the ball.

Did that mean their near kiss had come not from genuine emotion but from the roles they were temporarily playing? The thought depressed Callie, though it also gave her a chance to examine her own feelings toward Leo and his place in her life.

Her grandmother's warning from the other week soon repeated through her mind, making her question whether she'd unknowingly begun to believe that her arrangement with Leo could become something real. As she shakily worked to make another almond cluster, Callie feared she already knew the answer.

CHAPTER 5

SEATED AT HER vanity table, Callie twisted her head one way, then the other to view the artful arrangement of her hair. A sprig of flowers, compliments of Leo, ordained the elaborate knot. "Thank you for your help, Mary," she said sincerely to their maid. "You've outdone yourself this time."

The young woman blushed, but her pleased smile didn't wane. "You'll look as lovely as any of the other girls at the Patriarch Ball, Miss Callie."

She hoped so. Though in truth, Callie only cared about the opinion of one man. If she was fortunate enough to see Leo tonight, would he find her beautiful? Her pale-blue ball gown complemented the color of her eyes, and she liked the almost whimsical look of the puffed sleeves and long flared skirt. Tonight she felt unusually fanciful and happy, despite knowing she would face an entire room of people in less than an hour. And she had Leo to thank for her budding confidence.

Still, Callie had done her best to avoid a repeat of their

almost kiss from the other week. After all, their arrangement was only temporary, whether Callie wished it differently or not. So she'd kept her interactions with Leo as those of a close friend. Yet in spite of her efforts, she knew he claimed a little more of her heart with each exchange, each gift, each letter. Now the night they'd both been working toward had finally arrived.

The boxes Callie had ordered for the chocolate favors had been delivered to the shop two days earlier. Callie had also gone in that same day, and stayed as long as she dared without raising her mother's suspicions, to help prepare everything for the ball.

Leo's mother and sisters had also been there. And though their presence had thankfully made any private moment with Leo impossible, Callie had still felt tongue-tied, especially in the wake of their exuberance toward her and her assistance. But like their son and brother had once done, the three women had taken her shyness in stride, and after a time, Callie had felt more at ease, conversing and laughing with them.

Then this afternoon, her last gift from Leo had arrived. This one had included a spray of flowers for her hair, a small box filled entirely with almond clusters, and a letter that had scattered petals across her lap when she'd opened it. His words of admiration about her character, her smile, her willingness to help others, and her ability to treat everyone fairly had inspired tears of happiness to fill her eyes. Never before had she felt so accepted and cherished. It was as if a bright light had been lit inside her—she felt as if she glowed these days.

That feeling, thankfully, remained with Callie as she donned her coat and trusty scarf and joined her parents inside the carriage for the ride to Delmonico's, where the Patriarch Ball would be held. Callie tried to pay attention to her mother's speculations regarding who her daughter's admirer could be, but her thoughts kept wandering.

Had Leo and his family finished putting together all of the boxes of chocolate? Would she catch a glimpse of him tonight when he delivered the party favors?

Directing her gaze to the city lights beyond the window, Callie offered a quick prayer that all would go well this evening. That people would enjoy Leo's chocolates and that the shop would become busy once more.

Once they reached Delmonico's, their driver assisted Callie and her mother from the carriage. The cold night air swirled around Callie as she followed her parents inside. When they entered one of the ballrooms, the temperature was anything but brisk. People filled every available spot in the room. Callie gazed around at the decorations and glittering throng and felt a prick of fear. So many strangers. She wasn't sure which she dreaded more—being asked to dance or sitting out, alone, one song after another.

Before she could decide, the gentleman who'd complimented her smile at the dinner the other week approached her and asked for the first dance. Callie smiled in relief as she answered in the affirmative. Soon, much to her surprise, her dance card held no more empty slots.

Her dinner companion came to claim her for his dance when the musicians struck the notes of the first number. Taking his hand, Callie reminded herself to smile bravely. Though it wasn't until she again recalled the sweet words from Leo's letter that the gesture felt less stiff.

If Leo were here now, he would surely smile back at her with pride at how much she'd grown this past month. Callie still preferred tidiness and punctuality, and she would likely always be reserved in demeanor. Yet she'd also learned to enjoy the delightful mess that came with making chocolates and the ability to speak up, even when she felt shy.

With that reminder, her smile lifted anew as she and her partner began to dance.

Leo wanted nothing more than to sleep for days. But his fatigue stemmed from satisfaction. He and his family had succeeded in having everything ready for the ball, and the delivery of the chocolate and its distribution among the other party favors had gone well. Now it was time to return to his room above the shop.

Music floated outward from the open doors of the nearest ballroom as Leo passed by. He nearly kept walking, but his curiosity—and a desire to see Callie, if only from a distance—got the better of him. Keeping himself mostly hidden, he peered into the room. Women decked in fancy dresses and jewels conversed with men in expensive-looking evening clothes. Even the lights themselves seemed to blaze with wealth and prestige.

He glanced down at his worn coat and the frayed mittens he held in his chocolate-splotched hand. A wry sniff escaped Leo. No one would mistake him for a guest. This glittery world held no place for him, though after tonight, he hoped some of it would find its way to Hauser Chocolates.

As he started to turn away, the crowd in front of the doors shifted, allowing Leo a glimpse at the dance floor. There, directly ahead of him, he saw Callie. She wore a blue dress, and her dark-brown hair had been piled on top of her head. But it was her lovely eyes and smile that sent his heart pumping faster as he watched her. An aura of ease seemed to encompass her, even at this late hour, and he wasn't the only one to notice. Her dance partner stared at her, his expression a mixture of interest and surprise. Clearly her efforts to be more engaging had proven effective.

Leo knew he ought to feel relieved or happy for her. Together they'd saved Callie from having to leave New York for England. But in this moment, he felt no joy that their plan had worked. Surely it would only be a matter of time before she received the interest of some real suitors, and that likelihood settled in the form of a hard knot inside his stomach.

Because I love her.

The thought didn't surprise him, not completely. He'd been falling in love with Callie Sloan for weeks now; he'd just been more focused on the shop and the chocolates for the ball to fully realize it sooner. Yet somewhere in the midst of the gifts, the notes, and their time together, the fantasy of being her admirer had become something very real for him.

As he continued to watch her dance gracefully about the ballroom, Leo could hardly believe this was the same girl who'd willingly made chocolates with him in the shop's back room. Callie fit this setting perfectly. And that realization made the truth of their situation cut more deeply.

What did he have to offer Callie, beyond a home above the store and days spent working? Surely she deserved someone who could give her the life free of want that she'd always known.

At that moment, Callie's gaze locked with his. Her demeanor brightened even more, though Leo struggled to return her smile. She lifted her eyebrows in silent question, but he couldn't possibly convey everything on his mind. He settled for an acknowledging nod, then he turned his back on the room and headed toward the exit once more.

If only he hadn't given in to his desire to peek inside. Then again, maybe it was good that he'd stopped to watch. It meant no longer denying what could and couldn't be between him and Callie.

"Will you please excuse me?" Callie said to her dance

partner the moment the song ended. "There's someone I must speak with."

She headed toward the doors without waiting for the man's reply. If he found her break in decorum odd, it hardly mattered. The most important thing to her right now was reaching Leo before he left Delmonico's. *Why did he look so forlorn?* she wondered. A thrill had shot through her when she'd caught sight of him, but it had quickly transformed into alarm when Leo had failed to smile back.

Callie hurried from the room and felt instant relief to find Leo still in the hallway. "Leo?" she called out, ignoring the few loitering guests who looked her way. "Wait."

His shoulders visibly tensed, but he stopped and slowly spun to face her. The sadness in his blue eyes increased her worry.

"Is something wrong?" she asked when she reached his side. She placed her gloved hand on his sleeve. "Did things go badly with the chocolate?"

He shook his head. "Everything went well." He cut a glance toward the others in the hallway and added in a stiff tone, "Thank you for asking, Miss Sloan."

Hurt at his formality slipped through her as Callie lowered her arm. "Whatever is the matter?"

"I'm fine," he said, exhaling a sigh. "Are you enjoying yourself?"

Callie gathered her courage to answer with the truth. "I'm enjoying myself now." She stepped closer to him. "I'd hoped to see you tonight, and then I looked up and saw you standing by the doors."

"I shouldn't have looked in like I did." He slipped a pair of mittens onto his hands.

"Can't we talk a little longer?" she asked. She no longer felt the need to hide that she preferred being with him over anyone else she'd ever met or would meet.

The tortured expression that passed over Leo's handsome face made her fall back a step. "Callie, you belong here. I don't, and I never will. I'll always be just a humble chocolatier."

"But that's what I like about you . . . it's what I love about you."

Her cheeks flushed with heat at her bold words, yet she didn't wish them back. She didn't want to keep her feelings unspoken anymore—she wanted Leo and everyone else to know them.

Rather than delight or surprise, Leo appeared resigned. "We both fulfilled our arrangement. Now things can go back to the way they were—for both of us."

Confusion mingled with a growing ache inside her. Had she misunderstood him? Were his words and gifts and lingering glances truly all an act? Had there been no sincerity in any of them? She didn't want to believe it, yet Leo's goodbye could not be clearer.

"I don't understand. I thought we . . ." Callie couldn't finish, not when her throat felt as if it was closing.

Leo reached out and cupped her cheek. The warmth of his touch melted through his mitten to her face and all the way down to her heart. "We can't ever be more than friends, Callie. But I'll always be grateful for your friendship. You are an exceptional person. I hope you remember that."

He dropped his hand, sending a wave of cool air against her skin. "Let me know if you ever need me to play the part of secret admirer again," he said, attempting a light laugh.

"Thank you." It was all she could manage.

"Goodbye, Callie."

She lifted her hand in a limp wave. "Goodbye, Leo."

Watching him walk away, Callie felt the cold of the hallway seep deep within her. But she couldn't make her feet turn in the direction of the ballroom just yet. Instead she stood frozen, her hopes scattered about her feet like the petals from Leo's last letter. Thankfully the tears didn't begin until long after he'd disappeared from view.

Chapter 6

The parlor felt stifling with heat two mornings later, but Callie had chosen to read in here rather than in her room, among the reminders of Leo's former affection. She couldn't bear to throw away his notes, though. Yesterday she hadn't gone to the chocolate shop for her normal weekly visit, but she'd still seen her grandmother. Thankfully, Grandma Emelie had made no comment about the lack of chocolates at their tea.

Callie hadn't been able to face seeing Leo again, at least not yet. His dismissal at the ball stung just as fiercely today as it had the other night. She'd felt brave and excited to share her feelings with him, only to learn he wished for them to go back to being once-a-week friends.

Her mother soon wandered into the room. "I'm rather surprised your secret admirer hasn't sent you anything since before the ball and that none of the gentlemen you danced with have called."

"A few of them tried," Callie answered, turning her page

without looking up. "But I declined seeing anyone." Her time with Leo had given her confidence in more than social settings—she was ready to be the mistress of her own life, especially when it came to matters of the heart.

"Why would you do something so foolish?" From the corner of her eye, Callie saw her mother frown. "Are you hoping your admirer will make himself known?"

She shook her head. "I already know the identity of my admirer."

Agnes rushed to the settee and sank beside Callie. "Who is it?"

Breathing in some courage, Callie set down her book. "It was Leo Hauser."

"Leo Hauser?" Agnes repeated in a bewildered tone. "I don't recognize his name. Where do his people come from?"

"His people come from Austria." Callie rested her folded hands on top of her book. "And they own Hauser Chocolates."

The confused expression on her mother's face might have been humorous if Callie weren't still hurting. "I don't understand."

"He pretended to be my secret admirer, Mother, so I wouldn't have to go to England."

Agnes spluttered, clearly unable to form a coherent reply. Callie used the silence to finish explaining. "In exchange, I ensured his shop was the one to provide favors for the ball." She rose to her feet, her book in hand. "I also helped him make chocolate."

"Oh, this is horrible, simply horrible." Her mother collapsed against the cushions as if she might faint. "Did anyone see you?" She waved her hand impatiently before Callie could answer. "Oh, never mind. It hardly matters now. You don't have a suitor, and you've turned away the few who might have been potential candidates."

Suddenly Agnes snapped to attention, her back ramrod straight. "We'll have to go to England after all."

Callie clasped her book tightly to her bodice. "No, Mother. I am not going to England."

"Not going?" her mother said as she stood. "You are not in a position to decline, Callie Sloan, not if you wish to remain an heiress."

She'd expected such a response, but Callie wasn't without a plan of her own now. "Do what you wish with my money, but I'm not leaving New York."

Agnes dropped back to her seat, her mouth opening and closing in evident shock.

"I know you want what's best for me." Callie relaxed her posture. "But I've realized that if I do marry, it will be for love and not because I fear the ramifications of not marrying. If that's unacceptable to you, I'll understand. I can go live with Grandma Emelie if I need to."

The first glimmer of happiness she'd felt since the night of the ball sparked inside Callie as she left the room. She might never find again the love she'd felt for Leo, but she was no longer timid about the future.

Would Callie come into the shop this afternoon? Leo asked himself for the dozenth time that morning. She hadn't visited the previous Tuesday. And though he'd been unsure how he would feel at seeing her the day after the ball, Leo had felt disappointed and confused by her absence. Had she mistakenly thought he didn't wish for her to come to the shop anymore? He hoped not.

"You have the long face again, Leo," his father chided as Leo placed a batch of finished chocolates within the display case.

Their last customer had just departed, and another had yet to come through the door. A steady stream of people had visited the past week, proving that the chocolate favors at the ball had been a success. But not even that victory could pull Leo from his despondent mood.

"I'll be fine, Papa."

Simon leveled him with a pointed look. "You think I cannot tell what eats at you? I, too, was once young and in love myself, you know?" His expression softened as he continued. "Not until I told your mother what I felt for her did I feel better."

If only it were as easy as that for him and Callie. "Telling her won't do any good."

"Why?" Simon countered. "Because she does not return your affection?"

Leo recalled Callie's words outside the ballroom when he'd argued that he was just a humble chocolatier. *It's what I love about you,* she'd told him.

He shook his head in answer to his father's question. "I do think she cares for me." The admission did little to lessen his heartache, though. "But it doesn't matter, Papa. Her parents would never approve. I don't belong in her world, and I'm not sure she would want to belong in ours. At least not for the rest of her life."

"How do you know? Have you asked her?"

"Like I said, it won't change anything."

Simon clapped a firm but gentle hand on Leo's shoulder. "It may not change things. But which would you rather live with, regret or grief? The latter can heal in time, but the former . . . Well, that one sticks around much longer and eats away at our peace."

His father's words settled softly inside him as Leo mulled them over. "So you think I should just throw caution to the wind and tell her how I feel, even if it doesn't change our situation?"

"I'm saying you share what is in your heart, son." He tapped a finger to Leo's chest. "And then you let that delightful, intelligent girl decide for herself what to do with your declaration."

An inkling of hope stirred to life within Leo. Maybe his father was right. Once Callie knew how much he loved her, would it open a way for them to be together, a way that he couldn't see right now? Surely it was worth finding out.

"Will you excuse me, Papa? I'm going to wait to make more of the vanilla chocolates." A real smile tugged at his mouth. "I have another letter to write." And this one would be the most important of all.

CHAPTER 7

"ARE YOU GOING to your grandmother's?"

Callie nodded to her mother as she looped her scarf about her neck and evened the ends. It was Tuesday—once again—but she hadn't decided yet if she would visit Leo's shop before visiting Grandma Emelie. She'd missed his little gifts and letters this past week. But most all, she missed him, deeply.

Could she see him at the shop and not reveal in her words or countenance just how much she still loved him?

She hadn't told her parents her feelings for Leo, though she guessed her mother had suspected something, given her comments about Callie being more reserved than usual the past few days. The two of them had formed a silent truce, neither of them broaching the subject of suitors and marriage, but Callie knew the reprieve was only temporary. She had spoken the truth, though, when she'd told her mother that she would marry for love. If that required being cut off financially by her father and moving in with her grandmother, then she was prepared to do that.

A sudden knock drew their attention to the front door. "Are you expecting someone?" her mother asked.

"No." Callie shook her head and moved to answer the door herself.

Her grandmother smiled at her from the front step. "Oh, good. I caught you before you left."

"Grandma Emelie?" Callie's mouth fell open in shock. She couldn't recall the last time her grandmother had ventured to their house.

"Emelie?" Agnes exclaimed. "Whatever are you doing here?"

"I may rarely leave my house these days, Agnes dear, but that does not mean that I can't."

Callie recovered enough from her surprise to step back from the door. "Come in, please."

With a nod, her grandmother entered the foyer, and Callie shut the door behind her. "I was tasked with delivering this letter." She handed Callie an envelope.

There was no mistaking the handwriting. But why did her grandmother have a letter from Leo? "Where did you get this?"

"I wasn't entirely certain you would visit the shop before our tea," Grandma Emelie confessed. "And I've missed my chocolate caramels." Her eyes twinkled with enough mirth to signal the absence of her favorite sweet hadn't been her sole reason for visiting Hauser Chocolates. "I was also eager to learn the intentions of a certain secret admirer of yours."

Agnes cleared her throat. "He wasn't a real admirer."

"Is that so?" Grandma Emelie lifted an eyebrow. "After speaking with the younger Mr. Hauser, I discovered his regard for my granddaughter is quite genuine."

Callie's heart sped up. Could her grandmother be correct? She studied the letter in her grasp. "What did Leo say?"

"I believe he thoroughly declares his affections in his missive."

"But . . ." Agnes looked as if she'd swallowed something horrid. "My daughter can't marry a shopkeeper's son. It isn't right." She turned to face Callie. "I meant it when I said if you wish to remain an heiress, you must marry someone of our social class."

Callie squared her shoulders. "I don't love anyone of our social class, Mother. But I do love Leo." There—she'd finally stated the words out loud. "And if he loves me in return . . ."

Was it possible Leo truly felt the same, even after telling her that they could now go back to being friends? She opened the envelope and withdrew the single sheet of paper.

"Do you really wish to live a life of servitude?" her mother pressed. "Scraping for every penny?"

Grandma Emelie reentered the conversation. "She won't need to scrape for any pennies."

"She—she won't?"

Callie's grandmother shook her head. "After my lovely visit to the chocolate shop, I decided I must also see my lawyer this afternoon to make a few things official. You see, some time ago, I made the decision that Callie will receive the bulk of my fortune after my death." Agnes gasped aloud. "Until such a time, I'd also like to make arrangements for her to receive a substantial annual income."

Grandma Emelie offered Callie a full smile. "So you see, my dear, if you're willing to accept my offer, you may remain an heiress and follow your heart's desire as well. We can even visit my lawyer this afternoon to make it all official."

Callie's eyes welled with tears of relief and happiness. She no longer had to wonder what the future held—if needed, she would have more than enough to provide for herself. "I'll gladly and gratefully accept your offer, Grandma." She put her arms around her grandmother and embraced her tightly. "Thank you so much."

When Callie released her, Grandma Emelie sniffed as if clearing away her own tears. "It's you who deserves my thanks for your kindness and care towards me, especially these past few years. This was one way to show my gratitude."

"This is all too much," Agnes moaned. "What are my friends going to say?" She pressed her hands to her pale cheeks.

"They'll all be green with envy." Grandma Emelie gave Callie a conspiratorial wink. "Because your daughter, Agnes, is now fortunate enough to choose to marry for love."

A laugh slipped from Callie's lips. "I haven't married yet. I don't even know how Leo feels."

"Then I suggest you read that letter at once, my dear. For I believe your handsome chocolatier is eagerly awaiting a response."

Leo's gaze jumped from the customers at the counter to the clock. It was nearly six o'clock. He'd already told his father to go ahead upstairs to supper. If Callie didn't arrive or send a note within the next ten minutes, he would have his answer to his letter.

After confessing how much he loved her, Leo had asked Callie to come to the shop before closing—that is, if she felt the same way about him. He'd hoped to see her step inside by now, that soft smile on her face, but he was beginning to fear she might not come at all.

Earlier that day, he'd put on his coat in preparation to hand deliver his letter when a fashionable woman with white hair had entered the shop and announced she was Callie's grandmother. It had taken only a few exchanged words of greeting between them for Leo to recognize the same kindness in her that her granddaughter had always shown him.

Mrs. Emelie Sloan hadn't acted superior to him or his father. Instead she'd warmly complimented them on their work and purchased a large box filled with her favorite caramel chocolates. Then she'd surprised Leo by sharing her knowledge of his and Callie's arrangement. What she didn't know, she'd told him, was how he felt about her granddaughter.

With nothing to lose—and hopefully everything to gain by being honest—Leo had confessed how he'd fallen in love with Callie over the past six weeks. He'd even told the elder Mrs. Sloan about the letter he'd written and planned to deliver himself.

After listening to him, Callie's grandmother had offered to take the letter to Callie for him. And though she never gave Leo any indication of how her granddaughter might react to his declaration, Leo felt more hopeful, knowing he had one family member's support.

But now . . . It was nearly closing, and no Callie.

While he finished helping their present customers, the door to the shop opened again. Leo turned to see who had come inside, but it was a young couple. He tried to stem his pricks of jealousy over the adoring looks they gave each other. With their attention more on themselves than the chocolate, assisting them took longer than needful. By the time the pair departed, the clock showed seven minutes after six o'clock.

A sharp jab of disappointment cut through Leo as he moved to the door and turned the shop's sign from *open* to *closed*. He reluctantly twisted the lock into place, then faced the vacant room. The silence echoed with none of its usual comfort. Tonight Leo felt as if his future also stood empty before him, at least when it came to Callie.

The sudden rattling of the door handle and the rap of knuckles against the windowpane startled him. Turning, Leo tried to see through the half-fogged glass, but it was impossible to see who might be knocking. He did his best to tamp down his anticipation of it being Callie as he retraced his steps and unlocked the door.

"I'm sorry, but we're closed," he said as he inched the door open.

Cold air whooshed into the space, along with a familiar voice. "It's me, Leo. I'm sorry I didn't come sooner."

"Callie?" He widened the gap in the door and stared unbelieving at her. She'd come.

Her expression changed from apologetic to anxious. "Am I too late?"

"What? No."

Shaking his head, Leo waved her inside. She entered the shop and walked past him, looking much as she had the last time she'd been late, her scarf askew and her demeanor worried.

"I got your letter." Callie held it up as he shut the door. "Only I thought things at the lawyer's office wouldn't take so long. They did, however, and then I wanted to make sure my grandmother was settled at home before I left. And all of that meant I was later than I wanted to be."

Leo nodded, though this news wasn't exactly what he'd expected her to say if she came. "The lawyer's office?" he repeated as he untied his apron.

"Yes, my Grandma Emelie decided to name me as heiress to her fortune." Some of the apprehension faded from her face. "She's also gifting me an annual income."

Which surely put her even farther above him in station. Leo's excitement at seeing her crumbled a little, though he tried to hide it as he said, "That's wonderful, Callie."

Had this been her reason for stopping by? Maybe she hadn't read his letter after all.

"No, you don't understand." Unwinding her scarf, she took a step toward him. "My grandmother's gift gives me the freedom to do what I want with my life, without fearing that my parents will disagree or cut me off financially."

Something told him her words hinted at her true motive for being here. Keeping his gaze fixed on her, he set his apron on the counter. "What do you want to do with your life?"

"I want to invest in a certain chocolate shop that I love," she said, placing her scarf atop his apron and moving another step nearer. "Perhaps make it bigger or open another location somewhere else in the city."

Leo gave a thoughtful nod that belied his growing hope. "That sounds like a good plan."

"There's just one problem."

Her eyes didn't leave his, and the way they gleamed with courage set his heart thumping faster with expectancy. He took a step forward this time, narrowing the distance between them to almost nothing. "And what is the problem?"

"To be successful, I ought to know how to make more than three kinds of chocolate, and even those, I'm not very proficient at making yet." Callie visibly swallowed as she lowered her gaze to the letter she still held. "Do you know someone who'd be willing to take a chance on an unskilled heiress like me?"

Tipping her chin upward, Leo studied her lovely face. Did he dare believe that she still cared for him? "I don't see an unskilled heiress," he countered quietly. "I see a beautiful woman with skills of kindness, respect, and constancy. And if she's willing to take a chance, too, this humble chocolatier would like to spend the rest of his days at her side, making chocolates together."

"I'd very much like that." Her gentle smile finally made an appearance. "Which means, in answer to the question in your letter, yes, Leo Hauser, I do still love you."

"I love you too." He cupped her cheek as he had the night of the ball. But this time, the gesture held no sadness or final farewell, only joy and the promise of beginnings. "Will you marry me, Callie Sloan?"

She rested her free hand against his chest. "Nothing would bring me greater pleasure."

Grinning with happiness, Leo lowered his hand to her waist and angled his head near hers. "Just so you know, tonight's special is a free almond cluster for every kiss."

Callie laughed softly as she placed her hand alongside his jaw. "Then I hope you're prepared to give away a great deal of free chocolates."

"Gladly, and for the rest of my life," Leo murmured.

His lips eagerly met hers. Soon one kiss became many, each sweeter than any chocolate in creation and a testament to the genuine love and affection they would always share.

An Unlikely Spring Courtship

CHAPTER 1

Idaho City, Idaho Territory, April 1867

"WHERE IS THAT confounded ledger?" Tempest Blakely placed another stack of receipts and papers on the counter above her. If people didn't know better they might mistake her mercantile as a paper shop, given the mess she'd made this morning. But she was sure she'd placed the ledger under the counter next to her tin of pencils after closing up last night. And yet the book was nowhere to be seen.

The bells on the door tinkled as a customer entered. "I shall be with you in a moment," Tempest called out.

"I'll just look around," a male voice responded.

She blew a puff of air to dislodge one of her springy auburn curls out of her eyes and sat back on her heels, her wide skirts ballooning around her. Why couldn't she remember something as simple as where she'd placed the ledger? Squeezing her eyes shut, she attempted to retrace her steps from last night. Old Mr. Seymour had been her last customer—she could remember that because she'd finally succeeded in coaxing a smile from the ornery miner. A victory indeed, since he typically grumbled the entire time inside her store about it "not bein' right for a female to be runnin' this place like a man."

Then she'd made supper, though she'd come down before eating it to look through the crate of combs and hairbrushes she'd ordered. They were a bit of an experiment to draw more female customers to her store. She'd needed a hammer to pry open the box and she'd found the tool . . . under the ledger.

Tempest leapt up to find the hammer sitting innocently on top of the ledger at the far end of the counter. "Aha." She lifted the tool off the account book and brandished it in the air in triumph. She'd remembered after all.

"Do you greet all of your customers as if you mean to bash them over the head?"

Whirling around, she found a rather nice-looking man standing there, watching her, his hazel eyes lit with a hint of amusement. His blond hair stood attractively on end and his shirtsleeves had been rolled back to reveal muscled forearms.

"Only the impatient ones," she countered in jest.

When his gaze widened in surprise, Tempest blushed. Her scattered brain wasn't the only thing she had to try to rein in. "My apologies. I was simply looking for . . ." She exchanged the hammer for the ledger and waved it as proof. "For this. How may I help you?"

She moved serenely to where he stood opposite the counter. A look of hesitation crossed his handsome face. "I . . . um . . . could use . . ."

"Are you here to work in the mines?" His clothes suggested otherwise, but he might be newly arrived from the East, eager to make a fortune in gold from the Boise Basin.

She'd seen fewer of these men since opening her store last year, but still they came. "My store has everything you need in the way of supplies."

He shook his head. "I'm not a miner. I'm . . ." Stepping forward, he extended his hand. "My name is Bram Wakeman."

Tempest leaned forward to shake his hand. "Tempest Blakely."

"Tempest?" His eyebrows rose along with the corners of his mouth.

She pulled her hand away. "Yes, Tempest," she said with a frown as she began gathering up the strewn papers and receipts from off the counter. She knew what he would say next; she'd heard it all before. Even at twenty-five years old, she still couldn't escape the comments regarding her name.

Is Tempest your real name, not a nickname? It's rather different and unusual, isn't it? What prompted your parents to choose that one?

"I like it." The statement came out definitive, without a hint of insincerity.

She let her mouth drop open before she managed a strangled, "You do?"

"Yes. I like the name." Bram smiled and for a moment Tempest forgot what they'd been discussing. "Or rather, I like the play by that name."

"*The Tempest* by Shakespeare," she said at the same time he did. They both laughed.

"I hadn't thought of it as a first name per se, but it fits you."

Her pleasant shock disappeared at once. "It *fits* me?" She drew herself up to full height—all five feet six inches, though it was nowhere near his tall frame. "And how would you know it fits me? You've only been in my store for five minutes."

"Well, you know." He waved a hand at her as if it were obvious. "The wild hair, the mess on the counter . . ." He had the decency to look embarrassed as he added in a low voice, "Sort of like a tempest?"

She slapped her pile of papers back onto the counter, no longer feeling the need to clear away "her mess." "Perhaps you'd like to find a different mercantile to shop in, Mr. Wakeman. There's another about twelve miles from here. Good day."

"I'm sorry, Miss Blakely." He splayed his hand on the papers and bent forward. "I'm new in town, as of yesterday actually, and I've made a real blunder of my first official introduction. Can you forgive me?"

Those green-brown eyes regarded her with what appeared to be earnestness. And she didn't wish to drive away a paying customer. Business-wise things were going decently, but there was always the niggling fear that running her own store wouldn't work out in the end. Then she'd be forced to return home and throw her lot back in with one of her brothers and their large families. She'd be the pitied spinster aunt once again, spending her days overseeing someone else's children. Tempest shuddered. She liked her nieces and nephews and a part of her still held out hope for having children of her own. And yet she adored her freedom and her store and the life she'd made for herself right here.

"Very well." She offered him half a smile. "You're forgiven."

He dipped his head in a stoic nod, though she detected more relief in his demeanor than he was letting on. "I believe I've decided on what to buy. Do you happen to stock nails?"

She allowed herself to smile fully. "Of course. Which size do you need?" She swept through the opening in the counter to show him where she kept the nails inside a handful of wooden boxes. The various sizes tended to get mixed in with each other, but her customers had never complained about having to pick through several containers to find what they needed.

As he searched for the correct nails, they talked amiably about life in Idaho City, the beauty of the surrounding mountains, and the spring weather. By the time Bram was finished, Tempest had nearly forgotten his remarks about her hair and the scattered papers. It had been years since she'd spoken with a handsome young man who was more interested in talking to her than he was about her family's money.

And she greatly hoped to see more of him. Perhaps even tonight, at the party the Stanburys were hosting. She debated asking him to join them as she rang up his purchase. Would Bram think her forward, or see an invitation as her simply being neighborly?

"Seeing as you're new in town," she said, making a decision, "you might enjoy the musical party my friends Lydia and Calvin Stanbury are throwing this evening. Calvin is the postmaster. It'll be a small affair, but you'll have the opportunity to meet a few more of the townsfolk and enjoy a private performance from a visiting opera singer."

"Are you sure your friend won't mind one more?"

Tempest brushed another unruly curl from her eyes. "Not at all. You'd be more than welcome."

"Then I accept," he said, shooting another warm smile her way. "Thank you."

Pleasure at the thought of seeing him again, and soon, wound through her as she shared the details of the party and then watched Bram exit the store. Her day, and now the upcoming evening, had taken a definitive turn for the better.

Bram charged into the street, heedless of the traffic, his bag of unneeded nails gripped inside his hand. He hadn't expected his competition to be a woman. And certainly not one as passionate and pretty as Tempest Blakely. When she'd leapt up from behind the counter, brandishing that hammer like some fierce Roman goddess, he quite forgot his purpose in entering the store in the first place.

"Watch out," a voice barked.

He reared back at the last minute to avoid colliding face-first with a horse and wagon. Shaking himself to alertness, he nodded apology to the driver and moved at a more sedate pace to the building across the way from the mercantile. Tempest's mercantile. But in a matter of days it wouldn't be the only one serving the people of Idaho City.

Pausing on the sidewalk, Bram locked his hands behind his back and gazed at his wooden building, a sight he felt certain he would never tire of. The sound of hammering rang from inside, where several craftsmen were installing more shelving.

"Do you know what's goin' on with the old saloon?" A scraggly-bearded man who appeared to be in his fifties came to a stop beside Bram.

"It's being renovated," he answered with satisfaction.

The older man's gray eyes lit up. "Renovatin', huh? You gonna put a new saloon in?"

Bram chuckled until he realized the man was serious. "No, it's going to be a mercantile."

"But we already got one." He pointed a thumb over his shoulder at Tempest's store. "Even if it is run by a woman. A body can't never have too many saloons though."

A prick of conscience irritated Bram's excitement at the mention of Tempest and her store. He liked her and was more than pleased to accept her invitation to her friend's party. And yet, he had no intention of changing his plans or making his business anything less than a success. His mercantile would be the greatest in the Boise Basin—it had to be. More than his livelihood and entire life's savings were at stake. His self-respect was too. No one admired a man who'd served as a soldier in the war but hadn't seen a single battle. But a prosperous merchant would command respect wherever he went.

"Sorry to disappoint you, my friend." Bram hoisted the bag of nails and slapped them into his other palm, shooting the old man a grim smile. "But the old mercantile is about to meet her match."

Chapter 2

Tempest knocked on Lydia's door, then smoothed a hand over the waist of her blue silk dress. Her stomach roiled a bit with nerves and excitement. Would Bram come as he'd promised? She shot a surreptitious gaze down the street, but she didn't see him.

The door opened, and Lydia stood there, a warm smile on her face, her blond hair as perfectly coiffed as always. "Tempest, come in. Come in."

Sweeping through the doorway, she embraced Lydia. "I invited one more guest," she said, easing back. "I hope you don't mind."

"Not at all. If she enjoys opera, she is more than welcome." Lydia shut the door and gestured for Tempest to join the knot of guests already assembled in the parlor.

Tempest blushed. "I believe *he* does."

"He?" Her friend whirled around and stared at her with wide, twinkling eyes. "Who? Where?" She linked her arm with Tempest's and guided her to a corner of the room. Ever since

Lydia had married Calvin last year, shortly after Tempest had met her, she'd been intent on matchmaking. But none of the men her friend pointed out to Tempest had stolen her breath or her attention the way Bram had, especially in so short a time.

"Well, he's newly arrived in town." Tempest couldn't keep a smile from pulling at her lips. "And he came into the store earlier today. I was actually looking for my ledger again and I found it under my hammer. So I lifted it and . . ." Her gaze wandered over the faces of Lydia's guests, but it stopped on a now-familiar one. Bram locked eyes with her over the glass of punch he was drinking. Tempest's pulse began to sprint.

"And?" Lydia pressed. "What about the hammer?"

Tempest leaned close to hiss, "He's here."

"Who?" Her friend frowned in confusion, her voice rising. "Who's here?"

"Shh. The man I've been telling you about. He's over there talking to Calvin."

Lydia glanced in the men's direction, but instead of grinning, her consternation increased. "That can't be him."

Tempest turned to face her friend. "But it is. That's Bram Wakeman. I met him earlier today and invited him to the party." She threw another look at Bram. "He's really quite charming and likes the name Tempest, even though he did say it fit me. Something about my hair and the mess I'd made—"

"Tempest," Lydia said in a low voice as she squeezed her arm. "Do you know who Mr. Wakeman is?"

Their conversation was growing more puzzling and irritating by the moment. "Of course I know who he is. He's the man I met today who is new in town and who I invited to come this evening."

"I think you'd better sit down."

"Lydia, what's going on?" she asked as her friend steered

her toward a chair, away from Bram, and practically pushed Tempest into it. She crashed onto the velvet seat with a huff. "What is the matter with Mr. Wakeman and how can you possibly know him?"

Wringing her hands, Lydia shot a glance at the men. "I only met him tonight, but Calvin met him this afternoon. He invited him to the party and Mr. Wakeman said a friend of ours had already invited him. I didn't realize that friend was you."

Tempest shifted in the stiff chair—it had never been her favorite in Lydia's parlor. "I don't understand the problem."

"Did he tell you why he's here in Idaho City?"

She thought back over their conversation, but she couldn't recall Bram explaining his reason for coming to town—only that he was new and not a miner. "No, he didn't. But why ever should that—"

"He's renovating the vacant saloon." Lydia put a consoling hand on Tempest's shoulder. "And he's turning it into a mercantile."

Tempest blinked, certain she hadn't heard right. The town already had a successful mercantile—hers. There was no need for two. "Ar-are you certain? He didn't say a thing . . ."

She moistened her dry lips as a measure of panic crept up her spine. Competition could mean the loss of profits, and a loss of profits could mean the loss of her store, and the loss of her store could mean the loss of her independence, freedom, and solitude. She'd have little choice but to return to living like a permanent houseguest in the home of one of her brothers.

"I'm so sorry," Lydia said, her eyes snapping with the same indignation beginning to smolder deep down inside Tempest. "When Calvin asked about your store as competition, Mr. Wakeman said if Idaho City ended up with only one mercantile again, he strongly hoped it would be his."

Her anger surged from a slow burn to all-out flames. She'd been taken in completely by his handsome looks and appealing manners. And all the while, Bram Wakeman had only been a wolf trussed up like an innocent lamb.

Tempest charged to her feet. "Excuse me, Lydia." She set her sights on Bram's guiltless, smiling face across the room. The nerve of him to accept her invitation...

"What are you doing?"

"Advancing on the enemy."

Bram watched Tempest move through the small crowd with as much deadly force as her name warranted, her brown eyes as cold as frozen leaves. *She knows.* He'd hoped to ease her into a conversation regarding his true reason for coming to town, but it seemed Calvin's wife had beaten him to it.

Swallowing past his suddenly parched throat, as if he hadn't emptied his glass of punch just now, he set the cup down and made his exit from the conversation. He met Tempest halfway through her determined charge. Thankfully she'd left her hammer back at her store.

"You—you snake," she hissed, her cheeks nearly as flushed as her hair in the firelight. "You Benedict Arnold. There I stood making a goose of myself and you going on about how you didn't know what you wanted to buy. I ought to—"

He cut off whatever she felt she ought to do by taking her elbow gently in hand and steering her toward the door. Bram had no wish to cause a scene, especially in front of potential customers. "Let's discuss this elsewhere, shall we?"

"Unhand me, you villainous traitor. You... you..."

"Dastardly scoundrel," he supplied, feeling the truth of every single one of the cutting names.

She looked momentarily surprised that he would join her tirade before her expression hardened again. "Yes, that one works as well. Along with rogue, reprobate, and scalawag."

"Don't forget rascal, rake, and cad."

"And ungentlemanly, dishonest, sneaky . . ."

Each word cut a little deeper and obliterated any hope he'd entertained all day for coming to know Tempest better. But then again, he'd known that wasn't a possibility the moment he'd left her store, hadn't he?

Calvin's wife intercepted them as they reached the doorway, her chin tilted in defiance to him and protection for her friend. "Tempest. Mr. Wakeman. Is everything all right?"

Bram nodded stiffly. "I would simply like to speak with Tempest outside."

"It's all right, Lydia," Tempest said in a limp tone. "I've decided to let the *blackguard* have his say before we never speak to each other again."

Her friend swept aside, allowing them to pass. Bram dropped his hold on Tempest's arm as he slipped out the front door behind her. The instant it closed she spun to face him, her countenance furious. "You were spying on me this morning. Getting the lay of the land before you made your move."

There was no sense in denying it, though it pained him to see the hurt the moon revealed in her eyes. "Yes, I was. And it isn't an excuse, Tempest, but I didn't expect the mercantile to be run by a woman. You took me completely by surprise."

"Then that makes two of us," she countered. "I didn't take you for a cheat when I met you this morning."

"I'm not a cheat," he voiced with conviction. "I had every intention of telling the store's owner that *he* would have some competition and see what was not being offered to the townsfolk that I could supply."

Tempest crossed her arms over her blue dress, one that

emphasized a trim waist and heightened the color of her hair. "And yet you didn't say a word. That is lying by omission, Mr. Wakeman."

"Bram," he urged, wishing to at least keep that tiny piece of familiarity between them. "And you are right. I didn't say a thing." He plucked at his perfectly arranged tie for a bit more air. "And for that I am sorry. I should have told you myself."

"Don't think because I am a woman that I'm going to make this any easier for you." She speared him with her gaze. "This store is my life and I will not let it fail. And so it is you, Bram Wakeman"—she jabbed her finger into his chest—"who will have to bow out."

The smile that began to form on his mouth at her passion died at hearing her words. "And don't think that because I am a man and you are a woman that I won't be just as fierce in making my store a success. I, too, have reasons for needing my venture to prosper."

One eyebrow lifted in a haughty look that made Bram feel as if she were taller and looking down upon him rather than the other way around. "I'm not afraid of a little healthy competition."

"Nor am I."

"Good." She moved to the door and gripped the handle, her wide skirts swinging like a bell around her hips. "Then it will not come as a surprise to you when you're packing up your shelves and boarding up your newly opened store to return to wherever it is you came from."

He thought of the disheveled papers and disorganized shelving he'd observed in her mercantile this morning. She greatly underestimated his natural instincts for order and business and his desire to succeed. "Then let the best storekeeper win."

"Oh, she will," Tempest intoned in an icy voice as she swished her way inside.

Bram took in a great gulp of night air to ease the tension, and regret, lodged in his shoulders and chest. His eyes went to the stars above. They stood as cold and distant as Tempest herself did now. He didn't want to see her livelihood shattered, and yet, he wouldn't back down. He and his store weren't going anywhere.

Chapter 3

"There's another... eight, nine, ten customers." Tempest hugged her arms to her waist as she stared out the mercantile window at the commotion across the street. "If you count the little boy with his mother that makes eleven. And if she buys herself something and him some penny candy, then I would certainly count them both. Perhaps I ought to invest in more kinds of candy." She glanced at the glass jars behind the counter.

Lydia came to stand beside her, her expression compassionate. "Tempest, I know this is difficult. And perhaps it's best not to count the number of people going into Mr. Wakeman's store."

"But I've only had four customers this morning, Lydia. And he"—she motioned toward the other store, where another woman slipped inside—"has had twelve."

Linking her arm with Tempest's, Lydia gently steered her away from the window and back toward her customary spot behind the counter. "It's his grand opening. The townsfolk will likely soon grow tired of the novelty."

"And if they don't?" Tempest plopped onto the stool she used to access the higher shelves, making her skirts puff up around her. A despondency she hadn't felt since before she'd headed west bubbled up as well.

Her friend threw her an empathetic smile. "Then you will deal with that *if* it comes. Calvin and I still plan to only shop here, and I'm sure a great many people in town will continue to do so too."

She hoped Lydia was right, and hope was about all she had in abundance this morning. She'd managed to avoid Bram since the party the week before, but that didn't mean Tempest hadn't kept a keen eye on the goings-on across the street. Each night she'd peeled back the curtains of her two-room apartment above the mercantile and studied her competitor's building. She'd seen the carpenters finish inside, the sign hung above the door, and the display window filled with items. And each night she'd determined not to go down without a proper fight, which meant she had no time for wallowing in self-pity.

Climbing to her feet, she bustled around the counter, then stopped. She spun in a slow circle as she examined her various wares and the full shelves.

"I know that tempestuous look," Lydia said, tempering the teasing statement with a laugh. "What are you planning?"

Tempest put her hands on her hips. "There must be a way to draw his new customers back to my store. What do I sell that he doesn't?"

Lydia shrugged. "I don't know. Shall I go across the street and see?"

"Certainly not," Tempest declared with indignation.

"Would you like to go then?"

She frowned. "Lydia, I'm not going over there."

"Then how will you know what you have that he doesn't?"

Scowling at the shelves before her, Tempest considered the best course of action. "On second thought, yes. Why don't you go over?" Lydia nodded, picked up her hat from off the counter, and pinned it back onto her hair. "Just don't be persuaded by his charm or his merchandise." A ripple of annoyance, mostly directed at herself, accompanied her words. How foolish she'd been to fall for his polite manners and feigned interest.

A glint of humor and determination lit Lydia's blue-gray eyes. "I assure you, I am quite immune to both."

Tempest watched her friend leave, then scooped up a rag with the intention to dust. But after a few swipes at one shelf, she positioned herself in front of the window again. Her current display featured a variety of smaller farming and mining implements. Bram's window display held a rather lovely set of china dishes. Her frown increased, bringing tension to the muscles in her jaw and neck. So much for drawing more female customers to her own store.

The sting of Bram's betrayal pinched her anew, and her eyes swam with tears. Why couldn't he have been forthright when they'd first met? Then she wouldn't have naively believed she'd found a man to be her friend—and maybe, in time, something more. She would have seen him as a competitor then and nothing else.

Pressing a clean corner of her rag to her eyes, Tempest sniffed hard. There was no use wasting tears on a scoundrel like Bram Wakeman. If this was truly war, she had to keep her wits about her.

She returned with full force to her dusting, her curls soon falling back into her eyes. At the jingle of the bells on the door handle, she leapt up from cleaning behind a barrel. She was relieved to see Lydia entering the store. "Well? What did it look like? What is he selling?"

"It looks new," her friend said with a chuckle, "and it's very organized. And most of his customers, as you observed, are the women in town."

"Come to gawk at him or his wares?" Tempest mumbled darkly, causing Lydia to laugh harder.

Her friend's gaze swept the room. "He does seem to be selling quite a number of dishes and fabric. But again, I think the women will come back to one of their own when the newness wears off."

Tempest tapped her finger to her chin. "I can't wait that long. There must be something I have that would reengage their attention . . ."

Whirling around, she marched to the place where she'd set out the new combs and brushes. She picked one up and turned it one way and then the other as the light caught the lovely inlaid ivory. They'd cost her quite a sum to purchase, but she'd felt certain the women of Idaho City would appreciate owning such expensive-looking items.

"I've got it." She grabbed a nearby empty crate and went to the window. Taking everything from the display ledge, she called to Lydia over her shoulder, "Grab a piece of paper and something to write with. I need your perfect penmanship."

She could hear her friend rummaging for the needed articles. "What for?"

"I am going to have a sale, on all things related to women's hair."

Tempest began artfully arranging the combs and brushes while dictating to Lydia what to write. At the last moment she decided to add splashes of color to the display with a few yards of ribbon she'd ordered on a whim.

"Here you are." Lydia handed over the beautifully written sign with the information and price, but her expression showed dismay instead of approval. "I know what you paid for those, Tempest, and you're not charging enough. You'll barely make any money."

A smile lifted her mouth, her first real one in days. "It isn't about the money. I need to remind the townspeople, especially the female ones, that I don't just stock household or mining supplies." She stepped back and surveyed her handiwork with satisfaction. "I can offer them refinement too. And hopefully keep them from returning to the likes of Bram Wakeman."

Something wasn't right. Bram drummed his pencil against the counter and frowned at the numbers he'd finished penning into his meticulous ledger. Yesterday's grand opening had been a success. Customers had been frequent and all of them exclaimed over the new store and its painstaking tidiness. But he'd had far fewer people today than he'd expected. Which made little sense. The novelty of the town's second mercantile shouldn't have tapered off so quickly.

The bells on the door jangled as the old man who'd hoped for another saloon ambled inside. He'd introduced himself yesterday as Potter Seymour.

"Afternoon, Mr. Seymour," Bram called out. "Can I help you with something?"

"Sure, you can let me rest in here instead of outside with that gaggle of women"—he pointed across the street—"causin' a ruckus outside Miss Blakely's store."

Bram came around the counter and went to join the man near the door. Sure enough, he could see a feminine crowd gathered around the display window of Tempest's mercantile.

His uneasiness from moments ago returned full force. "What are they looking at over there?"

"Pshaw." Mr. Seymour waved a condemning hand at the lot. "Goin' on and on about paying pennies for combs and brushes and wee little bits of ribbon. Stuff and nonsense."

Paying pennies? For combs and brushes? The agitation in his gut multiplied. He was supposed to be supplying the town with the finer things in life and not just the staples he'd observed in Tempest's store.

"Will you excuse me, Mr. Seymour?"

Not waiting for the man's reply, Bram exited the store. He paused to let two wagons roll by, and as he did, the group of women parted, giving him a clear view of what had them in such a feverish excitement. Tempest was, indeed, selling fine hair accessories for near pennies.

"Of all the foolish business notions," he muttered as he crossed the street.

She'd be broke in no time, which ought to make him happy. But he didn't feel happy; he felt annoyed. No wonder he hadn't had many customers since yesterday afternoon, few of which had been women. Tempest had cleverly stolen his female customers.

He marched straight past the women into the mercantile, not giving them or the display another look. A line of customers waited for Tempest and her friend Lydia to accommodate them.

Ignoring the wait, Bram strode to the counter and plunked his fist against the worn surface. "You can't possibly make anything on those items, Tempest," he said in a fierce whisper. "You'll be out of business in no time."

"Ah, Mr. Wakeman," she said in a pleasant tone without slowing her movements. He guessed only he, and perhaps Lydia, caught the undercurrent of fierceness in her voice. "How is the new store working out for you?"

"Rather well." He bent toward her. "At least until my competitor decided to try something underhanded."

She slowed long enough to throw him a scolding look. "Not underhanded. I am simply weighing cost against loyalty. Something I'm quite sure you have no knowledge of."

Bram straightened, frustration tightening his jaw. He didn't like to think that Tempest saw him as dishonest or unreliable, and he hated that he cared about her opinion at all. "Apparently you know nothing about me. For I prize loyalty and *common sense* as some of the most important virtues in business."

Coming to a stop before him, the counter acting as a barrier, Tempest glowered at him. "Are you implying that I have no common sense?"

"Those prices would suggest that, yes."

"It's a sale, Mr. Wakeman. Merchants have them all of the time."

The room felt warmer and warmer, and Bram could tell from the corner of his eye that there were several women now watching them. "You are correct, but . . ." He paused to peer directly into her eyes. They were an extraordinary color of golden brown and were a striking combination with her auburn hair. And the green dress she wore fit her figure well, showing off her fluid movements as she practically waltzed about behind the counter, reaching for this or tying up that.

"But . . ." she echoed.

He shook himself back to the present and plucked at his tie. "But what?"

Her soft red lips drooped in a frown. "I don't know what. You said I was correct, but . . ."

"Yes." He desperately searched his mind for what he'd been saying before foolishly getting caught up in her gaze. "You are correct about the sale, but you have also laid down a challenge. And you should know, I never back down from a challenge."

"Oh, good." She smiled, though the gesture held little warmth. Which was a pity. He'd rather enjoyed her real smiles the day they'd met. "I'd hoped this business between us wouldn't be boring."

He gave her a grim smile in return. "It certainly won't be. Good day, Tempest."

"Good day, *Mr. Wakeman.*"

Turning on his heel, he moved with purpose toward the door. He could just as easily host a sale as Tempest had. Though he'd need to be strategic about what items to sell at cheaper prices. With any luck, he'd pull his straying customers back to his door.

As he stalked to his side of the street, a plume of guilt uncurled inside him. *It can't be helped, Lord,* he reasoned in silent prayer. *You know what this store means to me. And we both know, I won't give up easily.*

The next three weeks passed in a blur of exhaustion for Tempest. True to his word, Bram had countered her sale with one of his own. It required more energy than she would have suspected to stay ahead of her competitor. Each night she found herself almost too sleepy to finish eating her supper, but she slept fitfully, her worries and the troubling numbers in her ledger invading her dreams.

In spite of a steady stream of people coming into the mercantile, she'd noticed a decline in the number of staple supplies she was selling. Most of her customers seemed to be buying more of the items she'd discounted than basic necessities. Were they purchasing those from Bram's store instead of hers?

She'd been inside his store several times now. The first to see what had so many of the townsfolk clucking. Tempest had to admit the place was rather nice with its highly polished floor and counter and the smell of new paint and leather. After that she'd gone over twice more, to retaliate at Bram for sneaking into her store when it was busy and imposing his idea of order onto the way she arranged things. She'd gotten even by meddling with his alphabetized system. And had rather enjoyed sticking the pickles by the apples and the garden implements with the bags of sugar.

Now it was Sunday again, the third one since Bram's unfortunate arrival in town. Tempest yawned and sat up in bed to stretch. She didn't need to look in the mirror to know that if she didn't get more sleep soon, she'd have permanent dark patches beneath her eyes.

She swung her feet out of bed and started to rise before sinking back down. The temptation to remain home and slip back beneath her warm blankets held her captive for a moment. It would be so nice to rest, to pretend Bram, his store, and everything associated with both didn't exist. But she wouldn't beat him by staying in bed and she wouldn't miss church. Her parents had raised her and her brothers to be God-loving, Sunday-service-attending people. Of course they'd also raised the four of them to be compassionate, honest, and worthy of respect too.

A needle of guilt pierced her fatigue. Could she really call her actions of the last few weeks respectful or compassionate? Tempest let the question pinch a moment before pushing it aside. Her store meant everything to her. She would not give up living on her own or supporting herself. She would remain independent and fulfilled.

Satisfied with herself once more, she dressed in a soft brown dress that nearly matched her eyes and ate a quick breakfast. Morning sunshine lit up the streets and surrounding mountain pines as she walked to church. The grip of winter had begun to loosen on the town. Wildflowers were pushing their way up through the dirt and the chortle of birdsong filled the air.

Lydia and Calvin met her outside the church building, and she took her customary seat beside them in their pew. Behind and to her right, she caught sight of Bram already seated and waiting for the service to begin. He looked rather dashing in his dark suit.

Just remember, she chided herself, *that handsome physique hides a black heart.*

The organist began to play and Tempest turned her attention forward. As the service wore on and the temperature in the room rose, she found herself growing increasingly sleepy. She fanned her face with her hand to stay awake, wishing she was sitting closer to one of the open windows.

"Are you all right?" Lydia asked in a whisper.

Tempest nodded. "Just warm and a little tired." Her friend squeezed her free hand in a comforting gesture. Once the pastor's sermon ended, she could return to her room above the store, hopefully for a much-needed nap. Then she'd go to her friend's later and help Lydia and her cook prepare a delicious Sunday supper . . .

"Love your enemies, do good to them who despitefully use you and persecute you . . ."

The words pricked Tempest's thoughts, and she jerked upright as if she'd been stuck in the backside with a straight pin. Lydia shot her a concerned frown, which she waved off.

What are you saying, Lord?

The pastor laid his Bible on the stand before him and let his kind gaze sweep the audience. Tempest thought his eyes lingered on hers a moment longer than on anyone else's.

"Now, I don't believe that God is saying when we love our enemies that we condone violent acts. What I do believe he's saying is, 'That person who's offended you? Who's gossiped about you? Who's *wronged* you? Well, isn't that the person you've deemed to be your enemy?'"

Tempest squirmed in her seat, increasing the fanning action of her hand. Her cheeks felt twice as hot now.

"Isn't that the person God is asking you to love the most?" The entire congregation sat in silence, the pastor's voice rolling over them like a wave of quiet strength. "To choose not to take offense by their actions, however unkind, and remember they too are children of our God. What you're really seeing is their hurt and fear. That's what's spilling out in the offense, in the gossip, in the wrongdoings."

He paused and offered them a gentle smile. "What you need to remember then is that the second commandment is we love our neighbors as ourselves. So go spend some time with God and rediscover His love for you and your love for yourself. And then"—he waggled a finger at them for emphasis—"go show that love to your neighbor, to your enemy."

Flicking a glance over her shoulder, Tempest found Bram looking her way. Was he also thinking of them and their fierce competition in light of the pastor's words? She couldn't be sure. A frown formed on his mouth and he lowered his chin. She faced forward again, her mind swirling with thoughts.

She'd deemed Bram as her enemy—and had felt completely justified in the act. After all, he'd intruded into her life and her store. And yet if she was supposed to love her enemies, then that would most certainly include Bram Wakeman. She thought of her actions since his arrival and felt her heart squeeze with greater guilt. She'd been petty and vindictive and hadn't wasted much thought on what she was really doing until this morning.

The service ended and Tempest quickly excused herself, assuring Lydia that she was indeed fine and would be by later. Outside she drew in a deep breath of the fresh air and blew it out slowly. Catching sight of Bram coming down the church steps behind her, she hurried away from the building. She wasn't ready to see or speak to him yet. Not when she had some inward wrestling to do.

Back in her room above the store, she pulled her Bible from a nearby table and blew off the light coating of dust. She sat in her rocking chair and found the scriptures the pastor had referenced. Tempest read them through several times, and each time she felt greater regret for her actions and greater hope for change.

She'd taken Bram's presence here as a personal affront to her own dreams and ambitions. And while she still wasn't certain the town could support two mercantiles long-term, she could understand how badly he wanted to succeed, just as she did.

"What do I do then, Lord?" She didn't feel right about simply giving up or giving in. That wasn't what the pastor meant. To help her store continue to thrive, she still had to work hard and invite her customers to return again and again.

She flipped the pages of the Bible until she located the scripture in Ecclesiastes that had brought her comfort before she'd finally decided to head west on her own. "To every thing there is a season and a time to every purpose under the heaven," she read out loud.

She believed that truth, which meant there must be a purpose to this new and challenging "season" she was experiencing with Bram and his store. And even if she couldn't decipher what the purpose might be, she wanted to act with greater compassion and integrity from now on.

And I can do that best by not ruining Bram's attempts at

success. Their goals weren't likely to ever match up—not when they both desired to have the most successful mercantile in Idaho City—but she could respect his tenacity and no longer treat him as an enemy.

Her mind at peace, she couldn't keep her eyes open any longer. She shut them, along with the Bible, and blew out a soft sigh. And for the first time in weeks, she easily, and peacefully, drifted off.

Chapter 4

Bram couldn't get yesterday's sermon out of his mind. It couldn't be more applicable to anyone in the congregation than himself. He'd acted abominably toward Tempest and certainly not as the gentleman he'd been raised to be. Shouldering another sack of flour from the delivery cart, he carried the load into his store and dropped it onto the burgeoning pile. Then he returned for the final sack.

What to do now was still a matter of debate for him. He wouldn't give up his store, and he knew for certain Tempest wouldn't be giving up hers either. If only their clientele were different. But those who frequented Tempest's mercantile were largely the same people he needed to come to his. Could they agree in a way to disagree? To both simply operate their stores the best they could and suspend with the battling behavior?

He had noticed Tempest's display window featured a new sign this morning. It was for the same items as the week before but for a slightly higher price. It could be a good omen, though he didn't flatter himself into believing he was no longer on her blacklist.

For all of their competition, he liked Tempest and wanted her to think well of him. She was far savvier as a business owner than most, even if she tended toward disorganization. And he hoped to earn her respect as he hadn't yet done. He pictured how she'd looked yesterday in church, her determined demeanor softened by the open quality of her expression during the sermon and the brown dress that matched her eyes.

He was so lost in his thoughts that he didn't realize the flour stack had started to slip until it was too late. Scrambling to lower the sack in his hands as well as catch the others in the pile from sliding forward, Bram ended up kneeling in several inches of flour from three split bags.

"Oh, my," an older woman tsked from the other side of the store. She wasn't the only customer either. He felt the eyes of several others on him as he surveyed the damage.

Brushing flour from his shirt and pants, he swallowed the bite of disappointment at the ruined merchandise. There was nothing to do but clean it up.

A knock sounded on the door he'd left open for ease of transferring the sacks inside. Bram looked up and frowned when he saw Tempest standing there.

"Is everything all right? I saw a cloud of white billowing out the door just now."

He stood, gesturing at the mess near his feet. "Come to gloat?"

Her chin tipped higher, and yet her golden-brown eyes held nothing but open curiosity and compassion. "On the contrary, I'm here to help, if I may."

"Help?" he echoed in surprise.

She ignored his bewilderment. "Do you have a broom

and a dustpan? I'll clean this up while you tend to your customers." She waved at the counter, where several ladies were already waiting to pay for their purchases.

"You ... will?" His confusion and disbelief were beginning to give way to genuine gratitude.

"The broom?"

"Right," he said, nodding. He thumbed his finger at the storage room. "It's in there. I can get it if you like."

She smiled, a slow smile that made his heart expand. "I can manage. You go attend to your customers."

"What about yours?"

"Lydia is helping out for the moment." As she brushed past him toward the storage room, he caught a scent of wildflowers. It fit her perfectly. "They'll be fine."

Bram went to stand behind the counter to assist his store patrons. By the time he finished with them and helped another couple who came inside, he could see Tempest had the entire flour mess cleared away. She put the broom and dustpan back, then met him near the door.

"Thank you, Tempest," he said with every ounce of sincerity he could muster.

A pretty blush painted her cheeks. "You're welcome. After yesterday's sermon, I've been thinking . . ." She glanced down at her hands, appearing embarrassed.

"I've been thinking too."

She lifted her head. "You have?"

He smiled. "Yes, and I'd like to call an end to this little war."

Tempest laughed. It was a sound as wild and bright as her hair. Bram liked it, even felt eager to prompt it again. "Agreed." Her expression changed to one of somberness though. "I'm still going to keep my store open."

"As will I." He locked his gaze with hers and was relieved

to see understanding there. They could, hopefully, be friends, even if neither of them ever acquiesced their dream of a successful mercantile.

"I should be going." She moved to the door. "Good day, Bram."

"Tempest?" he called after her, an idea beginning to take shape in his mind.

She spun around as if she'd been waiting for him to say something more. "Yes?"

"I would like to repay you for your help."

Her eyes began to narrow. "That isn't wh—"

"Please. No strings attached. It's simply an expression of gratitude."

He watched the features of her pretty face relax. "Such as?"

"Would you agree to accompany me to the opera tomorrow night?"

She blinked in apparent shock at the invitation. It was the same emotion racing through him at that moment. What had compelled him to invite her to do something that smacked of "courtship"? He wasn't courting Tempest. There was no point. They'd both stated their positions. It was merely a chance to express his gratitude and possibly get to know her a little better too. Nothing more.

"I would like that." She offered him another smile, though this time the gesture held a trace of shyness, something he hadn't seen in her before. "Thank you, Bram."

"Thank *you,*" he said as she swept out the door. As he repositioned the stack of flour bags to prevent another spill, he found himself whistling.

"You're going to the opera with whom?"

Tempest rolled her eyes. "You heard me, Lydia. Bram Wakeman and I are going to the opera tonight."

"But why?" Lydia blocked her way to the bureau mirror.

"Because I helped him yesterday and he asked if he could thank me by joining him for tonight's performance."

Lydia frowned and stepped aside. "Are you certain this is a good idea? He isn't going to give up his store for you."

Tempest laughed and stuck some more pins into her artful hair arrangement. She'd taken more time than usual to wrestle it into submission. Not that it meant anything. She was simply anxious to achieve the higher standards going to an opera warranted. "Of course he isn't. And I won't give up mine for him. It isn't as if we're courting, Lydia. It's a friendly outing between colleagues, so to speak."

Lydia's arched look conveyed plenty without her uttering a single word.

"I'm not entering the lion's den," Tempest defended. "And besides, this is what the pastor was talking about on Sunday. About us loving our enemies and setting aside our offenses and wrongdoings."

"Don't you think you might be taking the *love* part a bit too far in this case?" Her eyebrows rose along with her smiling lips.

Whirling around, Tempest stared at her friend in irritated shock. "That is certainly not true. My intentions and Bram's are of a friendly, business-minded nature. That is all."

"Forgive me." Lydia took up her hand and squeezed it. "I presume too much."

"Yes, you do." But Tempest still cherished her friendship.

"I'm only concerned. I don't want to see you hurt by him again."

Tempest embraced her. "I understand. And I'll be fine. Now, how do I look?" She fell back a step and twirled in a circle to give her friend a full view of her cream-colored dress.

"Picture perfect." Lydia threw her a kind smile.

Tempest put on her gloves and hat and followed Lydia down the stairs and through the empty store. Slipping out the door, she locked it behind them. Bram stepped away from his door when he saw her.

"Enjoy your evening," Lydia said before waving to Bram and striding off toward home.

Tempest waited for him to cross the street, her stomach suddenly aflutter with nervousness. He looked every inch the handsome gentleman, and she was grateful she'd chosen one of her best dresses for tonight.

"I thought she hated me," he said, inclining his hat in Lydia's direction as he joined Tempest.

"No," she said with a laugh. "She may have strongly disliked you, on my behalf. But Lydia has never hated anyone."

He motioned for her to begin walking. "Have you known her long?"

"A year. She was one of the first people to come into my store when it first opened."

"You've only been here a year?" His tone revealed his surprise.

Tempest nodded. "And one month."

"You seem so established. I thought you'd been here longer." He took her elbow in hand to help her around a stack of crates, increasing the rapid trembling in her middle. "Where did you live before you came here?"

"New York—that's where my family still lives. During the war my widowed mother and I spent time with each of my brothers' families to assist my sisters-in-law." She pushed out a sigh as the cloistered feeling of the past rose inside her. "Once my brothers all, miraculously, returned home though, I felt restless and eager to do something for myself."

Bram fixed her with an understanding look that both surprised and pleased her. Even her own brothers had questioned her judgment right up until she'd left. They had softened their stance in their letters over the last year, though she suspected they still didn't fully comprehend her determination. "So you came out here and made a name for yourself with your store."

It was a statement, but she nodded just the same. "I did, and I've loved every minute of it. Even the ones when I'm not quite sure how the numbers will all work out."

"I can relate to that," he said with a chuckle.

"And you?" she prompted. "Where are you from? Did you serve in the war?"

His open, kind expression vanished, replaced by tense lines around his eyes and mouth. "I'm from the West, and yes, I was a soldier. But I didn't serve in the war as your brothers did."

Tempest stopped walking and turned to peer directly at him. "If you were a soldier, then you did serve."

Looking away, he pocketed his hands. "It isn't the same. You're not a real soldier in most people's eyes if you never saw or fought in a battle." He visibly swallowed. "They sort of look down their noses at you, even if they didn't fight themselves."

She boldly placed her hand on his sleeve until he returned his gaze to hers. "That isn't easy to swallow—the ill opinions of others. I understand that difficulty all too well. And yet . . ." Should she go on?

"And yet?" Bram repeated.

"Like the pastor said on Sunday, perhaps that's their own hurt. Maybe they feel less for having not even been a soldier or helped with the war in any way."

After a moment, he dipped his head in a slow nod, the guarded quality fleeing his face. "Perhaps you're right."

"Is that why you want your store to succeed?" she asked with sudden understanding.

"Yes." Bram shot her a humorless smile. "Apparently we both have strong reasons for succeeding with our ventures, don't we?"

Instead of answering, Tempest began walking again. A feeling of melancholy washed over her. She'd never been so honest with a man and felt that honesty returned. And yet, Bram had explained it perfectly. They both had compelling motives for digging in their heels and making their stores the best in the town.

He caught up with her. "Did I say something wrong?"

Should she tell him what she was really thinking? That after ten minutes in his company tonight, with their battle-axes set aside, she wanted to know everything about him. And share everything about herself in return.

But there was no point in saying it and no point in pursuing such a course. It would only lead to one or both of them giving up their dream and independence. For so long, she'd wanted love and a family of her own. When she realized those weren't likely to be hers, she'd turned her focus to other pursuits and fulfillments. To unbury such wishes now, on the thin chance of something happening between her and Bram, would be too painful.

"No, Bram." She gave him a full and sincere smile. "You said nothing wrong." He'd simply spoken the truth.

"If you're sure..."

"Yes," she said emphatically, linking her arm through his, "let's enjoy our night at the opera."

The tops of the dark pine trees stretched toward the stars as Bram walked Tempest back to her store. He'd liked the opera, though he was grateful she hadn't asked him his favorite parts. He was content to let her share what she thought of the costumes and the story.

Honestly he couldn't recall details of either. His attention throughout the night had been snagged again and again by Tempest. It wasn't just that she looked extraordinary in her ivory dress with her hair pinned up off her neck. It was the expanding feeling in his chest the longer he spent in her presence. Now that they'd agreed to end the war between them, he'd quickly come to see what a compassionate heart she possessed, even as he still admired her fierceness and passion. Her own brothers had fought in the war, and yet she hadn't condemned or belittled him for his own innocuous role. For the first time since he'd stopped being a soldier, Bram felt heard and understood. Such a thing was a new and intriguing emotion for him.

"Did you like it?" Tempest asked when they stopped beside her door. "I've been prattling on about what I liked and haven't stopped to ask you what you enjoyed." Her light laugh coaxed a smile from him.

"I rather like your prattling."

He meant it in earnest, but he realized she'd mistaken the remark for teasing when her eyes widened and she ducked her chin.

"I know I jabber on—like a tempest, a whirlwind, my brothers would say. But I am—"

Lifting her chin upward, he gazed into those lovely eyes of hers that appeared deep and dark in the moonlight. "I meant nothing unkind, Tempest. I really do enjoy listening to you talk."

"Thank you," she half whispered.

She said nothing more and Bram found his focus drawn to her slightly parted lips. Kissing her would likely be as energetic and full of feeling as the woman herself.

An image entered his mind of a storm he'd witnessed once where even the great trees had bent to its wild strength. Asking her for a kiss, when there could be no promises between them, would be like asking the wind to give up its independence and force. He'd been given a glimpse tonight of Tempest's deep determination and fulfillment when it came to her store. It was nearly identical to what he felt for his. And he suspected neither of them wished to relinquish that newfound freedom, even if they were now getting on quite well.

He released her chin, instantly missing the feel of her soft skin beneath his fingertips, and stepped back. "I very much enjoyed the evening. Thank you for coming with me, Tempest. And for helping me earlier with the mess."

"You're welcome," she said, giving him a tremulous smile. "I very much enjoyed the evening too. Good night, Bram."

Nodding good night, he waited for her to let herself inside before he crossed the street to his own building. He made his way through the shadowed store to the stairs and up to his room, where he lit a lamp. A glance out the curtains revealed a light glowing from Tempest's room as well.

Was he content to keep living a life that felt a bit like his store just now, he wondered as he sat on the bed and removed his tie. One that was empty and silent?

Since meeting Tempest, it was as if a bright light had burst into his quiet, ordered existence. But he couldn't have her and his store, could he? After what he'd learned tonight, he felt confident she wouldn't easily give up her independence for him. And while he felt a new appeal at marrying someone, especially someone as vivacious and passionate as Tempest, there was also the fear that he would never be someone great or respected if he chose that path too soon. Maybe in a few more years . . .

He tried to take some solace from that last thought as he prepared for bed and voiced his prayers, including gratitude for Tempest's friendship. But deep down he couldn't shake the realization that no matter what, his store would never, ever be his friend. Or love and respect him back.

Chapter 5

A WEEK LATER Tempest woke with a headache and a nasty cold. It had been slowly creeping up on her for several days, but she'd ignored it, choosing instead to focus on running her store and going for walks in the evenings with Bram. She relished his company and friendship, but despite continued teasing from Lydia, she knew there was nothing more between them. There couldn't be. Still, that didn't mean she couldn't enjoy walking and talking with a handsome, congenial gentleman like Bram Wakeman.

The room spun as she tried to sit up, and she placed a hand to her forehead with a moan. She couldn't afford to keep the store closed—not for a whole day. The numbers in her ledger were still troubling, though she had hope she could hang on a while longer. But an entire day without purchases would be too much of a setback.

Fatigue washed over her anew, and she collapsed back onto her pillow. Perhaps she could simply open a little later than usual. Clinging to that plan, she drifted off.

Sometime later a loud rapping at the store door jerked her awake. Tempest scrambled up, her head and heart pounding. She managed to get to her feet, throw a shawl around her nightdress, and start slowly down the stairs. The incessant knocking battled with the pain in her skull. She paused beside the counter to catch her breath, then pressed on. She could see a tall male figure through the glass in the door. Hopefully whoever the customer turned out to be, he wouldn't mind waiting a little longer while she returned upstairs to dress. Though the thought of climbing the stairs and wrestling into her petticoat and dress felt as long and difficult as a hike up the mountains would be in her present condition.

She opened the door a crack and drew in a sharp breath when she realized Bram stood there, looking agitated.

Dispensing with any greeting, he explained his presence at her door. "You didn't switch your sign to open earlier and I started to wonder if something was amiss." His eyes went wide when she opened the door a little farther and he saw her attire. "I was right. What's wrong?"

"Nothing that won't be better soon, I'm sure." She gritted her teeth against another wave of dizziness and gripped the door frame tighter. "I wasn't feeling well, so I decided I'd sleep in before I opened the store. I'm actually going back up to dress now."

"You don't look well enough for that."

She released her hold on the door and stepped back, waving away his concern. "I'll be just ... fine ..." But her knees wouldn't hold her up any longer. She began to crumble to the floor, when Bram leapt forward and grabbed her arm.

"Tempest, you're not well. You can't possibly stand at the counter all day when you can't even stand here."

Desperation crawled up her throat and spilled over into unshed tears. "I have to," she rasped out. "I can't afford to close the store today."

Before she knew what he was doing, Bram scooped her up into his arms. "You don't have to," he said, carrying her toward the stairs.

Her head felt so heavy, she gave into the urge to rest it against his shoulder. "But I have to, Bram. I have to."

"All you have to do today is rest," he soothed in her ear. "Because I'm going to manage your store today."

Tempest jerked her head up, then bit her lip against the ache such a motion caused. "B-but you can't do that. Who will watch your store?"

He slowed to navigate the stairs, making sure to keep her feet from bumping into the wall. "No one. Mine is new enough that I can afford to close it for one day."

She wanted to protest further, and yet she had no energy to do so, and the fog in her head made thinking up more arguments difficult.

When he reached her rooms at the top of the stairs, he carried her into the second and set her on her bed. "Get some more rest. I'll send a message to Lydia to come check on you."

He'd never looked more handsome to her than he did in this moment, even with the worry etched on his face. She ought to feel mortified at him seeing her in her nightclothes and with her wild, curly hair untamed. But she couldn't muster up any embarrassment. Instead, she felt only gratitude and an irrational hope that she might one day be cradled in his arms again.

Her cheeks flushed at her errant thoughts, but she hoped Bram would think it was her fever instead. "The ledger to note purchases and orders is under the counter."

He nodded and moved back through the doorway into her tiny parlor and kitchen. "Don't worry about a thing."

"Bram?" she called.

Turning, he waited for her to speak.

"I don't know what to say other than thank you for your help."

"My pleasure," he said, his mouth hiking up in a smile. And Tempest couldn't help thinking that smile might be the best medicine of all.

Bram snagged another bite of the sandwich Lydia had given him and recorded the purchases of the man who'd just exited the store. The last few hours had been rather busy, and he guessed some of that had to do with his store being closed. Anyone who wanted things from a mercantile had to get them from Tempest's today. It made him wonder how well she had done since he'd set up shop four weeks earlier.

Pushing the question aside, he dusted the counter and straightened the candy jars. Finally his curiosity got the better of him. He opened the ledger again and flipped through several of the pages, noting the daily and weekly totals before his store had opened. Then he carefully reviewed the numbers for the weeks since he'd come to town.

He frowned when he reached the page for the day before and closed the ledger. The numbers told the truth he'd been ignoring since taking Tempest to the opera a week ago. His store was mining profits from hers, and the longer his stayed open, the more hers dropped in income.

The sound of someone coming down the stairs reached his ears. It was too sure-footed to be Tempest, so he suspected it must be Lydia, who'd gone up an hour earlier.

Sure enough Tempest's best friend descended the stairs. She offered him the same kind smile she had when she'd come into the store.

"How is she?" Bram asked.

"She's resting again." Lydia came to stand opposite the

counter from him, setting her gloves and hat on its smooth surface. "She did eat well just now and managed to drink some herbal tea for her sore throat. I think she'll be on the mend tonight or tomorrow."

He nodded. "I'm glad to hear it."

"She was fretting about the store, but I told her it was in good hands."

"Thank you."

Lydia put on her hat. "It's me who must thank you. I misjudged you and I apologize." She pulled on her gloves. "What you're doing today for Tempest goes beyond gentlemanly behavior or neighborly kindness."

He chose not to respond to the not-so-subtle hint behind her words. His feelings for Tempest had grown immensely the last week, as they'd taken their evening walks and talked, but he needed to sort out those emotions before he voiced them to anyone else. "I gave you reason to misjudge me by not being honest with Tempest that first day, and for that, I am sorry."

"I'll check on her again at supper," she said, stepping toward the door.

"Has she told you how her store is really doing?"

Lydia turned back, her mouth turned down in a frown. "Not really. Why do you ask?"

"I looked through her ledger just now," he confessed, tapping a knuckle against the book. "There seemed to be a greater number of customers in here today, and I wanted to confirm a hunch I had regarding the reason."

Her gaze widened in understanding. "It's because your store is closed today, isn't it?"

"Yes," he answered simply and truthfully.

Bram wished it wasn't so. He was also grateful that Tempest's friend studied him with no condemnation in her expression. Neither Tempest nor Lydia nor her husband judged him for his minor role in the war. Instead they took his measure from his character, his honesty, and his actions. The realization poured through him with force and thankfulness, soothing his troubled heart. Was this why he'd felt the Lord nudging him to build a new life here? Not to find success solely in his store, but more importantly, in his relationships?

"I'm going to tell her I looked through her ledger."

Lydia dipped her head in a nod. "I think that's wise and truthful of you. What will you do after that?"

He sensed she meant much more in the question than merely relaying information to Tempest. "I'm not sure exactly," he said with a chuckle. "And that's rather new for me."

Her smile buoyed him up as a sister's would. "You'll figure it out, Mr. Wakeman. As we all must." She moved toward the door, where she paused to add, "And for me that usually starts on my knees."

Brushing a curl from her eyes, Tempest eyed the numbers in her ledger once more before setting her pencil down. Things didn't look good. With a weary sigh, she sat on her stool. She'd been well for four days, though she still felt tired after a whole day on her feet. The darkness outside the store and the shadows within pushed at her small circle of lamplight. The rest of the town was likely sleeping.

Bram had confessed to looking at her ledger, and she didn't blame him. She didn't think she could work in his store and record numbers in his log without taking a peek at some of the other pages. But she hadn't quite believed what he'd told her about his store stripping profits from hers. Now, after having his store open again for a few days, she'd seen what she hadn't wanted to acknowledge. Her mercantile was, indeed, on a steady decline. She could likely eek by for another few months, but there was no guarantee she would last that long. The newness of Bram's store would wear off completely, and yet she didn't know if she would be able to sustain business until then.

She offered the same prayer she had so often over the last five weeks. *What should I do, Lord?* She propped her arm on the counter and rested her forehead in her palm. An image of Bram's warm hazel eyes and genuine smile filled her thoughts. *I meant about the store.* Tempest chuckled, the sound echoing in the silence. *Though I suppose I need to know what to do regarding him too.*

Something had shifted between her and Bram since he'd come to her aid when she was sick. She felt it in her renewed energy when she saw him crossing the street to join her for their evening stroll. She felt it in the way her heart pulsed faster when their hands brushed as they walked. She felt it in the way her soul stirred at their shared conversations and mutual regard for the other's thoughts and perceptions. The one topic they largely avoided was about their respective stores.

Tempest lifted her head to gaze at the familiar, organized chaos around her. This place symbolized more than her livelihood—it represented her independence and her ability to make a life for herself. And she'd certainly accomplished that, whether her brothers recognized that or not. She, a woman all on her own, had opened and successfully operated a mercantile for more than a year. She'd also come to love this town and its people.

Including Bram?

"No," she told herself aloud as she shot to her feet and grabbed the lamp. She couldn't love him . . . could she? They'd known each other less than two months, and half that time they'd spent competing against each other.

She started up the stairs, turning the question over in her mind. There was so much she did love about him though—his kindness, his humility, his bursts of humor. Did that mean she loved *him?*

The answer came as softly as a kitten nudging at her heels. *I do love him.*

Tempest stopped halfway up the stairs and leaned back against the wall—the very one Bram had worked so hard not to bump her feet against when he'd gently carried her. She probably ought to sell her store, and soon, if she hoped to get a decent price for it. And yet, she couldn't imagine not seeing Bram anymore, of not living across the street from him. She wanted him in her life tomorrow and the day after that and on and on through the years.

"Is there a way to have both?" she half prayed, half hoped.

If she sold her goods to Bram and the building to someone else, she would have enough to stay in town for a time. Surely long enough to see if he felt more than friendship for her, especially once her store ceased to be a deterrent to a long-term relationship between them.

Determined to move forward with her plan, she continued up the stairs. She set her lamp down and readied for bed. Right before climbing beneath the covers, she caught the distinct smell of smoke. Perhaps she hadn't properly stoked the fire from supper.

She checked the stove in her kitchen area, but there was nothing inside except cold ashes. Perhaps it was the downstairs stove. Not bothering with the lamp, she descended the stairs to check the stove inside her store. It appeared as cold and lifeless as the other one. And yet, she could still smell smoke.

The muffled sound of shouting reached her ears, and Tempest hurried to peer out the display window. Her shocked cry shattered the quiet of the empty store, and for a moment she couldn't move as she stared in horror at the scene before her. Fire rose from the roofs of several of the buildings down the street, including the post office. In the reddish glow, she could see people doing what they could to fight the blaze. Surely Lydia and Calvin were among them, and that was where she should be.

Tempest rushed back upstairs and changed from her nightgown into an old work dress. She exited her store, sucking in a sharp gasp as a wave of heat engulfed her. Would they be able to stop the angry beast before it devoured most of the town? She'd heard Lydia, Calvin and other townspeople talk about the fire two years earlier that had consumed so many buildings.

"Tempest!"

She looked toward Bram's store to find him approaching her at a run. The sight of him brought an instant measure of courage. "It's already spread to the post office," she exclaimed.

"Then let's see what we can do."

Giving him a grim smile of gratitude, Tempest matched his racing footsteps down the street. The fire brigade was already on hand, but the post office's roof was still ablaze.

"Lydia," she cried out when she and Bram found her friend among those passing buckets of water up the line of people to the burning building. "What can we do?"

Her friend's smudged cheeks were streaked with what Tempest guessed were tears. Farther up the line Calvin dumped water onto the fire. "We're doing everything we can, but it might not . . ." She visibly swallowed. "It might not be enough. What about your stores?"

Bram answered, "Neither one has caught fire yet."

"Oh, thank goodness." She took the next full bucket,

tipping her head in the direction they'd just come. "Go keep them that way."

"Are you sure?" Tempest wanted to stay and offer comfort somehow. But Bram gently guided her back up the street.

"She's right," he said kindly. "We've got to take precautions."

"How?"

"Get every sheet and blanket and sack that you have, and meet me out front of your store."

Tempest ground her feet to a stop. "What about your roof?"

"We'll get to it second."

"Bram?" she protested. She appreciated his help, but he would need some too.

He urged her forward again, his expression full of resolve. "We've got to hurry, before it's too late for either one."

CHAPTER 6

HE'D NEVER FELT so warm. Sweat dripped into Bram's eyes and down his neck as he placed another wet sack on his store's roof. In the light from the nearby fire, he could see Tempest's damp hair clinging to her temples. Across the street her roof resembled a patchwork quilt with its hodgepodge of color and cloth.

"That's the last one," she announced, resting back on her heels. "Do you think it will do the trick?"

"I hope so." Bram pushed out a sigh. His muscles felt cramped and sore from kneeling on a second rooftop, but he didn't regret his decision to help Tempest with her store first. The thought of her losing her mercantile and disappearing from his life had prompted his decision earlier. If he lost his store, so be it. He wouldn't stand by and see Tempest lose hers too.

"What do we do now, Bram?"

He eyed the blazing rooftops down the street. "We wait . . . and we pray."

A hint of a smile lifted her lips. "I've been doing the second one already."

"Me too," he admitted with a half smile of his own. "We probably ought to get down." Offering her his hand, he guided her to the edge of the roof, where he'd placed his ladder in the alley beside his store.

Tempest climbed down first and he followed. "I think we work quite well together." She gestured to the roof above.

Her words matched the thoughts he'd had since she'd been sick. "We do."

Bram reached out and rubbed a smudge of ash from her cheek. There was no one else he preferred working beside like this. Or talking to. Or laughing with. No other woman he loved like this.

He'd come to a decision just the day before to ask Tempest to partner with him and join their stores. If she didn't love him as he did her, then he would accept a marriage of convenience with her and hope in time his feelings would be shared.

"What is it?" She studied him, her head cocked to the side.

Lifting his hand to cup her neck, he tugged her gently forward. "You are beautiful, Tempest," he murmured, "inside and out. And I would very much like to kiss you."

"Then I think you should," she murmured.

His timing might be off, given the fire and the fact that their stores might not survive, but he didn't want to wait another moment without giving her a glimpse into his feelings. He captured her lips and poured his gratitude and love into the kiss. And Tempest ardently kissed him back.

A cry from beyond the alley had him stepping back. Bram saw a man gesturing toward the fire. Was it in relief or terror?

"Come on," he said, reaching for her hand again. "Let's see what else we can do to help."

They emerged onto the street to see the fire's greediness had slowed, though not stopped altogether. "We can assist with one of the bucket brigades," Tempest said. Bram nodded agreement.

For what felt like several more hours, they passed buckets up the line. At last, flames no longer rose to the sky. Now there was only smoke and ash and the blackened shells of several buildings, including the post office.

Bram joined Tempest where she sat beside Lydia at the edge of the boardwalk, both women's faces dotted with soot.

"I'm so sorry we couldn't save it, Lydia." Tempest placed her arm around her friend's shoulders. "How are you and Calvin holding up?"

Lydia sniffed and wiped at her eyes with the back of her hand. "We'll be all right. Especially once we build a new building."

"You won't have to build a new building," Tempest said, her voice full of conviction.

"Why ever not?" Lydia asked, voicing the same question running through Bram's head.

Tempest lowered her arm to face Lydia directly. "Because I'm giving you my building."

"What?" he and Lydia exclaimed at the same time.

Looking a little less sure of herself, Tempest glanced down. "I want you and Calvin to have it. I was planning on giving it away or selling it, along with . . ." She looked toward Bram. "Along with selling my goods to you, Bram."

Did that mean she was leaving? He wasn't ready for that, would never be ready for that. "Why?" he asked.

She sighed. "I can't hold out much longer, but I am hoping to stay in town . . ." Her voice trailed off. There was clearly more she wished to say.

Climbing to her feet, Lydia smiled kindly at them both.

"I believe there are some things you need to discuss, in my absence." She reached for Tempest's hand and squeezed it. "Bless you for your offer, my dear friend. I'm going to talk to Calvin about it right now, and we'll let you know if we accept."

As Lydia walked away, Bram scooted closer to Tempest. "How come you want to sell me your goods but still stay in town?"

"Because I have some unfinished business," she said in a soft voice. "Regarding us."

Bram scooped up her hands, his heart drumming faster with hope. "You don't have to sell them to me, Tempest. I'd already decided tonight to ask you to partner with me, to join stores." Her eyes widened and he hurried to add, "In a marriage of convenience, if necessary."

She frowned and cocked her head, her lovely, wild curls framing her face. "Only a marriage of convenience?"

Tempest watched Bram carefully. Did he love her as much as she loved him? She wanted to believe it, given his wonderful kiss earlier, and yet, he was talking about marrying for convenience only.

He lifted his thumb and rubbed it against her bottom lip. Her pulse sped up at his touch. "I don't really want a marriage of convenience, Tempest," he said, his tone somber. "I only suggested it because I thought you might prefer that." A slow grin began at the corners of his mouth, the one she'd very much enjoyed kissing, and drove the solemnity from his handsome face. "But if you don't want that..."

A rush of happiness and love prompted her to edge closer so their knees were touching. "I'll tell you want I want, Bram Wakeman."

"I'm listening," he said with a light laugh.

She gazed into his eyes and felt clarity for the first time since he'd come to town. "I thought I still wanted a store and my hard-earned freedom." Tempest swallowed as she turned her gaze first to her mercantile and then to his. "But now I know what I want more than anything. It's what the Lord knew I needed all along, what *we* needed. And it isn't a marriage of convenience. We need a marriage of love."

Her face warmed with her boldness, but she didn't regret saying what was on her mind. She might not be the owner of a store after tonight, but she couldn't think of anything she'd rather do than work alongside Bram in *their* store.

"I couldn't agree more." He kissed the back of her knuckles, his lips lingering against her skin. "Together we'll have the best mercantile in Idaho City."

She bent forward and placed a quick kiss on his lips. "I love you, Bram. I think I have since that moment you first walked into my store."

He smiled, setting her heartbeat thrumming all over again. "I rather like the idea of marrying a woman who brandishes a hammer like it's a battle-axe."

"Is that a proposal then?" she teased.

"No, but this is." He went down on one knee in the ash and dirt. "Will you marry me, Tempest?"

She didn't hesitate with her answer. "Yes," she said with enthusiasm.

He drew closer for another kiss. Tempest closed the distance as well, then purposely paused a hairbreadth away. "Will you let me keep some of my organized chaos?"

Bram pretended to think the question over before nodding. "If I can keep some of my alphabetizing methods."

"All right," she said, adopting his thoughtful pose. "And will you try to tame the tempest out of me?"

"Never." His expression radiated tenderness. "'I would

not wish any companion in the world but you,'" he quoted softly.

"Ah, *The Tempest.*"

"No," he corrected, "my Tempest." And then he kissed her again as the songbirds began their early morning chorus.

A Summer for Love

Chapter 1

Bayocean, Oregon, August 1922

LORALEE LOVE CLASPED the ferry's railing tightly between her gloved hands as she watched the sand and tree-dotted shoreline drawing ever closer. She was nearly there.

"Is that where we'll be staying all summer?" a young girl excitedly asked her mother from their spot along the rail at Loralee's right.

"Yes," the mother answered, her voice full of equal delight. "That's Bayocean."

Bayocean. The name itself had the power to conjure up so many memories for Loralee, both sweet and bitter. Even this far from shore, she could see the resort town had changed since she'd been here eight years ago. There were more buildings and houses, and the beach appeared narrower than she remembered. Perhaps the ferry captain had been right—the jealous sea was greedily eating away at the town.

"Excuse me?"

Pulling her gaze from the resort, Loralee glanced at the girl's mother from beneath the wide brim of her hat. "Yes?"

"Are you by chance . . ." Her cheeks flushed. "What I mean is you look a great deal like Miss Loralee Love, the singer."

"One and the same," Loralee said with a genuine smile, swallowing a ping of disappointment. She may prefer watching the shoreline in solitude, but she wouldn't turn down a chance to talk with someone who recognized her. Her career would never have soared as it had without the support of those who appreciated her singing.

The girl slipped her hand into her mother's, furthering the feeling of disquiet within Loralee, and stared up at her with wide eyes. "You're pretty."

Keeping one hand on the railing, she crouched in her high-heeled shoes and drop-waist silk dress. She'd learned a long time ago the importance of looking someone in the eye, even if that someone was a child. The girl's unruly red curls reminded Loralee of her own light blond ones as a child, though she kept her hair cropped short and close to her face these days. "Thank you. I think you're quite lovely too."

The girl beamed. "Are you a real singer?"

"I don't always feel like one, but don't tell my manager I said so." The girl and her mother joined Loralee in a laugh. "Do you like singing?"

The curly head shook vigorously. "I like playing the violin."

"Then you keep playing, young one," Loralee said, rising to her feet. "And one day you just might be performing all over the world."

"Have you been all over the world?" the girl inquired.

Loralee nodded, her gaze drifting back to the shore. "I've visited a great many places, but I felt like it was time to return to Bayocean."

"Are you from here then?" the mother asked.

"No, not exactly."

Memories of living in the small, crowded cabin in central Oregon invaded Loralee's thoughts—the barren land, the hungry cries of her younger siblings, the peace she'd found in singing and in God. The memories bled together before coalescing on the day, eight years ago, when she'd watched her entire family drive away from the Hotel Bayocean Annex without her. She'd stood on the steps, tears tracing her cheeks, while fear and loneliness ate at her from the inside.

"This job is a good one," Loralee's mother had said. "You'll be paid a decent wage as a maid and have a house and food." She squeezed Loralee's hand, her fingers as cool as ice despite the sunny day. "It's for the best, Loralee."

After a quick hug and a peck to Loralee's cheek, her mother turned and climbed onto the wagon seat. Loralee's siblings watched her as the wagon moved farther and farther away, their expressions ranging from confusion to indifference. Her mother didn't look back once.

Loralee hadn't seen any member of her family since, though she'd tried for years to locate them, if only to send a portion of her earnings to help out. But they'd disappeared as quickly and completely as the scanty food of her childhood.

Breathing through the pain, which thankfully hurt less and less as the years passed, Loralee forced her lips upward. "I spent a summer here in Bayocean, a long time ago, but it was a happy time." Then her manager, Henry Love, heard her sing for the first time and had convinced her to come live with him and his wife—giving Loralee a home, a new last name, and a life as a professional singer.

"Have you come back to perform?" The mother's voice was as kind as it was curious.

"Yes." It was one of the reasons she was here and the

easiest one to share with Henry and Susan. But she sensed their suspicion that there was more to this trip than performing in Bayocean for old times' sake. Thankfully her adoptive parents hadn't pressed her with questions and agreed to let her travel unaccompanied.

After all, she wasn't a novice anymore, in life or in singing. She was twenty-four years old and had sung to audiences in London, New York, Paris, and Amsterdam. She'd even joined a tour to lift the troops' spirits in France during the war.

"Looks like we're docking." The mother smiled down at her daughter, then lifted her gaze to Loralee's once more. "It was very nice to meet you, Miss Love. We'll be sure to come hear you sing."

"Thank you." Loralee watched them walk away before hoisting her single piece of luggage, a large suitcase. Her heart knocked against her chest, faster and faster, as the shore loomed ahead. Was he here already? Would he come at all? Or had he found someone else to love during these intervening years?

The unanswerable questions pestered her like swarming mosquitoes as she disembarked from the ferry and made her way toward the Hotel Bayocean—they'd dropped the "Annex" part from the name at some point. Each step forward increased her hope and trepidation.

She'd thought of this reunion so many times during those first few years living with Henry and Susan. Then less and less as her singing career grew and she gained popularity with the public. But still, that long-ago promise she and Wyatt Noble had made remained with her always, like a treasured keepsake at the back of her mind, something to be pulled out every so often and lovingly reexamined.

She'd searched for his face among the soldiers during her time in France, but she never saw him. There'd been one man who looked much like his brother-in-law, but Loralee couldn't be certain. She had only met Wyatt's sister and her husband once. By the time she finished singing, though, she'd worked up the courage to approach him. Only she'd been swarmed at the end of the performance, and when she'd finally had a moment alone, the man with a possible link to Wyatt had disappeared.

Lost as she was in the past, she reached the hotel in no time. People bustled in and out of the main doors, their voices rising and falling in conversation. Loralee entered the busy lobby and wound her way through the throng to the front desk.

"May I check in?" she asked the young desk clerk, who was busy scribbling into a logbook.

"One moment." His tone bordered on the impatient. Loralee set down her suitcase, her gaze sweeping the room. The place exuded more permanence than it had nearly a decade ago, though the automatic fire sprinklers were still an original, and innovative, feature. "Now . . ." The young man glanced up, but his bland expression changed to one of flustered surprise. "Miss Love? So sorry to keep you waiting. I do apologize. Welcome to the Hotel Bayocean."

"Thank you."

"If you'll sign the register, please." He spun his book around to face her and handed her his pen. Taking it in hand, she signed her name. The young man eyed her signature with a grin. "Such beautiful penmanship."

"May I have my key?"

"Of course, of course." He fumbled a few moments behind the counter. "Here it is." He brandished the key. "Room twenty is ready and waiting, with a fresh bouquet of flowers, I might add."

It was Loralee's turn to flush at his starry-eyed

exuberance. What would he say if he knew that not so many years ago she'd also been an employee of this hotel? "I appreciate it, though it really wasn't—"

He continued on as if he feared she'd leave before he could finish his effusive speech. "As you can see, we hung the poster your manager mailed to us the other week."

He waved at the large drawing that depicted her in a long, rose-colored gown, hands cupped near her heart, lips parted in song. It was Henry and Susan's favorite portrait of her. But to Loralee, it was the picture of a different person. Someone far more confident and beautiful than the orphan girl she was inside. Only onstage did that girl and the poised singer become one.

"We want all of our guests to know you'll be performing here this weekend."

Loralee managed to return his smile, though hers felt suddenly tired and drooping. "Again, thank you. I believe I'll head to my room now."

"Oh, yes. Your key." He presented it as if it were a trophy. Loralee pressed her mouth over a chuckle. "If there's anything you should require during your stay, please let us know."

She tipped the key at him. "I will." Picking up her luggage, she started for the stairs, but a new thought made her turn back. "Actually, a friend of mine is coming ..." She swallowed, tamping down the hope. "That is, he might be coming into town. Could you tell me if he's already checked in?"

The clerk nodded. "Certainly. What is the name?"

"Wyatt Noble." The words felt strange leaving her throat after holding them in silence for so many years.

The young man's eyebrows rose to his thinning hairline. "As in the owner of Noble Logging?"

Wyatt is now the company's owner? She felt a measure

of pride at the news but also a twinge of sadness. Something must have happened to his formidable father to make Wyatt the owner of his family's large and profitable logging business. "Yes, I suppose so."

A few seconds of silence passed as the clerk perused the list of hotel guests. At last he lifted his chin and shook his head. "No, it doesn't appear that he has checked in yet. Shall I let you know when he arrives?"

If he arrives. "No, that's all right. I simply thought I'd check. Thank you again for your assistance." She nearly asked if he knew whether Wyatt was married or not, but she didn't wish to hear such news from a stranger.

She turned away, willing back the unexpected press of tears. Wyatt's absence at the moment didn't mean he wasn't coming at all. There was still an entire day to go until the date they'd agreed upon to meet would be here at last.

Still time for their dreams from that long-ago summer to yet become reality.

CHAPTER 2

Bayocean, Oregon, Summer 1914: Eight years earlier

LORALEE SMOOTHED HER hand over the bed linens, eliminating any creases or wrinkles, and stood back to survey her handiwork. Satisfied, she dipped her head in a nod. While her days as a maid were nearly as tiring as the ones she'd spent on the homestead, at least now she was earning wages, had a non-leaky roof overhead, and plenty to eat at mealtimes.

But even the measure of pride she felt in her position couldn't completely eradicate the homesickness and loneliness that still crept over her, especially at night. Only then, in the dark of the bungalow she shared with two other maids, would she allow the tears to come unchecked as she thought of her parents and siblings. She missed them and she missed having a place to call home, even though life on the homestead had been difficult. She hadn't made any real friends in Bayocean yet. And while the other members of the hotel staff treated her kindly, the wealthy patrons ignored her.

"You are invisible to them," the hotel manager had instructed her on her first day. "Keep your gaze down and avoid conversation with the guests unless you're directly asked a question."

She'd followed his counsel thus far and it had served her well. Although she couldn't help wondering at times why money, or the lack thereof, meant one person was "seen" and another merely faded into the background. Wasn't God the Father of each of them, regardless of wealth, position, or birthplace? At least that was something no one could take from her. She often reminded herself of that after a long day of picking up after people who viewed her in such a lowly light.

After gathering up the bundle of towels and clean linens to deliver to the next room, Loralee slipped out the door—only to crash into a firm chest clad in a damp bathing shirt. A hand clasped her elbow to keep her from joining the towels and sheets that had spilled onto the carpet.

"Sorry about that. Didn't know anyone was in the room. Are you all right?"

Loralee didn't look at his face as she nodded and dropped to her knees to pick up the mess. If she moved quickly, perhaps she wouldn't have to take everything back down to the hotel laundry to be cleaned again and risk getting in trouble.

"Here you go." He knelt beside her and passed her a folded sheet. "Thankfully it doesn't look spoiled from my mishap."

As she accepted the sheet, she couldn't resist glancing at him. He'd clearly come from the beach or the pool inside the natatorium, his towel draped casually around his neck. He was handsome and at least a few years older than her. And not only was he helping, he'd taken responsibility for the collision.

"Th-thank you," she managed to stammer out.

His light brown hair stuck up in tufts here and there, though not unattractively so, and appeared to still be wet at the ends from swimming. His skin was tanned a golden brown, and his eyes were the color of coffee.

But it was his smile, when he trained it on her, that robbed her of breath, more than colliding with him had. "You're welcome."

Loralee sucked in a gulp of air. She wasn't supposed to be conversing with the hotel guests, let alone staring openly. "I appreciate the help, but I can manage now." Balancing the bundle once again, she slowly rose to her feet. She'd inspect the linens for dust or dirt inside the next room, away from his open gaze.

"Are you certain? I smacked you pretty hard. You aren't seeing stars or anything, are you?" He bent to study her eyes, an expression of mock seriousness on his face.

She tried to hold back her chuckle, but it escaped her lips. "I'm fine, truly. I apologize for not seeing you." She moved past him, but he matched her steps.

"I likely put you behind schedule, though. Which isn't easily forgivable." His brow furrowed a bit. "Believe me, I know."

Loralee allowed herself a full laugh now. Nice as he was, what did this rich young man know of schedules, especially in a place like Bayocean, where life was all about leisure, at least for the guests? "I'll make it up on this next room."

"Why do I get the feeling I've just been insulted?" His tone sounded more amused than annoyed.

Turning to face him, the next room's door at her back, she shook her head. "Not at all. We all have work to do in this life. Some of us just get more hours off than others."

"And when are your hours off?"

She raised her eyebrows in surprise. Why wasn't he leaving or ignoring her? "Not until five o'clock this evening."

"Then what do you say to my making things up to you"—he held the ends of the towel around his neck—"by taking you to dinner in the hotel dining room?"

Dinner at the hotel? The only dinner she planned to eat was in her bungalow, not in the hotel's dining room, trying to pretend she was a guest and not a servant.

"Not an adequate repayment?" he voiced into the silence.

She glanced down the hall, grateful no one else had happened by and seen them deep in conversation. "It's not that."

She ought to refuse, even if spending time with hotel guests outside of work might be permissible. They were from two completely different social backgrounds. And yet, the idea of doing something so out of the ordinary from what she'd known the last sixteen years of her life was more than a little appealing. This was the first time she'd ever been asked to accompany a young man anywhere.

"Tell you what." She shifted the pile in her arms. "I have yet to swim at the natatorium . . . and, well, I'd really like to."

His disarming grin lit up his face again. "Say no more. I'll meet you there at six. My treat."

Loralee offered him a genuine smile. "Do I get to know the name of my benefactor?"

"Wyatt Noble, at your service."

Noble indeed, she thought. "I'm Loralee Brown."

"Loralee." The way he said it reminded her of a beautiful poem or a stirring song. "I'll bid you adieu then, Loralee." He gave her a smart bow as if he were the servant and she a high-society woman. "Until this evening."

Loralee pulled at the ill-fitting bathing suit and sighed. It might as well be a gunnysack with how loose it lay around her middle, but it was the only one available that covered her long legs to her knees. Would Wyatt think her even more of a country bumpkin in such a suit?

"It can't be helped," she muttered to herself. "Not if you want to swim." And she did. She'd heard nothing but praise for the newly opened natatorium and she'd been eager to try it out. Even if it meant paying forty cents for a suit and towel and a day of swimming. But as he'd promised, Wyatt had covered the cost. Now there was nothing more to do but enjoy her time here.

The minute she exited the dressing room, she forgot all about her baggy suit. Instead she gazed in wonder at the giant indoor swimming pool. Two stories of grandstands rose into the air on either side, and even at this hour they were half filled with people.

"It's huge," she said as Wyatt approached her.

He grinned as if he'd constructed it himself. "Pretty incredible, huh? The salt water is heated and the band"—he motioned to one side of the grandstands—"plays while you swim."

"Are those waves?"

"Sure are," Wyatt said with a laugh. "They manufacture them, so you can get the ocean experience without actually dipping a toe in the frigid water outside."

Loralee shook her head in amazement. "Incredible indeed."

"You ready to go in?" He took a step backward toward the pool's edge, his smile teasing. "The grandstands are the place to watch, you know. Not the pool."

"Of course I'm coming in." She joined him in the water, the warm waves rolling over her feet. When she was in up to her knees, she stopped and watched Wyatt disappear beneath the surface several yards ahead of her.

He popped up a few seconds later. "Don't you want to swim?" he asked, shaking water from his hair.

Loralee ventured a few more steps forward. "I would, but I don't know how."

"What?" Wyatt's eyebrows shot up as if she'd proclaimed she didn't know how to walk. Slicing through the water, he swam back toward her. "Where did you grow up?"

"Central Oregon."

"And you don't know how to swim?"

She lifted her shoulders in a shrug. "I never had to learn."

When he reached her, he stood, water dripping off his suit. "If you want to learn, I can teach you." His encouraging smile made her insides feel as pleasant and balmy as the water.

"You'd teach me?"

"Of course. If you trust me as a teacher."

Loralee gazed up at him. While she hadn't interacted with him for more than a few minutes today, she'd taken an instant liking to him the moment she realized he didn't see her as a servant and nothing else. "Yes, I trust you."

"All right then. I'll teach you how to float first." With that, he scooped her off her feet and carried her toward the deeper water. Loralee clung to his neck, fear pushing at her desire to learn. Now that she was out of the water, the cool air made her skin goose-pimple and the shadows in the deep end caused her to shiver. "I promise I won't drop you," he murmured near her ear. "At least not on purpose."

Chuckling, she relaxed her grip. "What do I do first?"

He eased her into the water, so it lapped around her hips. "Just stretch out on your back in the water. I'll still hold you, so all you have to do is get a feel for floating."

Loralee nodded and he gently placed her in the water. Gazing upward and holding herself stiff, she fought through pricks of panic as the waves pushed at her ears and arms and legs. True to his word, though, Wyatt kept a strong hand beneath her back and knees.

After a few moments, she calmed her tense muscles. She'd never floated on her back before, but the sensation was nice and peaceful. And the chance to look at Wyatt made the experience all the more pleasant.

"When you're ready, I'm going to move my hand away from your knees."

She exhaled through another spike of fear. "Okay."

"You're doing well. Just keep relaxing."

Closing her eyes, she listened to the water lapping around her face and the muffled sound of the band's music.

"Now I'm going to let you float by yourself," he said. Loralee opened her eyes, no longer relaxed. "It's okay. You can do it, and I'll be right here. Let's just see if you can float a second or two on your own."

She pressed her lips together and dipped her chin in agreement. If he thought she could do it, she would. She squeezed her eyes shut once more then breathed in and out slowly. She could do this. It would be wonderful to know how to swim, to be able to do so whenever she liked. Perhaps she'd try the ocean itself, once she mastered the natatorium . . .

"Loralee." His whisper prompted her to lift her eyelids. "You're floating by yourself and have been for at least twenty seconds."

"I am?" She hadn't realized he hadn't put his hand back beneath her.

He grinned. "You're a natural."

A genuine smile tugged at her mouth. "That or I have an excellent teacher."

"My guess is both," he said, his brown eyes lit up with amusement. "Want to try something else?"

"Yes."

Before she could ask what to do, he lifted her up and out of the water again. He carried her back to where the water's depth reached below his waist then set her down. "I know you can touch here, but it'll make it easier to practice moving your arms and kicking your legs. Then if you need to rest, just put your feet down."

"I like the sound of that." Though she had very much enjoyed being in his arms.

After watching Wyatt's demonstration, Loralee mimicked his movements by scooping her arms and paddling her feet. Her first trip across the pool took some time, and she stopped twice to catch her breath. But each time she moved from one side to the other, her movements became more confident.

She wasn't sure how long they'd been in the pool when she noticed the band had stopped playing. Lifting her head, she saw the musicians putting away their instruments. "It's time to go already?" she said, standing. She shivered and folded her arms against her sopping bathing suit, but she felt happy with her progress and with the company. She'd enjoyed every minute with Wyatt.

He came to stand beside her, his gaze on the band members too. "You've done really well. I hate to stop now."

"Thank you, but there will be time another day to keep learning." She started for the pool's edge.

"Loralee, wait." She turned to find him running his hand through his wet hair, his expression hopeful. "We could stay."

She eyed him in confusion. "But the natatorium is closing."

"But it doesn't have to for us." He walked toward her through the water. "My father is . . . well, you see . . . he's a powerful man. If I tell them that I'm his son, they'll let us stay. Probably as long as we like."

Disappointment cut through her at his words and she glanced away. It was nice to know he wanted to spend more time with her, but his statement about his father had only served to remind her that they still came from two vastly different worlds. He lived a life where the rich could command anything, and she lived where others dealt with the consequences of those demands.

"No, thank you, Wyatt." She started forward again. "I'm done for today."

He caught up with her, a frown pulling at his mouth. "You don't want to stay? I thought we were having fun."

"We were; we did." She stopped to face him, though she kept her gaze lowered. "Thank you for the lesson and for inviting me to come with you."

"But?" he pressed.

Loralee lifted her chin to study his handsome face before looking away. "Just because you are in a position of power to make something happen doesn't always mean you should." She gestured toward the band members, some of whom were watching them. "Many of these people have been here, working, all day. They're ready to go back to their homes and bungalows to eat and sleep, so they can get up tomorrow and do it all over again. So as much as I would enjoy more time to swim with you, I don't want to be a part of something that forces them to stay here longer than they wish."

The distant mutter of conversation and the splash of the waves were the only sounds to meet her ears. Had she offended Wyatt with the truth? She hoped not, but if she had, then it would be easier for her to make the choice not to see him again.

After the pause between them lengthened even more, Wyatt wiped at his face with his wet hands and chuckled. "That was well said, exactly right, and I do apologize." He offered her a contrite smile. "What do you say we change and then I'll walk you home?"

"You don't have to do that."

"I want to." He shifted his weight. "Actually, if we're being honest, what I really want is to see you tomorrow and maybe the day after that and the day after that . . ."

Loralee stared at the water around her knees, hardly daring to hope. He, the son of a powerful and obviously wealthy man, had not only listened to and accepted her honesty, he also wanted to see her again. Her own wish to spend more time with him, however foolish, beat as strongly as her heart did.

"Are you sure?"

"Absolutely," he said with a confident tone. "But I have a question first."

What did he wish to know? she wondered. "Yes?"

He stepped closer to her and tipped her chin upward with his finger until their eyes met. Loralee's pulse stuttered and sped up. "Why won't you look me in the eye?"

"I do."

Wyatt shook his head. "A few times, yes, but then you look away. Like you're doing right now."

She dragged her gaze back to meet his. "I'm a servant, Wyatt. We're not supposed to look the guests in the eye."

"Am I just a guest?"

"No."

"And you're not just a servant." His voice sounded husky, and she noticed he kept glancing at her mouth. "Can I say something else?"

"Yes," she repeated in a half whisper.

Wyatt lowered his finger, to her regret, but he took hold of her hand. "You have the most extraordinary blue eyes, Loralee. And everyone should get the chance to see them." She opened her mouth to protest, but he kept going. "Besides that, you are a confident, well-spoken young lady. It doesn't matter what your job is, look everyone in the eye. It shows your confidence, and it's an acknowledgment of others' humanity."

"Where did you learn that?" she asked, touched more than she would likely ever be able to say by his compliment and admonition.

Giving her hand a squeeze, he led her out of the pool. "Looking others in the eye is one thing my father has modeled that I do admire."

"Do you not get along with him?"

He laughed, but the sound held none of his earlier merriment. "You could say that. He's the owner of one of the largest logging companies in the Northwest and doesn't want anyone, including his only son, to forget it. Someday I'll take over for him, but I pray every night that I won't lose my faith and integrity in doing so."

She squeezed his hand in return. "I don't think you will." And she meant it. What she'd seen in Wyatt today was starkly different from what she'd observed in most of the other rich people at the resort. Or really in any person she'd met thus far in her life. He was kind and funny and optimistic. Best of all, he'd seen her, the real her.

Singing to herself as she changed back into her clothes, she realized for the first time since coming to Bayocean that she couldn't wait to see what tomorrow would bring. Because Wyatt Noble would be a part of it.

Chapter 3

August 1922

THE SCENT OF freshly milled lumber permeated every inch of Wyatt Noble's office. It clung to his clothes when he went home each day and filled his dreams each night. But the smell was both familiar and welcome, a tangible connection to his past and to those he'd lost—his mother, father, sister, and brother-in-law.

He drew in a full breath of the calming aroma and returned his gaze from the large picture window to the contract on his desk. Even though the demand for lumber to build airplanes and ships had eased with the end of the Great War, the Noble Logging Company still continued to be successful and profitable. His father would likely be proud of that fact, though Wyatt had discarded the man's underhanded, ruthless tactics when he'd taken over. He regretted never having had much of a relationship with his father until the very end, but Wyatt would never be sorry for choosing to run the company from a position of faith and honesty. And apparently his customers felt the same, judging by the new contract before him—the second this week.

The memory of a conversation he'd had years ago, one he hadn't thought of in a very long time, replayed inside his mind. A conversation with a beautiful, compassionate young lady, regarding his fear of losing his faith and integrity once he became president of the logging company.

"I don't think you will," Loralee had said in that singsong, confident voice he'd loved from the moment he first heard it.

While this particular recollection hadn't entered his thoughts in years, the woman herself had more times than he could count. *Loralee Brown,* he thought, tapping his desk with his pen. *Or rather, Loralee Love.*

She was a famous singer now—and a very talented one at that. Wyatt hadn't heard her sing since the summer they'd shared in Bayocean when he was twenty, but he'd been given a glimpse back then of her amazing gift. And he'd followed her career through the newspapers.

Not for the first time, Wyatt wondered if she had a beau. He figured he would have read about her wedding if she'd married, but she might wish to keep the relationship of a sweetheart as private knowledge. Something akin to regret pierced him at the thought, bringing a frown to his mouth. No other girl had captured his heart the way Loralee had eight years ago, though he'd made a concerted effort to get to know other young women since then. At least until taking over the company. His work, and becoming guardian to his niece at the death of his sister and brother-in-law, had taken over his life, leaving him little time and energy to pursue romantic attachments.

Wyatt tried to focus on the contract before him once more, but his mind refused to let go of the memories of his first love. The summer they'd spent together had been the happiest time of his life. But she'd been so young, four years his junior, and his father had refused to condone the match. So Wyatt and Loralee did the only thing they felt they could—they'd promised to meet in Bayocean in eight years if neither of them were married or attached by then.

"What day was that?" he murmured to himself, spinning in his chair to view the calendar pinned to the wall. He recalled they'd chosen August 1922, but what day . . . Climbing to his feet, unsure why he felt driven to remember such a detail in this moment, he peered hard at the calendar.

"Daddy Wyatt!"

He turned, a ready smile erasing his frown as his niece burst into the room. She was followed at a more sedate pace by his housekeeper and Nellie's nanny, Mrs. Harper. "Nellie girl. How are you today?"

The four-year-old bounded up to him and he caught her in a hug. "I learned more letters and a new scripture today. So Mrs. Harper said we could come see you at your office."

The older woman smiled at him over the dark curly head of her charge. "I hope that's all right, sir."

"Of course." He returned to his seat and settled Nellie on his knee. The shock of losing his sister so soon after the death of his brother-in-law had been compounded by his sudden role as a father to his young niece. But he'd found great joy in caring for someone else. He may have come to fatherhood in an unexpected way, but he relished their little family. "Let's hear your scripture."

Nellie's face scrunched in concentration. "To every thing there is a season, and a time to . . . to . . ." She shot a look at her nanny.

"To every purpose," Mrs. Harper prompted with a smile as she took the seat opposite the desk.

"Yes." The girl clapped her hands. "A time to every purpose under the heaven."

Wyatt embraced her. "Well done, Nellie girl. You'll have the whole Bible memorized by the time you're ten."

She giggled and rested her head against his chest.

"Have you decided yet where you will vacation this year?" Mrs. Harper asked him.

Wyatt shook his head. "No." With the steady flow of new contracts, his mind had been more on work than on his and Nellie's annual vacation.

"I'm going to cut wood for a hotel," Nellie announced, sitting up to the desk. She grabbed his pen and a nearby pad of paper and began writing out her own version of a contract. It was her favorite game when she came to his office.

"That will require a lot of wood. And when do they need all that lumber?"

Her brow furrowed again. "Tomorrow. What is the day tomorrow?"

Wyatt glanced at the calendar once more, but as he rattled off the date for Nellie, a sudden jolt of realization shot through him. Tomorrow was the day he and Loralee had promised to meet.

"Is something wrong, Daddy Wyatt?" Nellie stared up at him, her brown eyes wide.

"No, nothing's wrong," he said absently. Should he go to Bayocean? Would Loralee be there? Eight years was a long time, and yet, if there was the slightest chance that she hadn't found someone either . . . He glanced down at Nellie, who had returned to her "work." Whomever he married would have to accept his niece as a daughter. The two of them were bound together now. And yet, would someone as established in her career as Loralee Love wish to be an instant mother?

He couldn't say, but the thought of seeing her again, of

speaking with her, filled him with a hope he hadn't entertained in years. *To every thing there is a season,* he repeated in his mind. Maybe this would be his and Loralee's season.

"What if we go to the ocean for our vacation this year?"

Nellie spun to face him. "Oh, yes. I love the ocean."

"Me too," Wyatt agreed with a chuckle. "How does that sound, Mrs. Harper?"

The woman smiled. "Quite lovely, sir."

"When will we go?" Nellie begged.

Making a decision, he scooped her up as he climbed to his feet, eliciting a happy squeal from her. "How about tomorrow?"

Bayocean, Oregon, Summer 1914: Eight years earlier

Wyatt whistled to himself as he strolled away from the hotel. Today was Loralee's day off, and he was meeting her in front of her bungalow. She'd progressed far enough in her swimming that she wanted to try out the ocean this afternoon.

Spending time with Loralee the last three weeks had been the highlight of his vacation and the highlight of his year. He'd enjoyed teaching her how to swim and seeing her confidence grow, not only in her abilities but also in herself. She no longer refused to meet his gaze when they spoke, which meant Wyatt had lots of opportunities to look into her beautiful blue eyes.

He had yet to introduce her to his father, and he hoped to put it off as long as possible. Not because he didn't think Loralee the greatest girl he'd ever met. He simply hoped to stay the row between him and his father that would follow such an introduction. Mr. Noble made no pretense about who he wanted his son to marry—a lady of social standing and breeding. And while there were a number of young women vacationing in Bayocean this year who fit that description, none of them elicited the admiration Wyatt felt for Loralee.

His sister had already married the son of another logging tycoon, and while Wyatt respected his brother-in-law, he wasn't blind to the reality that the marriage had been built on mutual interests rather than love. And whatever his father might say or demand, Wyatt wished to spend his days with a woman he loved.

Approaching Loralee's bungalow, he overheard someone singing. It only took a few seconds to realize it was Loralee. He stopped to listen, intent on waiting only a moment or two before knocking, but he found himself completely caught up in the magic of her melodic soprano voice. It reached inside him, laying bare all his former heartaches and pains, and then binding them up with fervent hope.

He was still standing there, enveloped in the spell of her singing, when she opened the door. "Wyatt," she said, smiling. "I thought I'd poke my head out and see if you were here."

Shaking himself back to the present, he nodded. "I've been here for a few minutes."

"You mean you heard . . ." She blushed.

He stepped toward her. "I didn't know you sang."

Her blush deepened. "It's just something I pass the time with."

"Loralee, you have an amazing singing voice." He stopped beside her and took her hand in his. "Better than anything I've heard before."

She smirked until she seemed to understand he spoke in earnest. "Thank you, but it isn't as if there's any sort of job in it for me." Swinging her towel over her shoulder, she tugged him forward. "The ocean awaits."

"But you could make a go at singing," he said, unwilling to let it lie. He was no expert when it came to singing, but even he recognized she had real talent. "How else do you think the men and women who sing in those clubs get started?"

"I don't know. I've never been to a club or a musical performance." They struck up an easy stride, her hand still clasped in his. After a few moments of quiet, she turned to him, an inquisitive expression on her face. "You really think I have a voice for performing?"

He chuckled, bumping her shoulder with his. "I know it. I was awestruck just listening to you."

She bumped him back. "Perhaps it's something to think about"—she wagged a finger at him—"but only to think about, mind you. My life is here now and I'm content with that."

They talked of other things as they wound their way to the beach. When they reached the water, Loralee dropped her towel on the sand and took off at a run for the waves. "You ready to go in?" she called over her shoulder, an echo of the words he'd said to her that first evening at the natatorium.

Her radiant smile hit him square in the chest, and Wyatt knew in that moment that, unlike her, he would likely never be content again. Not when he would have to say good-bye to Loralee for good at the end of the summer.

CHAPTER 4

Bayocean, Oregon, August 1922

IN SPITE OF a light drizzle the next day, Loralee ventured forth from the hotel. Her cloche hat kept her hair mostly dry and she didn't mind the damp on her cheeks. She wasn't the only one out and about either. Even with the less-than-ideal weather, there were plenty of people outdoors, enjoying the resort town. Loralee moved among them, grateful when no one seemed to recognize her. Today she wanted to get lost in the crowd.

She made her way to the bungalows and wandered past the one she'd once lived in. The afternoon Wyatt heard her sing played through her mind. He'd recognized her gift long before she had. His words of encouragement that day had inspired her with the self-assurance to eventually accept Henry's offer to make singing her new life.

The beach, the natatorium, the dance hall pavilion—each place held such treasured memories. The smell of the ocean and the tug of the breeze reminded her of the many walks she and Wyatt had taken along this stretch of beach. Would they ever do so again? She wanted to believe he would come today—that if free to do so, he would keep his promise. But she had no assurances. While she was a well-known singer now, he was still the son, and owner, of a very prosperous logging company. Perhaps his father had succeeded, before his death, in convincing Wyatt that he would do better to marry someone of similar social standing. The Loves might be well-enough off, but they weren't pretentious. They'd never been anything less than genuine, honest, and eager to surround themselves with people of sincerity. Loralee wanted to believe the same was still true of Wyatt, and yet, eight years was a long time.

She wandered the town the better part of the day, reliving the bittersweet memories that were as entrenched in this place as the salt and the spray. If she kept away from the hotel, she wouldn't have to know just yet whether he'd chosen to come or not.

By late afternoon though, Loralee could stay away no longer. It was time to prepare for her performance.

"We are looking forward to hearing from you tonight, Miss Love," the same exuberant clerk called out as she passed by.

She inclined her head and smiled. "I'm looking forward to performing."

"Oh, and Mr. Noble still has not checked in. I thought you'd wish to know."

Sadness settled in her chest, making it hard to hold her smile. He still hadn't come. He would if he could, she reminded herself. Which meant he must be attached or married. And it was no surprise. She'd never met another man like Wyatt, even through all of her travels and performances.

Straightening her shoulders, she smiled kindly at the clerk. "Thank you for letting me know." She would give the best performance she could in this place she'd loved, and in the morning she would leave. And do her best to forget the man she'd loved.

Bayocean, Oregon, Summer 1914: Eight years earlier

"Loralee"—Wyatt held her closer as they danced to the music—"are you still crying?"

Her chin bobbed up and down against his shirt, her cheek pressed to his shoulder. The dance pavilion, crude as it might look on the outside, was full of other enamored couples. But he felt as if they were dancing alone—the only two people in the world, encircled in a cloud of sadness and falling hopes.

"Is it about my father?"

Loralee nodded again, this time sniffling. "He doesn't like me, Wyatt."

"It's your bank account he doesn't like," he countered bitterly.

He'd been unable to put off the dreaded introduction any longer. His father had demanded to meet the girl whom his son had been spending all of his time with for the last month and a half. Loralee had met Wyatt on the terrace where his father, sister, and brother in-law were taking in the air. To her credit she hadn't cowed one bit. Instead she'd acted with grace and confidence, all the while looking his father in the eye.

Mr. Noble had asked to speak with Wyatt in private, but the man's words had easily carried to where Loralee stood waiting at one end of the veranda. "Have you lost your senses? She's a servant at a hotel. Not a young lady suitable to spending time with the future heir and owner of Noble Logging."

Wyatt straightened to his full height, giving him a few inches over his father. "Be that as it may, I won't stop seeing her."

"You would defy me?" his father roared.

"Only if you make me choose between the two of you, for the remainder of this trip."

His father's eyes narrowed. "So you will give her up once we leave?"

Everything in him wanted to answer no. But he wouldn't lead Loralee on with false promises for the future. She was still too young to marry at present, and his father had been tutoring him to take over the logging business for more than a year now. He couldn't turn his back on his family. "Yes, you have my word."

Loralee heard the entire conversation, and while she expressed understanding of the situation, she remained as visibly troubled as Wyatt felt. He had hoped dancing would cheer them both up, but his heart wasn't in it either.

"Let's go for a walk," he said, stepping back.

Tears trailed her cheeks, though she braved a smile. "That sounds nice."

Outside the pavilion, away from the music, the crashing waves could once again be heard. The moon shone overhead, lighting up the water. Mindful of her shoes, he led her a short distance across the sand and took a seat. Loralee sank down beside him. He put his arm around her shoulders. There wouldn't be many more nights like this. The realization filled him with intense sadness. He didn't want to imagine his life without Loralee. And yet, he knew he needed to.

Give me strength, Lord, to do and say the right thing. A nudge deep inside pushed words to his tongue that he'd contemplated saying for more than a week or two. "I love you, Loralee. And I'd love nothing more than to marry you right now, impossible as that may be."

She lifted her chin, her blue eyes dark and shining. "I love you too, Wyatt."

He tightened his arm around her as she nestled her head against him again. Letting her go from his life would be every bit as painful as losing his mother to sickness and then to death.

"I'm glad we still have a week," she murmured.

Only a week before he said good-bye to her forever. Unless . . . Wyatt twisted around on the sand so he faced her. Her brows rose in silent question. "What if we meet, right here?"

"What do you mean?" She shook her head in confusion.

He was thinking fast now, his plan forming as he voiced it. "What if in . . . let's say eight years . . . when you're all grown up and I'm getting old . . ." He got the smile he'd been hoping for with that remark. "We meet back here at Bayocean."

"But what if one of us should be married by then or has a sweetheart?"

Wyatt couldn't imagine ever loving anyone else, but he wasn't a fool. Loralee would likely be scooped up the minute she turned eighteen. "If neither of us is attached or married by then, we'll meet right back here."

Her mouth quirked up in a half smile. He could tell she was warming to the idea. "What day?"

"Today. Eight years from this day."

"It'll be 1922 in eight years," she said with a voice tinged with wonder.

Surely it would feel like eighty years to him, but he would be here. He felt certain of that. "So do you agree, Loralee Brown? Will you meet me here on this day in 1922 if you are not otherwise engaged or married?"

"Yes." Her expression registered her quiet determination. "I will. And will you agree to meet me here, Wyatt Noble, on this day in 1922 if you are not otherwise engaged or married?"

Wyatt held her face between his hands. "Most assuredly, yes," he stated emphatically. Then he pressed his lips lightly to hers. Loralee breathed the softest of sighs, encouraging him to kiss her fully. It was the first time he'd kissed her, though not the first time he'd entertained the idea of doing so. The reality of it was twice as splendid as he'd imagined.

The kiss solidified something he'd known, nearly since their first accidental meeting—he would not forget Loralee. And he hoped that she would not forget him either.

Bayocean, Oregon, August 1922

Loralee looked out at the crowded room, her heartbeat kicking up faster beneath her beaded evening gown. Everything was ready for her performance. The musicians were in position, and she had taken extra care in arranging her hair and her elaborate headband. Wyatt, though, was nowhere to be seen. Which meant he wasn't coming. A wave of sadness set her stomach churning even more.

The nameless faces stared back as the hotel manager announced her. She searched the room more closely, her gaze stopping on a mother and daughter waving at her from one of the tables. Loralee recognized them as the ones she'd chatted with on the ferry. Their smiles eased some of her nervousness, and she offered a small wave back.

It was time. Stepping up to the microphone, she smiled. "Thank you all for coming this evening. It is my deepest pleasure to be in Bayocean. I have many fond memories from my time here, years ago, and I hope tonight's performance will be a happy memory for each of you."

With a nod to the musicians, the room filled with the notes of her first song. Loralee waited for her entrance, her eyes sweeping the audience once more. A latecomer and his daughter drew her attention. Removing his hat to reveal brown hair, the man took a seat at the back table. At the moment she was supposed to begin singing, her gaze locked with his across the crowd. Loralee's breath caught in her throat. It was Wyatt. Looking older and more distinguished, yes, but she knew that face.

He came! Her pulse thudded faster, horribly out of step with the languid music. The realization that Wyatt had kept his promise was quickly followed by the recollection that he wasn't alone. Even as she watched, the girl he'd led into the room climbed onto his lap, her cheeks lifted in a grin. Wyatt had a daughter. Did that mean he also had a wife? Loralee mentally shook her head in confusion. He wasn't supposed to come if he was married.

Only then did she realize the musicians had repeated the opening bar of the song. She'd missed her cue. Feeling herself blush, she tilted her chin upward and opened her mouth to begin. Her voice carried across the space, sounding far more confident than she felt. Whatever her questions about Wyatt, she would at least have them answered in person when the performance was over. Channeling that hopeful emotion, she sang with all of her heart.

CHAPTER 5

OBLIVIOUS TO NEARLY everything else around him, Wyatt gazed openly at Loralee. He could hardly believe she stood only half a room away from him after all of these years.

"Who is that, Daddy Wyatt?" Nellie whispered in his ear.

"Her name is Loralee Love," he answered softly. "She is a famous singer . . . and someone I knew a long time ago."

"She's very pretty."

Wyatt murmured agreement. Loralee's lovely face, her blue eyes, her blond hair, worn short now, was so familiar to him. As if it were only yesterday they'd been wandering through Bayocean, laughing and talking, and not nearly a decade ago.

Her soprano voice still held the power to enthrall. One glance at the audience members around him was proof of the way she could command their rapt attention with her singing. He'd seen pictures of her in the newspaper, but seeing her in person, he could hardly believe the girl he'd known eight years ago was now a star.

"Daddy Wyatt, did you love her?"

He pulled his focus from Loralee to his niece. "What do you mean?"

"You look at her like you look at me. And I know you love me."

Giving her a squeeze, he cleared his throat of emotion before he could speak. "You are right, Nellie girl. I do love you." He lifted his eyes to Loralee again. "And yes, I did love her."

I still do, he thought. The realization didn't jolt him as much as he'd expected. Isn't that why he'd come? To see if he felt the same? There was no doubt in his mind of the answer now. He hadn't yet spoken to her, but his feelings hadn't changed. If anything, they'd grown in the eight long years of being apart.

"She loves you too," Nellie announced with adult-like conviction.

Wyatt started to chuckle at her self-assured tone, then stopped when a woman seated nearby threw him an annoyed look. "What makes you so sure?" he asked in a low voice.

Nellie pressed her nose to his. "Because she keeps looking at *you.*"

A spark of hope ignited inside him at his niece's words. He turned back to watch Loralee, intent on seeing if Nellie was correct in her assertion. Sure enough, Loralee's gaze seemed to gravitate back to his again and again. Each time he felt an electric current surging in his chest. But did that mean she still loved him? Or was she simply curious about his presence? She might not even remember they were supposed to meet today. Perhaps she was only here in Bayocean to perform, for old times' sake, and nothing more.

The song ended and the audience burst into enthusiastic applause. Loralee inclined her head, her smile full and sincere.

It reminded Wyatt of sunny days, strolling hand in hand with her along the beach. If she did return his feelings, could they pick up where they'd left off? Doubts crept in, especially around her willingness to be Nellie's mother if they were to marry. Seeing Loralee tonight, like this, he wondered again if she would wish to give it all up—not just for his niece but for him as well.

The possibility that he might have to say good-bye to her all over again pained him, but whatever happened, he would at least stay and talk with her. She might not feel the same, and yet, he would relish the chance to be with her one more time, even if it was his last.

Loralee finished her encore number to the enthusiastic applause of the audience. After motioning to the wonderful group of musicians, she made her final bow. The performance had gone well, in spite of her distracted thoughts each time she glanced at Wyatt. Now if she could just talk to him . . .

People swarmed her, effusive with their compliments. She accepted their praise and handshakes as she slowly made her way across the room. When she reached Wyatt's table, though, he and the little girl were no longer seated there. Panicked, she glanced around. Had he left already, before she could speak with him? Fighting tears, she excused herself and turned to walk away, intent on escaping upstairs to her room.

"Loralee, wait."

How long had she dreamt of hearing him say her name one more time? She spun around and found him standing there, his hands in his pockets, his gaze intent. "Wyatt. You're here."

"That was . . . incredible." He shook his head, a grin brightening his handsome face. "No wonder you've been asked to sing all over the country. And to think I knew you when the audience was just one." He pointed his thumb at himself.

"I thought you... and your daughter... might have left." She wouldn't think too hard about the fact that he must have loved another to be a father now. It was perfectly reasonable—they'd made no promises, other than meeting here again today.

He glanced back over his shoulder. "I was handing her off to her nanny, my housekeeper actually. I wanted to talk to you, alone."

Her heart raced as she nodded. "I was hoping to talk to you too."

"Shall we?" He gestured to a side door that led to the veranda.

Mustering her courage, to hear whatever he had to say, Loralee led the way outside. The night was perfectly temperate, the stars glittering above. She moved to the railing and leaned forward against it.

"Did you remember our promise?" he asked as he came to stand beside her, so close she felt the warmth of his presence through her elbow-length gloves.

"Of course."

He glanced at her. "Is that why you're here?"

She turned to face him, surprised. Wasn't that why he was here? "Yes. I thought it might be fun to do a performance as well." Swallowing hard, she pushed the question she most needed answered out her lips. "Why did you come to Bayocean, Wyatt?" Even if his answer didn't match her own, she longed to know it.

"I'm here ..." He rested his hand lightly over hers, reminding her that his touch still had the power to wield her pulse. "Because I made a promise and I want to honor that."

"What of your wife and daughter?"

Instead of chagrin or regret, Wyatt smiled. "Nellie isn't my daughter. Well, she is now."

"I don't understand." Loralee held her breath, certain his next words would either confirm her hopes or scatter them for good.

"Actually she's my niece, and I'm now her guardian and father. That was my sister's wish before she died."

Releasing her breath, she felt a mixture of relief and sadness. "I'm so sorry, Wyatt. And what of your brother-in-law?"

"Also gone." He gazed toward the sea, his expression wistful in the lights from the hotel. "He was killed in France."

"I thought I saw him, when I was there singing to the troops." She covered both their hands with her free one. "I'm sorry for all of your loss."

He smiled in gratitude. "Thank you. It's just me and Nellie now. She is a bright and exuberant little girl, and I feel lucky that we have each other."

Loralee waited for him to say more. Was he content in his new life with just him and his niece?

When Wyatt faced her again, she saw a mixture of hope and uncertainty in his brown eyes. "I would like the two of you to get to know each other. That is, if you wish . . ."

"I would very much like that," she said, giving him a full smile. There might just be room for her in his life after all.

"We can meet you here tomorrow morning. Say ten o'clock?"

Loralee nodded. "That would be lovely."

"You did splendidly tonight, Loralee." Leaning forward, Wyatt brushed a quick kiss to her cheek that made her stomach twist with delight. "I'll bid you adieu. Until tomorrow."

A happy laugh spilled from her at the realization his words were a near perfect echo of those he'd voiced when they first met. "Until tomorrow."

"One . . . two . . . three," Loralee counted. Lifting Nellie by her hands, she and Wyatt swung the little girl in front of them as they made their way toward the beach. Wyatt's niece squealed with glee.

The happy sound matched the feeling in Loralee's heart throughout the day as they'd shown Nellie their favorite places in Bayocean. And while Loralee had seen them all the day before by herself, she relished the chance to see them again alongside the man she loved. Her time with Wyatt after the performance last night had been short, but she hadn't needed more than a few minutes in his company to know she loved him still.

"I like you, Loralee," Nellie said, looking up at her. "You're as funny as Daddy Wyatt."

How she adored the girl's nickname for him. "I like you too, Nellie. Very much." Loralee exchanged a smiling glance with Wyatt.

When they reached the sand, all three of them sat to remove their shoes. Then Nellie asked if she could wade in the water. Wyatt agreed and he and Loralee strolled after her as she raced toward the waves.

"Reminds me of another girl," Wyatt said in a teasing tone, "who couldn't get enough of the water."

Loralee chuckled. "She's a darling little girl."

"I'm glad you think so." She didn't miss the hopeful tone to his words, and it caused her heart to race, especially when he captured her hand in his.

He tugged her to a stop at the edge of the water where

Nellie darted back and forth, giggling as the waves rushed at her feet.

"This has been a perfect day, Loralee."

She murmured agreement, sensing he had more to say.

"You were never far from my thoughts all these years, but I have no expectation that you'll suddenly give up your successful singing career for us."

He still wanted a life together! Loralee felt tears of joy and gratitude on her cheeks.

"I do have hope that you might feel as I still do." Wyatt brushed a tear from beneath her eye in a tender gesture that elicited several more tears. "And perhaps one day you'll wish to be with us. With me."

Releasing his hand, she placed hers alongside his clean-shaven jaw. She still couldn't quite believe he was really and truly here, standing before her again.

"I've loved singing and I'll be forever grateful for all that Henry and Susan made possible for me." She gazed at his handsome face, thinking how he looked older and yet familiar at the same time. "I'm also ready for a new life, Wyatt, with you and Nellie."

"Even if she isn't your daughter?"

Loralee smiled. "Yes. Because I know what a blessing it can be to have someone else step in as a mother. And I would welcome and cherish the opportunity to do the same with Nellie."

Placing his hand on her waist, he drew her close, causing her pulse to flutter with anticipation. "How soon would you be ready to start this new life? It has already been eight *long* years."

"Are you asking me to marry you?" she said, unabashedly looping her arms around his neck.

Wyatt grinned. "I already did that, a long time ago."

Contentment filled her heart and she sent a silent prayer of gratitude heavenward for their second chance. "I will marry you, Wyatt Noble. Just as soon as we can get Henry and Susan here." She nodded in the direction of the hotel. "I'd like the wedding to take place in Bayocean. If that's all right."

"I can't think of a more fitting place."

He kissed her then, deeply and fully, and in that moment the years melted away. She was sixteen again, and yet the bond between them felt stronger and deeper than what they'd known before.

When they parted, she caught her breath, only to have it stolen again by his next words. "I never stopped loving you, Loralee. I want you to know that. Not for a single minute."

"Nor I."

She peered into his expressive brown eyes, feeling more jubilant than she could ever remember. Seeing the tenderness she felt reflected in Wyatt's loving gaze, she realized she'd finally come home.

Romance in Autumn

CHAPTER 1

―――――――――――――※―――――――――――――

Newport, Rhode Island, October 1905

THE SMELL OF wood smoke and damp leaves greeted Phoebe Hill as she exited the town car in front of Baywood House. She paused, sheltering her eyes with a gloved hand as she gazed at the white stone mansion from beneath the short brim of her plumed hat. The house hadn't changed at all, not even in the fifteen years since she'd last seen it. She let out a breath of relief.

"I'd like to look around," she told the cabdriver, who stood at attention beside her open door. "Then we can return to the hotel for my mother."

The man gave a polite nod. "Very good, miss."

Phoebe ascended the wide steps, one hand lifting the skirt of her blue pinstriped dress, her heart beating wildly with excitement. She'd often thought of this house and dreamt it were hers. And now, because of her late employer's benevolence, if all went well, she would soon be the mansion's new owner.

Not surprisingly, she found the front door locked. Phoebe moved to a side window and wiped away the dust to peer inside. Sheets blanketed the furniture, but the parlor's ornate wallpaper and intricate ceiling moldings were wonderfully familiar and fueled her desire to find a way inside.

She strolled around to the side of the house, beneath a canopy of trees. Unlike the summer days she'd once spent here, when her mother worked for the Austin family, the trees now sported red, orange, and gold leaves. Phoebe drew in a full breath of crisp autumn air laced with saltiness from the sea. This was where she and her mother belonged, in the country. No more city life, no more adhering to someone else's schedule or social events or whims. She was now the proprietress of her own life with the means to provide her and her mother with a real home again.

Reaching the servants' entrance, she tried the worn knob, which turned easily beneath her hand. It was unlocked! Phoebe grinned and pushed through the door. Dim light and shadows made her blink after the bright sunlight outdoors, but she didn't need to see to know her way around. She strolled through the kitchen, her gaze wandering over the old stove and preparation tables. How often had she slipped inside this room to sneak a berry or dollop of cream from some confection her mother was making?

The memories trailed her like a gauzy evening gown as she made her way through the house to her favorite room of all—the ballroom. The Austins were never able to achieve as much wealth as the Vanderbilts or the Astors had, nor was their Newport mansion as large or lavish. And yet, Gwendolyn Austin had spared no expense when it came to decorating her ballroom. The walls had been adorned with gold paneling and painted scenes of the French countryside, while the large chandelier in the center boasted hundreds of real diamonds.

Outside the room's double doors, Phoebe stopped. She'd only ever been allowed in here to clean up after a party—never when guests were present—but she'd spent many happy hours pretending she was the hostess of her own ball inside the ornate room. Never would she have imagined that those girlish dreams might actually come to fruition.

She went to open the door and saw that it already stood ajar. Perhaps the servants who were hired by the Austins to clean the mansion once a year hadn't closed it properly the last time they were here. Slipping inside, she gazed with wonder at the ceiling and walls until her eyes fell on a tall figure standing by the French doors at the opposite end of the room.

A startled cry leaked from Phoebe's lips and echoed in the vast space. She'd been told the mansion was unoccupied. The man clearly heard her, for he turned around, but she couldn't see his face with the light at his back.

"I beg your pardon," she said, keeping her tone friendly and polite. Perhaps this was another interested buyer. "I was told I would find the place empty and that I wouldn't disturb anyone if I looked around."

The barest hint of an English accent laced his words as he said, "You are correct. I was admiring the place myself." With his hands tucked into the pockets of his stylish trousers, he approached her. "And may I ask who you are?"

He appeared every inch the gentleman from his straw boater hat, to his tailored suit, to his shiny black shoes. Phoebe nearly dropped a curtsey before reminding herself that she was an heiress now, which put them on the same social standing.

"I'm Phoebe Hill." She offered him a genuine smile. "I spent a great deal of time here as a child," she added honestly.

No need to mention her plans to buy the house just yet, in case he proved to be a competitor.

The man tilted his head, his expression puzzled, as he stopped a few feet away from her. "I lived here every summer as a boy, but I'm afraid I don't remember you, Miss Hill."

He'd come here every summer too? Phoebe felt as confused by his confession as he clearly felt at hers. Had he been the child of another servant or the son of one of the Austins' guests? She searched his face, hoping to recognize the boy from years ago in the man standing before her now. He was rather handsome, with brown hair and green eyes. Familiar green eyes.

"James?" she murmured in shock. "James Austin?" Was he here because the family wasn't going to sell the house after all? Her heart rapped out a staccato rhythm at the thought.

He reared back slightly. "You know me?"

"Of course." Phoebe gave a light laugh. "You taught me how to play marbles. And when you broke your leg, I sneaked a kitten into your room to entertain you."

James's mouth quirked up at the corners, though he still regarded her blankly. Would he recognize her at all? Her hair was the same shade of black, her eyes still the color of hazelnuts. But they'd both changed since the last time she'd seen him. He'd been fourteen and she'd been ten that last summer in Newport before his family had moved to England.

"I remember that kitten," he said with a nod. "Your name is Hill? Are you related to our former cook, Mrs. Hill?"

He didn't remember her—at least not yet. Phoebe didn't know whether to feel disappointed or relieved by that fact. "That was my mother. I'm Phoebe," she repeated.

This time his green eyes widened as he studied her more carefully. "Phoebe? The little girl with the black braids and impish smile?"

She laughed again as a flicker of happiness shot through her. He hadn't forgotten her. "Yes. That would be me."

James shook his head, looking dazed. "Y-you've changed."

"So have you. I thought you were still in England."

"I was. I am." He unpocketed his hand to wave at the room. "My mother sent me back to oversee the sale of the house."

Fresh relief accompanied his explanation. His presence wouldn't interfere with her plans. "I'm surprised I didn't see an automobile or a carriage out front . . ."

He shrugged. "I walked." His expression turned wistful as he glanced around them. "I didn't realize how much I missed this place until I stepped inside."

"I know," she agreed in a reverential voice.

This house had always been more than just a building to her. It was a place of magical summer days and wishes that might come true, even for the fatherless daughter of a servant.

"What are you doing here?" James asked. "Do you live in Newport now?"

"No." *Not yet.* "My mother and I are still living in New York. I . . ." How much should she tell him? She clasped her gloved hands together, hating how she suddenly felt like an impostor. "I came into some money, a rather great sum," she admitted, "when our recent employer willed the bulk of her inheritance to me."

Lifting her chin, she met his level look with one of her own. She would be forthright and honest as her mother had taught her to be, even if she feared his response. "I'm planning to buy the mansion. That's why I'm here."

A moment of silence accompanied her words. Phoebe resisted the urge to take them back. She had enough money to purchase the house, whether James felt she was worthy of such a residence or not. Deep down, though, she secretly hoped he would approve of her plans. James had always treated her kindly, unlike his sisters or the Austins' high-society guests.

"That is . . . marvelous, Phoebe." A full smile lit his face. And spurred a repeat to the rapid thumping of her heart. "About the inheritance and wishing to buy Baywood."

She had a sudden urge to embrace him in gratitude. Here stood the eldest son of George and Gwendolyn Austin, and he wasn't scoffing at her or looking down his nose at her as others back in New York City had done.

"I'll be rooting for you at the auction."

Phoebe's happiness shattered like glass. "The auction?" She'd been told the sale of the house would be handled by the accountant of the late Mr. Austin.

"Yes, Mother recently decreed she wanted the sale to be conducted through an auction. The event will take place at the end of the month."

The blood rushed to Phoebe's head, making her feel faint. She reached out to steady herself, but there was nothing to hold on to. Her plans had been contingent on acting swiftly in purchasing the mansion. Pitting her newly acquired fortune against those of far wealthier buyers at an auction would likely prove disastrous. She didn't have as deep pockets as many of them, and she had to hold a sizeable sum in reserve to comfortably provide for herself and to assist her mother.

"Are you all right, Phoebe?" James took her elbow gently in hand. "Do you need to sit down?"

Shaking her head, she gathered what little remained of her courage and composure. Her dreams had been foolish after all. "Thank you. I'll be well enough in a moment." She took a step toward the door, breaking his kind grip. "It was wonderful to see you, James. I . . . wish you all the best."

"Shall I see you at the auction?" he asked.

Tears stung her eyes. "Perhaps." It might be worth still coming, but then again, she couldn't stand the idea of being laughed at for bidding everything she had, only to lose to someone with more money.

He trailed her out the door and into the shadowed hallway. "Are you staying at one of the hotels?"

"Yes, but my mother and I are only here for a day," she replied, instinctually turning back the way she'd come. Through the servants' entrance. Even in that, she couldn't maintain her new position as an independent, wealthy heiress. "I need to return to the hotel. My mother's waiting there." Margaret Hill had been hoping to see the house too, after her rest from traveling, but Phoebe wasn't sure there was a point now.

James dogged her escape through the house and outside. "I'm thinking of staying here, while I get things ready for the auction."

"That sounds nice," she murmured. She drew in a cleansing breath, but the tears wouldn't leave her alone. "I've got to go, James. Good-bye."

With that, she rushed forward, ignoring how un-heiress-like she must look. The tears wet her cheeks as she reached the canopy of trees. At least she'd been able to see inside the mansion one last time, before relinquishing her plans and consigning the beautiful place to her dreams once more.

Bewildered, James tabbed his shoe against the gravel pathway as he watched Phoebe's flight toward the front of the house. He'd never expected to run into someone he knew from his boyhood days, least of all little Phoebe Hill.

Who isn't quite so little anymore, he thought with a rueful shake of his head.

She was all grown up, a beautiful and poised young woman, and an heiress to a fortune apparently. He was pleased to see her delightful, down-to-earth demeanor and mischievous smile hadn't changed with her altered circumstances. He could recall, in the past, how her smile had always coaxed him to return the gesture. Only just now in the ballroom, when she'd smiled, he'd felt more than a desire to smile back. He'd felt as if the autumn sunshine had taken up residence inside his chest.

He'd dreaded coming here today, knowing that in less than a month the mansion would be sold. But God had clearly answered his repeated prayers for strength in the sudden appearance of Phoebe Hill. Not only did she represent a friendly and familiar face, but she was also someone who clearly loved and cherished Baywood House as much as he did.

So why had she blanched when he'd mentioned the auction? James slowly began walking after her, his mind awhirl. Phoebe had sounded happy and excited at the prospect of purchasing the place—and truth be told, he would prefer she owned the mansion than anyone else. But something had upset her, something to do with the auction.

After a minute or two, his thoughts merged into sudden understanding, a reason as to why she was no longer thrilled about buying the house. He couldn't know if it was the truth, though, until he spoke with her again. And if he didn't catch her, he might not have another opportunity to do so.

James broke into a slow run. He rounded the front corner of the house and saw Phoebe slipping into the backseat of the automobile parked in the drive.

"Phoebe, wait." He jogged toward the vehicle. "Wait up a moment."

She thankfully didn't slam the door shut and order the

driver to speed away. Instead she glanced up at James with a drawn expression. Her lovely brown eyes appeared wet with tears.

Gripping the door frame, he leaned forward. "You don't wish to come to the auction, do you?"

Phoebe pressed her lips closed and shook her head, her gaze falling to her lap, where her gloved hands were clasped together. No one peering into the car would ever suspect she'd grown up in his family's household as the only child of their exceptional cook.

"You fear you'll be outbid." It was the only reason he could think of for the abrupt change in her behavior.

"Yes," she confirmed.

He could relate to the loss and defeat emanating from her. "If I could change my mother's wishes and allow you to buy the mansion, I would."

She lifted her head to look at him. "Really? Why?"

Why indeed? James swallowed, trying to understand his reasoning himself. "I think it only right and fitting that someone who adores this place should be its rightful owner. Someone with memories of what it once was." He turned to look over his shoulder at the grand house. "What it can be again."

He and his mother had shared numerous heated discussions throughout the last five years about the fate of Baywood House. Gwendolyn Austin wanted it gone and no longer draining money from her children's fortunes. The mansion represented her old life, not the one she now had in England with James's stepfather and their children. For James, though, the house represented a time of happiness when his father had still been alive.

As the eldest and the only one of his siblings with an affinity for the house, James had been commissioned to ready it for auction and oversee the sale. A task he no longer wanted.

If he could buy Baywood House for himself, he would. But the yearly stipend from his stepfather and his inheritance from his own father wouldn't be enough to purchase the mansion. Phoebe likely had more funds at her disposal than he did at present. Besides, his mother was likely to throw an apoplectic fit if he didn't return to England after the auction.

"Will you at least consider coming to the auction?" he asked, focusing on Phoebe once more. "Better yet, if you wished to, you and your mother could come a day or two early and look the place over. I'd very much like to put the furnishings and rooms back to rights—as they once were."

She peered up at him, her head tilted in thought. Her eyes no longer glimmered with tears but with undisguised interest. "You're auctioning off all of the furnishings as well?"

"My mother believes that will bring more buyers to the event."

"And you want everything to look as it did?" When he nodded, she continued in a gentle but teasing tone, "Do you remember how it all looked?"

James chuckled as he fell back a step from the car. "If that isn't simply pulling the sheets off the chairs and wiping away some of the dust, then I'm sunk."

Phoebe's wonderful smile reappeared. "You could do that . . . or . . . you could solicit the help of two people I know who are very well acquainted with each and every room of the house."

"Is that so?" he countered, enjoying their banter. "And how are these two people so familiar with the place?"

She twisted to the side to face him directly. "Because they were part of a larger group who traveled ahead of the family and readied the place for their arrival."

Relief mingled with hope inside him. "What would these two people require in exchange for providing such important help?"

Phoebe pretended to look thoughtful. "A place to live, rent-free, until the auction." A shadow flitted over her pretty face, erasing her merriment and furrowing her brow. "And a chance to spend a few more weeks in a place they dearly loved."

James tasted the bite of sorrow and regret on his tongue. If he could hand over the house to her, he would. Other than himself, he couldn't recall anyone else ever looking at it with such fondness as Phoebe was at this moment. He might not be able to grant her wishes to buy the house without an auction, but he did like the prospect of spending more time with her. And ensuring the house looked as it once had.

"As an authorized representative of the Austins," he said, with mock formality, "and a fellow servant in this endeavor to ready the house, I accept the terms you've outlined, Miss Hill."

Reaching out his hand, he waited for her to shake it and seal their agreement. Phoebe hesitated a moment, then placed her hand in his in a firm handshake. James grinned. "And may I be the first to say, welcome back to Baywood House."

Chapter 2

New York City

"Phoebe Christine Hill," her mother intoned in a firm voice as she sank into the nearby armchair, her cane propped between her hands. "Will you kindly stop moving about this room like a thundercloud?"

Grabbing up another pile of clothes from the bureau drawer, Phoebe remarked, "We'll be late for the train, Mother. I told James we'd be back in Newport today, which means we need to finish packing up both of our hotel rooms—"

"Phoebe . . ." Her name came out as much a command as a kind entreaty. There'd be no budging until she stopped and listened.

With a sigh, she shut the drawer and turned around. "Yes?"

Her mother regarded her with curious concern in her blue eyes. They shared the same hair color, or had until

Margaret Hill's turned gray, but Phoebe's brown eyes were a gift from the father she'd never known. She loved that she shared one thing with the man who had adored her mother and her, however briefly.

"Why are we going to Baywood House now instead of waiting for the auction?"

"I told you earlier. James needs our help to ready the house." She moved to place the clothes inside her suitcase. They only had four pieces of luggage between them, a far cry from what a typical heiress would own. But after purchasing a few new dresses, Phoebe didn't wish to spend any more of her inheritance on frivolities. Especially after learning Baywood House was for sale.

Her mother rose and moved with a slightly limping gait toward the bed. After years of service—as a maid, then a cook, and until their employer's recent death, as a housekeeper—her knees were no longer what they'd been in her youth. She sat on the edge of the bed and placed her hand on Phoebe's sleeve.

"I understand why James wants us there. What I don't understand is why *you* want to be there for so long before the auction?" She gave Phoebe a sad smile. "He already told you he can't change his mother's wishes and sell you the house outright."

Phoebe flinched at the reminder as she stared down into the half-full suitcase. "I know that," she murmured. The heaviness she'd felt the other day after learning about the auction stole back onto her shoulders. "But it will be nice to live in Baywood House for almost a month. And not as servants this time, Mother, but as guests. I've enjoyed these last few months on our own, but like you, I want a home we can call ours."

Releasing her sleeve, Margaret placed her palm on

Phoebe's cheek and gently turned her face. "Is that the only reason you agreed to James's plan?"

She couldn't quite meet her mother's eyes. Truth be told, it was James who'd agreed to the arrangement, not the other way around. And Phoebe did have another reason for wanting to help him restore Baywood House to its former inner glory.

"Phoebe?" her mother prompted again.

After pushing aside the suitcase, she sat on the bed. "I was the one to suggest to James that we could help him. And I did it for more than just living in the house."

Silence met her confession, but it wasn't censoring or unkind. Her mother would let her talk before voicing her own thoughts. Phoebe glanced down at her hands. They'd known less work while she'd served as the companion to the elderly Mrs. Tanley, a widowed heiress with no children. But still, her hands weren't exactly the same as those of other wealthy young ladies, and she hoped to keep them that way. If Baywood House became hers, she planned to live and work there, employing only a small staff of servants to help alongside her and her mother. She would be as independent as she'd longed to be for years.

"I'm hoping our help might mean an advantage over the competition." Phoebe turned to look at her mother. "I know James said he can't do anything, but he's an Austin. Perhaps he can pave the way for us so we still have a fighting chance at buying the house."

Margaret frowned. "And if our help doesn't change anything in the end?"

"Then we still get to live for nearly a whole month, rent-free, in a place we both adore." She rested her hand on top of her mother's where it gripped the cane. "Nothing may come of our helping James or even bidding everything I have at the auction, but I'm not ready to give up on this dream completely. Not yet."

Her mother's troubled expression eased. "As long as you understand the situation may not change, even with our help, I'm willing to lend a hand."

"Thank you, Mother." Phoebe hugged her tightly.

"You're welcome," she said softly when Phoebe sat back. A sly smile appeared on her lips a moment later. "James must be about twenty-nine years old now. You haven't yet said what he looks like. Even as a boy he was rather handsome."

Laughing, Phoebe climbed to her feet and resumed packing. "He is quite handsome, but it doesn't matter. So there's no use matchmaking."

"Oh?" She knew her mother was feigning innocence. "And why is that?"

"Because he lives in England, Mother, and Mrs. Austin would never condone her son marrying the daughter of a former servant. We are there as his guests, and possibly his friends, but nothing more."

Margaret stood, an impish glint in her blue eyes. "Be that as it may, James is his own man, my dear. And far more unsuitable marriages have taken place and thrived."

Phoebe shook her head at the futile conversation and felt relief when her mother dropped the topic to help her finish filling their suitcases. The thought of seeing James again and spending time together was more than a little appealing to her. But she was going to Newport for the house, not the man. A fact she felt certain she wouldn't soon forget.

Newport, Rhode Island

James strode down the front steps as the automobile pulled to a stop in front of the mansion. Deciding not to wait for the cabdriver, he opened the door for the two women.

"Welcome to Baywood House, Mrs. Hill." He handed her out of the car, noting the cane she used to steady herself on the gravel drive. It wasn't something she'd needed when he'd known her as a boy.

"Thank you, James." Her lined face radiated mature beauty and kindness from beneath her large hat. "It's wonderful to see you again."

"And you," he said, nodding. Reaching back inside the car to help Phoebe, he felt a familiar jolt of warmth in his chest when she smiled up at him and clasped his hand. "Phoebe. Welcome back." She wore a wider hat than the last time he'd seen her, and he liked the way the green color offset her dark hair.

"Thank you, James." She slipped out the door and released his hand to grip the skirt of her long dress. A sliver of disappointment moved through him at no longer having her hand in his. Tipping her head back, Phoebe gazed up at the house as if she hadn't seen it just three days earlier. "Isn't it as lovely as you remember, Mother?"

Mrs. Hill murmured agreement. "Which rooms should we put our things in, James?"

He'd been watching Phoebe and the way the afternoon light played with her cream skin. Clearing his throat and pushing aside his embarrassment, he turned his attention to Mrs. Hill. "How about two of the guest rooms?"

"Really?" Phoebe exclaimed, her brown eyes as bright as a child's on Christmas morning.

Had they expected him to put them up in the servants' quarters? "You are here as guests, both of you. So please, feel free to make the place your home too."

He motioned for the two women to enter the house, then started after them. From the corner of his eye, he caught sight of the cabdriver unloading their bags. With no other able-bodied men about, he didn't see why he shouldn't help, though his mother would likely have plenty of objections over such a menial task. James hefted two of the suitcases, leaving the other two for the driver.

The man's eyes widened with surprise. "Thank you, sir."

James led the driver inside, where Phoebe and her mother stood waiting. Then he guided the group up the grand staircase. The red plush carpet muffled their footsteps as they made their way to the second floor. He stopped in the hallway to indicate which two guest rooms the women could use. Neither of the bedrooms had been cleaned, which would likely be the first order of business.

Once he'd escorted the driver back downstairs and paid him, James returned upstairs to find Phoebe and her mother hard at work in their respective rooms. Both women had already changed into simpler dresses and aprons, their sleeves rolled back to work. They were pulling sheets off furniture and making the beds. He watched the activity from the hallway, feeling both fascinated and a bit inept. Every house he'd ever lived in or visited had been ready and waiting before his arrival. He'd never observed the frenetic preparations beforehand.

"What about your room, James?" Phoebe asked when she saw him standing there. "Has it been set to rights?"

He rubbed a hand to the back of his neck. The last two nights he'd slept at a hotel in town. It hadn't taken him long after Phoebe's departure the other day to realize he knew nothing about preparing a house like Baywood for daily living.

"No, not yet," he admitted. "I was going to sleep in my father's old room."

Phoebe stopped her bustling about to glance at him, her expression gentle. "When I'm done in here, would you like some help?"

No laughing, no condemnation, no spoken irony at the

reversal of his role from heir to servant. He smiled. "I would be ever so grateful for some help."

He moved down the hallway to his father's room. The idea to stay in here had come to him in the same moment he'd voiced it to Phoebe. Pushing through the door, James peered at the shrouded space. Whatever work was required, his tidy suit would likely be a hindrance.

He removed his jacket and vest then rolled up his sleeves and loosened his tie. A breath of stale air filled his nostrils, presenting a problem he knew how to solve. He crossed to the window and opened it. Fresh autumn air, laced with the smell of dying leaves, rolled into the room.

"Seems you do know what you're doing," Phoebe said from behind.

James turned. "What do you mean?"

She waved at the window as she set down a bundle of linens. "First order of business when readying the house, open the windows and air out the rooms." Moving to the twin armchairs before the fireplace, she yanked off the sheets that covered them.

Unsure what to do next, he waited until she approached him with a smile and pressed a rag into his hand. "Swipe this over every flat surface."

"Done," he said, chuckling. He walked to the bookshelves and began wiping at the dusty leather covers. "I'd forgotten how much my father loved books."

"The library downstairs is certainly a testament to that." Phoebe began making the bed.

"He loved his library, yes, but he also wanted books closer to his room. That's why he had these shelves built and stocked here at Baywood and at our house in New York."

James pulled out a slim volume and opened the cover to see his father's name scrawled inside along with a single-sentence quote. George Austin had penned little sayings or phrases onto the first pages of most of his books. This one read, *To every thing there is a season.* James recognized the Bible verse from Ecclesiastes. One he'd always liked. Though lately, he'd been wondering more and more what he ought to be doing with this season of his life.

Shutting the book and replacing it on the shelf, he continued dusting. "If my father had a wish to read in the middle of the night, he didn't have to go all the way downstairs to find a book. He could simply walk over to the shelves here. I've done the same in England."

"I think that's lovely." Phoebe straightened the blankets and asked, "Do you miss him?"

"Very much." The confession surprised James. He hadn't voiced to another person, in years, how much he missed his father. "He was a good man."

"I don't remember much about him, but he had very kind eyes," Phoebe said. James smiled at her memory and perception—it fit his own. "Do you miss living in America?"

Moving on to dust the windowsill, he considered the question. "There are a great many things I miss. I do enjoy playing cricket, and the English countryside is breathtaking."

"What do you do there?"

He sensed no judgment in the question, only curiosity. And yet the old resentments he'd harbored at feeling useless crept into his voice as he replied, "Most of the time I'm staying at my stepfather's estate in Yorkshire or Scotland, overseeing the upkeep of the house and lands and addressing any problems the tenants might have."

"Do you enjoy it?" Phoebe asked with uncanny perception.

James glanced out the window at the red and gold trees and the waves beyond. The ocean was something else he'd missed. What would he do for a living if he had the choice? A demanding voice in his head protested he had no choice, not if he wished to please his family. But for the first time in a long while, he ignored it and instead searched his heart for a different answer.

"If I had my wish, I think I'd be a gentleman farmer. That's the part I enjoy the most, working alongside the tenants."

"A farmer?" she repeated, her tone surprised. "You'd wish to give up a life of ease for one of daily work and toil?"

"There are days I think I'd like that." Something about Phoebe prompted him to answer her curious questions with truthful responses. Their open, honest conversation was a welcome change and a sharp contrast to what he'd experienced speaking to other young ladies back in England.

He took a seat on the edge of the sill, the dusting rag dangling between his knees as he leaned forward. "I've repaired roofs and built stone walls. I've helped bring in the harvest and planted gardens. I've even milked a cow, though rather poorly, I'll admit." He chuckled at the memory. "And I rather enjoyed every one of those days."

"No time like the present then to learn something new." A pillow arced across the room toward him, but he caught the object before it bludgeoned him in the head. "Ever fluffed a pillow as lord of the manor?" Phoebe's teasing gaze and smile reminded him of the feeling he'd had of soaring when he stood atop a towering peak in Scotland.

His gaze locked with hers as an invisible, kinetic energy leapt between them. "I am no lord of the manor, Phoebe. And no, I have never fluffed a pillow."

"If you can repair a roof, you can certainly fluff your own pillows." Her eyes lit with that impish spark he well remembered from his youth.

Dropping his rag, he rose to his feet. "Is that a challenge, Miss Hill?"

"Perhaps," she said with an upward tilt of her chin. But James thought her voice sounded a bit breathless. Did he have the same effect on her as she did on him? "Here's the other pillow."

She tossed it at him, but he'd anticipated her move this time. He lobbed his pillow in her direction. It bounced off her hip at the same moment hers struck his leg. Phoebe dissolved into laughter and sank onto the bed, clutching at her sides. James laughed right along with her. He couldn't recall the last time he'd done something a bit unruly. Probably not since his childhood days here each summer.

At that moment, Margaret Hill appeared in the doorway, leaning on her cane. "What is going on in here?"

Another round of giggles consumed Phoebe, so James volunteered an answer. "We are fluffing pillows, ma'am," he said with a smart bow. Phoebe clapped a hand to her mouth, and James could see her shoulders were still shaking with hidden laughter. Laughter he'd inspired and hoped to inspire again.

How many heiresses of his acquaintance enjoyed working and laughing and conversing about meaningful topics? None, except Phoebe. Once again he found himself admiring the fact that even with her newfound wealth she hadn't changed who she was inside.

Mrs. Hill arched an imperious eyebrow at them before her face relaxed into a smile. "If you two are finished fluffing pillows, I could use your help in the kitchen."

"We're coming, Mother."

Phoebe stood as James scooped up the pillows from off the floor. After he handed them to her, she placed them back onto the neatly made bed. "You really milked a cow?" she asked as he followed her out of the room.

He grinned. "I really did. Though I think I'm better at fluffing pillows."

"That poor cow," she quipped as they walked side by side down the hall.

James shook his head in mock solemnity. "You mean my poor pillows."

He solicited another laugh from her, as he'd wished. And as they made their way down the back stairs toward the kitchen, he couldn't help thinking this last trip to Baywood House might prove to be his favorite one yet.

Chapter 3

Armed with a list of foodstuffs to purchase and tasked by her mother to find someone to assist with the cooking during the next four weeks, Phoebe changed back into her nicer dress and hat for a walk into town. She was pleased when James asked to join her. Their conversation and witty banter earlier as they'd straightened his father's room had been more than a little enjoyable. Especially the intense way James had regarded her when she'd challenged him about fluffing pillows.

None of the other young men she'd met during her time as Mrs. Tanley's companion had left her feeling as delightfully off-kilter. Or were unthreatened by her need for independence. But she wasn't so naïve to believe her and James could ever be more than friends. He lived in England and she wished to live here. He was the son of "old money" and the stepson of an earl, and she would forever be the daughter of a servant.

"I never thought any season here could be as nice as summer," James said as they strolled toward town, the sea at their backs.

Phoebe murmured agreement. "Spring and winter are probably just as lovely as autumn seems to be." She hoped she'd be here to see those seasons as well.

"I should like to see those too," he said, echoing her thoughts.

"And why haven't you?" She tempered the question by adding, "Seeing as you love Baywood House so much."

James pocketed his hands, his straw boater shading his handsome face, which furrowed in a contemplative expression. "My family is no longer here, for one. Although all four of my sisters have married Englishmen now, which leaves just my mother, stepfather, and three half siblings in London." He kicked at a pebble with his shoe and sent it skipping ahead of them. "There have been plenty of times through the years, though, when I wished to come back. This place is in my blood, in my soul. It's . . ."

"Magical," she supplied, resisting the urge to touch his sleeve in a show of understanding. She felt the same about Baywood House.

"Yes, magical. But as the oldest and my mother's only son until my half brother Edward came along, I felt it was my duty to care for her. Even after she married Winston." The lines around his green eyes pinched with what looked like resignation. "I suppose that's why I never came back, even when I was old enough to do so. At least not until now."

"I'm glad you came back, James." She meant it. He wasn't to blame for the auction, and she liked getting to know him better. Four years between them had felt like a large gap when she was a child and he was a young man. But now the difference in their ages wasn't a hindrance. Other things might be, things that hadn't been a challenge when they were younger, and yet, she still savored the thought of spending time with him over the next month.

He glanced at her and smiled. "I am equally glad that you've come." His words filled her with warmth, which spilled over into her cheeks. "And your mother," he hastily added, making her smile.

Once they reached the shops and hotels, they agreed to divide tasks. Phoebe headed off to purchase the needed food items, while James, who'd had more experience with hiring servants, went in search of a temporary cook. Several of the older shopkeepers recognized Phoebe and made a fuss over how much she'd grown and what a lady she had become. The compliments and friendliness pleased her and increased her desire to remain in Newport—at Baywood House, if possible.

She exited her last shop some time later, hefting a wooden crate she'd been given to carry her purchases. A young clerk followed on her heels with the rest of the food. Even though the zenith of wealthy summer guests had fizzled out this late in the year, there were still plenty of carriages and motorcars about. At the sound of a horn, she looked up to see an automobile maneuvering toward her. James sat in the backseat of the open car.

"Did you find a car and a cook?" she asked with a laugh as the vehicle pulled to stop alongside the curb.

James hopped out to assist her. "We'll have the cook much longer than the car. It's just for getting everything back to Baywood."

She smiled, thankful for his thoughtfulness. With plenty of hands, the items were loaded into the car in no time, and Phoebe took a seat beside James. The breeze picked up as the automobile increased in speed. Clamping a hand to her hat, she held it in place, in case her pins didn't do the trick.

"Do you mind the open top?" James had removed his own hat and held it securely on his knee.

Phoebe shook her head as she tipped her chin up and

shut her eyes. "Not at all." She relished the feel of the sun and wind on her face. "Perhaps I'll buy my mother and I a car like this. Though I'd want to learn to drive it myself." She could imagine the thrill it would be to drive through the countryside.

"Then perhaps I can teach you how."

Opening her eyes, she glanced at James. "You know how to drive one of these?"

"Yes, but to be fair, it was only recently that I learned."

"Driving cars, milking cows, and fluffing pillows?" She arched her eyebrows at him. "I never knew you were a man of so many talents, James Austin."

He rewarded her teasing with a smile that made her breath catch. "Thank you. I think." She joined in his light laughter. "And you continue to surprise me as well. Though I can't say I'm shocked to learn the independent Phoebe Hill wishes to own a motorcar. As I recall you were never afraid of trains or boats and were always the first one in line to sled."

Phoebe nodded in surprise. She hadn't expected him to remember those details about her. "I would love for you to teach me how to drive an automobile." She turned her attention forward. "Except you won't be here. Not after the auction." And truth be told, she might not be either. The purchase of a carriage or motorcar would have to wait until after she knew what the future held.

Clearing his throat, James studied his hat. "You're right. I won't be here."

The air between them tensed as they rode the rest of the way to Baywood in silence. Phoebe nearly wished she hadn't said anything about his leaving—she enjoyed their conversation and easy banter. But they both needed to remember this friendship couldn't last. James wasn't staying. And as much as she appreciated his company and his willingness to allow her and her mother to live at the mansion at present, she must tread carefully. Otherwise she was in danger of losing the house and her heart.

Though Phoebe's mother protested eating supper in the dining room that night, James insisted. The two women were both his guests and an immense help, and he wanted them to feel as such. The simple meal they shared reminded him of those he'd eaten in the homes of his stepfather's tenants and was every bit as delicious. Mrs. Hill's talents in the kitchen hadn't dimmed over time. He also enjoyed the lively, sensible conversation that easily flowed between them.

He was grateful the earlier tension with Phoebe had eased. When they'd arrived back at the mansion, he'd helped her bring everything inside. Then she'd excused herself to help her mother clean the drawing room. James had sensed she wished for some distance so he'd settled on straightening up the library by himself. The smell of books and the sight of his father's favorite armchair brought back a flood of memories. He hated to think of someone else possessing the cherished items.

As he'd moved about the room, wiping down tables and shelves, he couldn't help thinking back to the way Phoebe had looked on the ride home, her face turned up to the sun, her lips curved in a candid smile. It was a memory he'd take back to England with him and one he'd pull out on cold, rainy days when the feeling of not belonging anywhere would creep inside him.

"A lovely supper, Mrs. Hill," he said, pulling his thoughts back to the present and setting aside his napkin.

The older woman's cheeks pinked. "Thank you, James.

Then again, I remember you seemed to like just about anything I cooked."

He chuckled. "Almost. I did conceal a great deal of onions in my napkin as a boy."

Phoebe gave a soft snort and lifted her glass. "I don't believe it." Her rich brown eyes held his as she took a drink.

Her uninhibited sniff and teasing challenge were far too attractive to him. And reminded him again of how different she was from the aloof and rather snobbish women he'd met through the years in London, and Yorkshire, and Scotland. Most of them expressed interest in him until learning that his inheritance was rather small in comparison to that of his English compatriots or his younger half brothers.

"Am I being accused of embellishment?" he countered good-naturedly.

She feigned an innocent expression he could see right through. "I'm only saying I find it hard to believe that the dutiful James Austin would refuse to eat his onions."

He knew she meant the words to be playful, but they pricked instead. Dutiful was how he'd always been described. And yet, hadn't he done enough out of duty? When would he feel free, at last, to pursue things that had nothing to do with what others wanted or expected?

"We all have our foibles," he replied.

Phoebe frowned as she studied him. Had she heard the note of regret and frustration in his tone?

"Shall we retire to the drawing room?" he said before she could comment on what she may have observed. She nodded and he came around to help her and her mother from their chairs.

"I'll see to the dishes," Mrs. Hill said.

James had completely forgotten the need to clean up. "No. I can do them." Though he couldn't recall ever washing a dish in his life. "Please relax in the drawing room or the library. I'll join you when I'm done."

Ignoring their objections, he gathered up the plates and cutlery and made his way through the servants' hall to the kitchen. He was relieved to find only a few more dishes there that needed cleaning. The large sink seemed the logical place to start his task. He placed everything inside, suddenly grateful for indoor plumbing.

"I can help."

He looked over his shoulder to see Phoebe entering the kitchen with the drinking glasses in hand.

"I'm capable of doing something as simple as washing dishes," he said with greater irritation than he'd meant to. In truth he felt a bit out of his element, in more ways than one, around the grown-up Phoebe Hill.

She stopped beside the sink. "I know you're capable. You're like no other lord of the manor I've ever met. And believe me, working as Mrs. Tanley's companion, I observed a great many gentlemen."

He met her gaze and realized she spoke with absolute sincerity. "And you are unlike any other lady of the manor."

"I'm not a lady of the manor, at least not yet." Her blush accentuated the pretty features of her face. "And I might never be." She leaned back against the counter. "Sometimes I feel as though I'll never quite belong anywhere, now that I have this inheritance. I'm too independent for some and too rich for others."

Her concerns were so similar to his own it was as if she'd heard his thoughts aloud. The melancholy of her expression reached out to him, inviting him to share. "It's not an easy position to be in, Phoebe. And I think you're doing marvelously well at it."

Her lovely smile wrapped itself around his heart. "Thank

you." Turning, she faced the small mountain of dishes. "Will you allow me to at least wash them, then you can dry?"

James welcomed the plan. Cleaning up would go faster with help, and he felt more confident with drying dishes than washing them. He'd also have the added benefit of Phoebe's company. "Agreed."

It wasn't long before the conversation flowed between them as it had earlier in the day. There were also pleasant moments when Phoebe's fingers brushed his as she handed him a damp plate or glass. Too soon, the dishes had all been washed, dried, and placed back inside their respective drawers or cupboards.

He trailed Phoebe back upstairs, enjoying the sound of her laughter and her occasional snort of exclamation. They hadn't yet spent a full day in each other's presence, and yet, he felt a real kinship with her. And, if he were truly honest with himself, something deeper too.

He was leaving, though, as Phoebe had pointed out on the drive back to the mansion. His mother and stepfather expected him to return to England and to his duties there. Yet, for the first time in years, James no longer wished to do what was expected, but what he wanted.

CHAPTER 4

THE DAYS FELL into a predictable pattern after that, a pattern James quickly came to anticipate. Daytime hours were spent cleaning inside the house. In the evenings before the sun set, he and Phoebe would stroll along the rocky coastline or join her mother in the drawing room for reading and card games. On occasion he and Phoebe would see to the supper dishes, giving Mrs. Hill and their temporary cook, Sylvie, a reprieve.

By the end of the second week, the inside of Baywood House had been restored to its former splendor. James conducted a thorough inspection of each room and felt a mixture of pride at his contribution, joy at the memories that surrounded him, and sadness at leaving the mansion behind.

With the house set in order, he'd turned next to the grounds. His experience in England and Scotland had given him confidence regarding soil and plants. But after he and Phoebe had mistakenly torn up most of the remnants of the herb garden, she'd suggested he invite a gardener from one of the neighboring estates to tutor them. Which James had done.

The old man with whiskered jowls who'd come over the last week had been more than willing to share his decades of knowledge with the young pair. He'd also lent them his assistance in clearing away the dead plants and shrubbery and readying things for winter.

James thoroughly enjoyed his time with Phoebe but especially outdoors. While he'd come to see cleaning the house as more agreeable, he felt most comfortable and useful outside among the trees and dirt, where their interesting conversations continued.

A week before the auction, which he'd advertised in town and in the newspapers as far away as New York and Boston, James awoke to rain pelting against the window. A flicker of disappointment dogged him as he got dressed. The glorious days of fall sunshine wouldn't last much longer. Not that he would be here to see cold weather come and cover the grounds in white. His regret at leaving deepened as he made his way downstairs for breakfast. The longer he stayed in Newport, the more he couldn't imagine being anywhere else.

With anyone else.

Phoebe greeted him with her typical smile. "When was the last time someone went through the attic?" she asked after he'd served himself from the sideboard and sat at the table.

"I don't know." He buttered his toast as he mulled over the question. "Is there anything up there?"

"I'm not sure. I haven't been up there in years. Do you know, Mother?"

Mrs. Hill sipped her usual morning cocoa, then set her teacup on its saucer. "I remember Mrs. Austin had us store a few things in there years ago."

"Shall we go through the attic today?" Phoebe turned to James. "At least until the rain clears up to work outside again?"

The idea of going through the attic sounded intriguing. "I think that's an excellent idea."

"I'll find something to do down here," Mrs. Hill volunteered. "These knees of mine aren't meant to climb all the way to the attic anymore."

Once they'd finished eating and Sylvie had cleared away the dishes, James lit an old lamp and followed Phoebe to the second floor, where a narrow staircase led to the attic.

"Did you come up here often as a child?" He tried to recall whether he'd ever spent much time in the attic and couldn't remember.

Phoebe nodded. "When you and your family went to town, the maids and I would see who could sit in the dark attic the longest." She cast a mischievous look at him over her shoulder that made him grin. "I won, every single time."

He wasn't surprised. Phoebe had gumption and determination, both then and now. She was also resourceful, independent, competent, witty, beautiful . . . James reined in his thoughts. They would only weaken his resolve to do his duty and return to England in another week.

They reached the attic door and Phoebe pushed it open. The space wasn't large; it didn't even span the entire second story of Baywood House. But there were plenty of shadowed corners and only a little light from the single window. He could understand the frightened fascination Phoebe and the maids had felt for the room.

"There doesn't seem to be as much here as I remember." Phoebe moved between some old and broken pieces of furniture to stand before one of several large steamer trunks. Lifting the lid, she peered inside. "These must be some of your mother's old ball gowns."

Something that wasn't likely to fetch much of a price at an auction. James opened one of the other trunks. Wooden blocks, china dolls, and other toys were tucked inside. These were things he hadn't seen in years.

"It's my trick pony," he exclaimed, pulling out the painted tin horse that stood proudly on top of a rectangular penny bank.

Phoebe joined him beside the trunk. "I remember this mechanical bank." Her fingers trailed the words "Trick Pony" on the shiny red surface. "You let me try it out on your birthday."

"I turned ten that summer and was so excited when I opened this." He turned the horse over in his hands. "It was the last birthday present my father selected for me." The memory brought both pleasure and pain.

Her hand on his arm was comforting. "It's still a lovely present. And surely something you can keep. It doesn't need to be sold at the auction."

He dipped his head in a nod of agreement. Perhaps there were other small things he could keep, such as his father's most beloved books.

"Should we see if it still works?" Phoebe asked with a smile. "I can run downstairs for a penny."

"There might be one in here." He fished around among the toys, handing out some of the larger ones to Phoebe, before he located a forgotten penny at the bottom of the trunk. "Aha."

Taking a seat on the floor, he placed the toy in front of him. Phoebe settled down next to him, her expression mirroring the anticipation he felt. He dropped the penny into the designated slot, and to his elation, the tin horse began to rock back and forth, kicking its wooden hooves in indignation.

"It still works," he declared. "After all this time, it still works."

As he stared in fascination at the once-treasured toy, something inside him clicked into place, bringing sudden clarity. It was as if an important yet forgotten piece of himself had been dusted off and given attention, much like his trick horse.

James rested his elbow on his lifted knee and picked up the now motionless toy. "I'd forgotten about this horse until I saw it again, and yet, there was a time when it meant everything to me." He ran his thumb over the horse's head. "I accidentally left it behind after my birthday, and I remember crying on the steamer when I realized my mistake. I couldn't imagine living without the horse, but by the next summer I don't recall even looking for it."

He glanced at Phoebe, grateful to see understanding in those charming brown eyes of hers rather than confusion or pity. "It's been the same with the house, all these weeks," he continued. "I thought I'd moved on, and yet, being back here has reminded me how much I love this place and how greatly I will miss it once it sells."

"Can't you buy it yourself?" He knew how much it cost her to ask the question, and he admired her all the more for it. Her friendship had become as precious to him as Baywood House itself these last three weeks.

"Unfortunately, no. My annual income from my stepfather, which is mostly contingent on managing his estates, combined with my father's fortune wouldn't be enough." He set the toy horse back down. "My mother did state the proceeds from the auction will be mine."

Phoebe leaned back on her hands. "Perhaps you can buy yourself a farm in England then with that money."

James laughed lightly, although there was a certain appeal to her suggestion. "I would prefer a farm here."

"Then why not buy one?"

"You mean not go back to England?" he countered.

"Yes," she said, nodding.

A few tendrils of her dark hair had fallen loose and rested along the high collar of her dress. Would those strands be as silky to the touch as he imagined?

"My duty is there, not here."

"Then perhaps it's time to rethink your duty, James." The conviction in her tone pierced through his desire to dismiss the idea as preposterous. "We have other duties besides those to our families. We also have a duty to God and to ourselves."

He wasn't surprised by her comment. She'd shared her own unwavering faith with him as they'd worked alongside each other the past few weeks. But her words in this moment struck him more deeply than any others and silenced the ready excuses he might have tossed out.

"I know that's probably bold to say," she admitted into the stillness, her gaze lowering to her lap, "too bold for an heiress." She gave a self-deprecating chuckle. "But I see how happy you are when you talk about Baywood House and Newport and farming. It's how I feel about this place and this town. Minus the farming, of course."

Climbing to his feet, he reached out both hands to help her up as well. She placed her bare palms against his, and as he pulled her gently to her feet, he tugged her a step closer. The familiar spark of electricity hummed between them as it had over and over again since she'd come to stay at Baywood.

"I like your bold words," he said in a low voice, his heart banging like a hammer in his chest. He released one of her hands to touch her hair beside her ear. It was, indeed, as smooth as he'd guessed. "And you are absolutely right about my duty." He intertwined his fingers with hers; they fit perfectly. "May I ask your permission to do something in this moment that has nothing to do with duty?"

When his gaze dropped to her lips, Phoebe knew exactly what he wished to ask her permission for. Her pulse wound faster. "Yes?"

"May I kiss you, Phoebe?"

"Yes," she repeated in a whisper.

His hand moved from touching her hair to cupping her face with his palm, his thumb caressing her cheekbone. Closing her eyes, she waited, her breath coming faster. She'd dreamt of this moment often after spending so many wonderful days working alongside James inside the house and out. His lips dusted hers, shooting feeling down into her toes and up to the crown of her head. He paused as if gauging her reaction, then he kissed her a second time. Her heart sprang into her throat at the gentle and hopeful touch within his kiss. She didn't want him to leave, not next week, not ever. Because she was starting to fall in love with him.

After a few marvelous moments—or were they minutes?—James ended the kiss and pulled her into his arms for an embrace. "I don't want to leave you," he murmured against her hair, voicing her own thoughts out loud.

"Me neither." She tightened her hold around his waist.

"I can't tell you, Phoebe, what your help has meant to me. That you would selflessly sacrifice to help with the house shows what a true friend and a remarkable woman you are."

Rather than inspiring joy, his words felt as abrupt as a slap. She hadn't agreed to help him out of complete selflessness. Her heartbeat picked up again, but not from happiness or anticipation this time.

"I don't know how everything will work out next week," James was saying, "but somehow I want to find a way to still see you." He eased back to touch her chin. "I think I'm in love with you, Phoebe."

The tender light in his green eyes only fueled her guilt.

She had to say something. Clearing her throat, she fell back a step, though she still kept hold of his hand. "James, there's something I need to tell you."

"What is it?" His expression conveyed nothing but curiosity.

Phoebe swallowed hard. "I did want to help you. I love this house and I remembered how kind you were to me when I was a child." She licked her lips, wishing she could go back to kissing him instead of hurting him with her confession. "That wasn't my only reason for wishing to help you though."

His brow furrowed. "What was the other reason?"

"I . . . I hoped that by helping you I could somehow help my chances at buying the house." How bitter the words tasted against her tongue.

The consternation on his handsome face as he pulled his hand from her grip cut into her. "But I told you that first day, Phoebe, there was nothing I could do. There still isn't."

"I know." She clasped her empty hands together, feeling small and selfish.

"And yet you still thought there was a chance if you helped me?"

She nodded meekly before lifting her eyes to his. "I'm so sorry for not telling you sooner. And even if that was my main reason for coming, it isn't why I've stayed, James. I've stayed because . . . well, because you've come to mean a great deal to me."

"As much as the house?"

Phoebe wanted to say yes, but she couldn't lie to him. Her dream of owning Baywood House, of living here permanently, was still a possible reality. A life with James seemed less so. "I don't know."

"I see." The finality of his tone provoked further regret inside her. Lifting his hand, he brushed his fingers along her cheek in an achingly gentle gesture of farewell. "I'm disappointed. And yet I appreciate your honesty."

He moved to pick up his horse from off the floor. "I think I'll keep this after all," he said, tipping it toward her. "The new owner of the house is welcome to everything else up here." With that he exited the attic.

Phoebe waited for the door to shut behind him before she sank onto one of the trunks. Even as uncertain as her future was, it had felt hopeful and bright only minutes ago, especially while kissing James.

But now . . . Now her tears fell as steady and quiet as the rain outside the tiny window, the dusty space and old furnishings a silent witness to her grief over what might have been.

"You live in England, but you want to buy a farm—my farm—here?" The middle-aged man scratched at his thinning hairline.

James shook his head. "I won't be returning to England to live. And yes, I may purchase your farm. I like what I see." He waved a hand to encompass the clapboard house, large barn, and plenty of acreage. It was a smaller farm than the one he'd viewed yesterday, but perhaps it would be wiser to start small in his new venture.

Just saying the words aloud to a stranger reinforced his decision. He'd come to it two days ago—he would remain in America, and with the funds from the sale of Baywood House, he would purchase his own farm.

Reaching out his hand, he shook the other fellow's. "I'll be in touch in a day or two."

The farmer nodded, still looking perplexed.

James strolled down the lane, crunching leaves beneath

his feet. The auction was tomorrow. In a way it couldn't come soon enough, and yet, he also wanted to put it off. Things had been strained between him and Phoebe ever since their kiss and her confession. He'd talked out his disappointment and frustration to the old gardener the day before, and the man proved as good a listener as he had a teacher and groundskeeper.

"Do you forgive her?" he'd asked James, his gaze keen.

After a moment, James had answered in the affirmative, "Yes, and I understand why she thought her help might further her cause to buy the house."

And he did. What he couldn't fully stomach was that she might feel more for his family's summer mansion than she did for him. She hadn't said as much but she hadn't denied it either. Her answer had simply been that she didn't know.

His own growing feelings for her were evident to himself and had become even clearer after he'd kissed her in the attic. James loved her, plain and simple. But his decision to live in America again and buy a farm had been his own. He wasn't staying for Phoebe, though he hoped to continue seeing her, whether she secured Baywood House or not.

He'd know for certain tomorrow where her heart lay. The realization filled him with both anticipation and anxiety. Whatever happened, he would be forever grateful for Phoebe's surprise entry into his life. And hopefully, God willing, he thought, slipping his hands into his pockets, she wouldn't be permanently exiting it after the auction.

"You're buying a farm? Near Newport?" Phoebe gaped in shock at James. The glow of sunset lit up the eager expression on his handsome face. He'd asked if she would walk to the cliff side after supper and she'd nervously agreed, wondering what he wished to say to her. The purchase of a farm hadn't been one of the topics she'd considered.

James nodded. "I haven't decided which one yet, but I'm going to be a gentleman farmer after all."

"That's . . . that's wonderful, James." And it was. His dream was coming true, and she hoped that after tomorrow's auction hers would too.

Her surprise deepened further when he reached for her hand. She'd missed his touch, however briefly she'd experienced it the other day. "Would you ever consider making a farm your home instead of a palatial mansion?"

Phoebe glanced away, her thoughts a snarl inside her head. Was he asking what she thought? Now that he was staying, could they have a life together, if she chose the same kind of life as him? "I suppose there is a certain freedom that comes with farm life that is appealing."

He squeezed her hand in obvious hope, but Phoebe wasn't finished. "But I'm also trying to better my life and my mother's, James." She turned to look at him again, willing him to understand. "Would a farm provide a better life? More so than Baywood?"

"I think it matters most who you share that life with," he said not unkindly, even as he released her hand. "To me this is a chance, Phoebe. A chance to live an independent life by my own rules." His eyes softened as he studied her openly. "A chance to live by *our* own rules, if you so desire."

A part of her longed to fall into his arms and accept, and yet . . . Baywood House had long been her dream, even before she'd had the means to secure it.

"I'm happy for you, James. I really am." She blew out a sigh of regret, then squared her shoulders. "But I still want to see my dream come true too."

A frown pulled at his mouth, the one she'd enjoyed

kissing the other day, but he dipped his head in a nod of understanding. "Then I will see you at the auction tomorrow, Phoebe."

Chapter 5

Nearly all of the furniture had been claimed. Phoebe couldn't even recall which buyer had just purchased Mrs. Austin's buffet cupboard. After today, the rooms of Baywood House would be as bare as they'd been when the mansion was first built.

Phoebe's heartbeat spiked again as it had over and over since the auction had begun. Inside her gloves, her palms felt clammy. Her mother sat beside her, a picture of calm. At the front of the ballroom, James was seated in a stiff-back chair, his demeanor growing more and more sorrowful as his family's furnishings were sold off one by one.

"Only a few pieces of furniture left, which means we're almost to the house," her mother murmured in her ear, squeezing her hand.

Phoebe nodded stiffly as her gaze strayed to James again. Before drifting off to sleep last night, she'd thought more about their kiss, the hopeful look in his green eyes as he'd told her about his plan to buy a farm, and his question that day in the attic. Did he mean as much to her as Baywood? Frustration and confusion pinched her anew as she considered the inquiry again. How did she really feel about James?

Ignoring the auctioneer's cries, she focused her attention on all she and James had shared the last month. She'd thoroughly loved spending time with him and coming to know him as a friend, and then something more. From that moment fluffing pillows, she'd felt a pull, a connection, between them. He was a man of loyalty, integrity, and kindness. His face was the one she couldn't wait to see each morning and the one she pictured each night. She loved knowing his thoughts and sharing her own, loved teasing and laughing with him, loved how he appreciated and encouraged her independence.

In short, she'd been falling in love with him for weeks now. But in this moment, she knew what her heart had been trying to tell her since their kiss. *I love him. I love James.*

She couldn't imagine living in Baywood House without him. Her memories of this place would always be magical, but what made this place so wonderful was James. The mansion would never embrace her, or tease her, or watch her in adoration. It was merely a beautiful façade, especially now that it was bereft of all its furnishings.

Perhaps, like James and his farm, it was time for her dreams to change and evolve.

"Who will start the bidding on this magnificent gentleman's chair?" the auctioneer drawled. "Genuine leather, folks, and years of life still left in it."

Phoebe saw James flinch. He'd mentioned to her that this was his father's favorite chair. A new idea bolted through her mind like a comet. A way to show James that what, and more importantly whom, meant the most to her was him.

The auctioneer threw out an opening bid, and Phoebe

immediately raised her number card in the air. James reared back a bit, his expression puzzled.

"What are you doing?" her mother whispered. Phoebe had already explained to her that she wouldn't be acquiring any of the furniture in order to put more money into her bid on the house.

Phoebe kept her voice low as she answered, "Something I should have thought to do much sooner." Her mother didn't question her; she simply clasped Phoebe's hand again in a show of understanding.

Gratitude and love filled her. Looping her arm through her mother's, Phoebe kept a vigilant focus on the bid for the armchair. In the end the auctioneer pronounced it hers. She smiled at James, who tentatively returned the gesture, though he still looked unsure.

When the last of the furnishings had been sold, the auctioneer announced it was time to bid for Baywood House itself. James visibly cringed before his countenance settled back into steely resolve. The opening bid was named, lower than Phoebe had anticipated. But it no longer mattered.

Seated up front, she couldn't see those bidding behind her, but the price began to creep higher. She met James's gaze and watched him tip his head toward the auctioneer. His silent question was obvious—wasn't she going to bid? Phoebe gripped her number card tightly between her gloved hands. She could feel them trembling, but she didn't know if it was from lack of courage or the presence of it. Everything inside her whispered she was doing the right thing.

Her mother tensed beside her, though she didn't urge Phoebe to bid. Her silent trust bolstered Phoebe. She could do this. The bidding price rose up and up until finally reaching a sum far beyond what she could've afforded. A few minutes later the auctioneer declared the winner of the bid and the new owner of Baywood House.

Phoebe exhaled a long breath—it was over. The other buyers rose from their seats, their conversations rising and falling like ocean waves inside the vast room. Setting aside her number card, she stood, eager to speak with James.

"You didn't bid," her mother said, lovingly regarding Phoebe.

She watched James shake hands with the auctioneer. "No, I didn't. I couldn't."

"Is that because you've possessed the most precious thing inside Baywood House for some time now?"

Phoebe glanced down at her mother, wondering what she meant. "What would that be?"

Margaret smiled. "His heart."

Bending down, Phoebe gave her a kiss on the cheek. "Thank you for understanding, Mother. And I promise we'll get a house soon."

"I can afford my own small place, my dear, if that's necessary." Her gaze went to James. "And something tells me it might be. Now go on."

Her heart thumping chaotically, Phoebe went to stand calmly beside the only thing she'd purchased today—the armchair. James caught her eye and slowly approached. Would he forgive her for taking so long to understand her heart? She hoped and prayed so.

"You didn't bid on the house." There was no mistaking the confusion in his tone.

"No. But I did win this wonderful chair." She rested her hand along the leather back. "It's a gift for someone I know. Someone very special." Her voice caught and she hurried to swallow. "He's come to mean the world to me, far more than any house here or anywhere else."

James studied her for a long moment. "Any house?" he said as he placed his hands over hers. Phoebe linked her fingers with his. "Even Baywood House?"

"Yes, James. Even Baywood House."

A hopeful glint lit his green eyes. Throwing a glance at the buyers still milling about the room, he led her by the hand out through the ballroom's French doors. He didn't cease walking until they reached the canopy of trees outside. Then he stopped her beside one glowing with golden leaves. "Thank you for buying my father's chair." He brushed his knuckle against her cheek, renewing the swift thrumming of her pulse.

"I knew what it meant to you."

"Why did you change your mind, Phoebe? Why didn't you bid on the house?"

She glanced at the mansion, suddenly afraid he might have already changed his mind about her. "You asked me the other day which was more important, you or this house." Licking her dry lips, she pulled in a breath for courage. "Sitting there during the auction, I realized Baywood House is only a place that holds wonderful memories, if you aren't here to make new ones with me."

Looking at him again, she bravely continued. "I love you, James Austin. With all of my heart. You mean far more to me than a hundred mansions."

A slow grin brightened his face. "How do you feel about living on a farm now?"

Phoebe squeezed his hand as joyful tears pricked her eyes. He still loved her. "I find the idea far more appealing today than yesterday. If that's where you'll be, James, then I want to be there too."

His gaze intensified along with his smile, filling her stomach with flurries of anticipation. "In that case, will you be my wife, Phoebe Hill? I'll have only a humble farm to offer. But it will be ours, a place to make a life together."

Winding her arms around his neck, she drew close, feeling as bright as the leaves swaying above their heads. "I would be honored to be your wife, James." She offered him an impish smile. "You can milk the cows while I fluff the pillows."

He grinned. "I can't think of anything I'd rather do."

"I can," she said teasingly, bringing her mouth near his.

Understanding lit his green eyes right before he indulged her with a long kiss. Phoebe kissed him back—soundly, firmly, and with all the love in her heart. She'd come to Newport to purchase Baywood House, but God had other plans for her and James. And she couldn't think of anything more magical than that.

Five years later

Phoebe jostled little James against her hip and smiled encouragement at her husband. Their little family, along with her mother, stood facing the small white house. The wind from the ocean whipped the ribbons of Phoebe's hat and scattered colored leaves across the expansive lawn.

"I christen this house Woodbay Cottage," James said in a commanding voice, his hand gripping the smaller one of their daughter, Maggie. "May you reside here through storm and calm for generations to come."

"Hear! Hear!" Margaret Hill clapped her hands. They'd picked her up in the family motorcar, with Phoebe at the wheel, and drove her from her modest house in town to their new seaside cottage. James's mother would also want the details of the informal ceremony in Phoebe's next letter, especially since she, her husband, and children would be coming to stay with James and Phoebe next summer.

Mrs. Austin had been reticent about her son's marriage and his plans to stay in America as a gentleman farmer. But time, and plenty of letters back and forth across the ocean, had soothed and overcome her hesitation.

Phoebe stepped forward and kissed James's cheek. "A beautiful speech."

"Will we get to live here next summer, Daddy?" Maggie asked, tugging on his pant leg.

James tousled her dark locks. "All summer, Mags. Just as your mother and I did a long time ago." He exchanged a tender glance with Phoebe.

Setting their son on his feet, she watched as he toddled after his sister and grandmother, who took his hand in hers. Then Phoebe turned to face the little house. "It's a wonderful cottage, James."

"It's no Baywood," he said in a playful tone. The cottage and the mansion were situated only a few miles apart, and Phoebe still liked to walk past it every chance she got. James put his arm around her waist and pulled her snuggly to his side. She would never regret choosing him over the grand house.

"This cottage is something better. Because it's ours to make new memories in."

"Like the farm," he added, pressing a kiss to her brow.

"Yes." She leaned her head against his shoulder, relishing the happiness of the moment and the love she shared with him. "You're here with me, James, and I'm here with you. And there's still no other place I would rather be."

A Long Winter Kiss

CHAPTER 1

Michigan, May 1861

THE BARN DOORS had been thrown open, allowing the night air to cool the overly warm structure and the eager crowd of dancers. Samantha Whitefield fanned her flushed cheeks as she maneuvered through the onlookers toward the barn's opening. She'd danced every song so far, and while she happily planned to continue until the farewell party was over, she hoped for a moment to catch her breath.

The need for fresh air drew her all the way outside, where a pleasant breeze pushed the heat from her cheeks and played with strands of her dark blond hair. The nearby budded trees were silver in the bright moon. The beauty of the evening contrasted so sharply with the knowledge that somewhere far away men had begun fighting—and dying—a fight that the young men of the town would soon join. Including Rexford Montgomery. A tremor of misgiving, the first she'd felt all evening, rocked through her and hardened in her stomach.

"There you are."

Samantha knew the voice without turning. It was Rex. Her best friend. Her longtime neighbor. And the boy she'd bested as many times as she'd lost to during their shared years at the one-room schoolhouse up the road. Their competitive dares hadn't ended, either, when Rex, two years her senior, had graduated. Though Samantha had enjoyed being the shining star of the classroom for those two years.

Except now that she was eighteen, she'd noticed things about Rex that she hadn't before. Like the way his jaw bristled with tiny dark hairs in the late afternoon. Or the way his blue eyes matched the sky when he was happy. Or the way his arms muscled beneath his shirt when he worked around his family's farm.

"What are you doing out here?" He came to a stop beside her and nudged her shoulder with his broad one. "Thought you'd dance till dawn."

Samantha shot him a haughty look, if only to cover the rapid footfalls of her pulse. When had the beat of her heart become tied to his nearness? "I will, soon as I rest my feet a moment."

He folded his arms loosely across his chest and stared up at the moon. "Sure is pretty. I hope the moon looks the same down South." He threw her a grin. "Can't wait to find out."

His arrogant tone jerked a frown from her lips. "You sound happy to go."

"Of course I am." Rex turned to face her. "I want to see more of the world than just our tiny corner. Remember all those places Miss Rogers taught us about? New York? New Orleans? Paris? London?"

"But you aren't headed south to travel, Rex. You're going to be a soldier."

The uneasy knot inside her tightened at her own words. She couldn't imagine her life without him. They might be too old for their dares, as her older sisters were constantly reminding her, but their competitive friendship had been something Samantha could always count on, something that would always be there.

"I'm going to come back, Sammie." His hands came to rest on her shoulders, firm yet comforting. Only he and her father still called her by her childhood nickname. In the moonlight, his eyes were oddly serious. "Which is why I've been meaning to ask you something all night."

Her heart picked up a quick tempo again. "What is it?"

Rex glanced around, then taking her hand in his, he led her around the side of the barn. "This is better."

"Better for what?" Samantha moistened her lips. She expected him to release her at any moment and restore order to her pulse. But instead he placed her hand against his chest and covered it with his own.

"For what I have to say." Though the shadows obscured most of his face, his intense gaze was hard to miss. "I've wanted to ask you this for a month. Ever since I decided to volunteer." He emitted a half growl, half cough, the telltale sign he was nervous. "I want you to be my girl. I have for a long time."

Samantha blinked. Surely this was all a lovely dream, not unlike the ones she'd had over the last six months. "Wh-what do you mean? Be your girl?"

"You know, wait for me. Promise your heart to me, and no one else. Until I get back." He placed a gentle kiss on the pad of her index finger, causing shivers up her arm despite the temperate night. What would it be like for her lips to meet his?

Her muddled brain finally began to work, and her first thoughts were of incredulity. "Why me?" He could have his pick of any girl in town, any girl in the county. He had for years.

"Is it so hard to believe," he answered in a low voice, "that all this time I've been trying to win our dares, I'd already lost my heart to you?"

The words rang through her, as inspiring and appealing as church bells. Had their longtime friendship turned into something more, for both of them?

Before she could decide, Rex leaned toward her and brushed his lips over hers. It was as if she were dancing again, her heartbeat thumping as fast now as her feet had earlier. Samantha sucked in a sharp breath of surprise, but she didn't move, afraid she'd break the hypnotic spell of the moonlight and Rex's entreaty.

Her patience was rewarded. Rex tugged her closer, and this time when his mouth met hers, it was with greater confidence. A thrill traveled the length of her, from her bare head to her pinched toes inside her too-small shoes. She lifted her free hand to rest it lightly against the back of his neck, where his hair curled slightly. This was her first real kiss, and she wanted it to last forever.

Too soon he eased back with a chuckle. "Didn't know you knew how to kiss."

Samantha shot him a half-hearted glare. "You don't know everything about me, Rexford Josiah Montgomery." He cringed, as she knew he would, at the use of his full name.

"So what do you say?" His thumb caressed her cheek. "Will you wait?" His eyes shone as bright as the moon as he added in a husky whisper, "I dare you, Sammie. I dare you to wait and be mine the moment I return."

How many times had those words prompted her to act in the past, with no real thought to the consequences? But this dare wasn't about racing to the creek or hurdling a fence or getting a better mark in spelling than him. This dare involved their hearts and their longtime friendship. If she accepted, there would be no going back to the way things had been.

Another niggling fear made her hesitate. What if Rex didn't return? Nearly everyone else dear to her had left—her mother and baby sister in death and her older sisters in marriage and setting up their own homes. The pain of never seeing Rex again would surely leave her gutted and empty.

Or what if he lived but met and fell in love with some Southern belle instead? Samantha didn't want him returning to her out of obligation.

"Are you afraid?" he asked softly when she continued to stand there silent.

Tears blurred his face for a moment. "Yes," she whispered. "What if . . ."

He cut off her question with another lingering kiss. "We'll make it through, together, Sammie. I'm not going to forsake you." He pressed his forehead to hers. "But more importantly, God isn't going to forsake you either."

How many times had he reminded her of that through the years? She wanted so much to believe it, but didn't that require effort on her part?

Hiding her smile, she pretended to eye him thoughtfully. "Will you write me every day?"

A full grin brightened his face. "Every chance I get." He took her other hand in his. "Does that mean you'll wait for me?"

Please keep him safe, Lord. Help me take this leap of faith.

She pushed out a soft sigh and nodded. "Yes, Rex. I'll wait for you."

He let out a whoop that surely the dancers inside the barn could hear before he clasped her close and swung her around. Samantha laughed. The worry in her middle diminished some.

"I'm the luckiest man around," he said, setting her on her

feet again. "And I promise to let you know that every day. In letters now but in person later. I promise."

She placed her hand alongside his jaw as she tried to memorize this moment and the beloved features of his face. "I'm going to hold you to that."

Virginia, December 1862

Another deep cough slashed through Rex's lungs. He pulled the ends of his blanket closer, but he guessed the temperature inside the tent wasn't much warmer than that outside. On his knees he balanced pencil and paper to write a reply to Samantha's recent letter. The page remained blank, though, the words that usually poured out of him as frozen in his mind as the surrounding landscape.

He would soon commemorate another Christmas as a soldier. Another Christmas away from Samantha and his family. It wasn't difficult for him to picture the festivities at home. His mother would decorate the house with pine boughs and tie ribbons to the jars of her carefully prepared jam. Those jars would be added to the pile of presents Samantha and her father delivered to their neighbors and friends on Christmas Eve.

A longing to be there filled him with sharp pain. As deep and visceral as what he'd felt after losing his two closest friends during the regiment's recent battle at Fredericksburg. His life had become a kaleidoscope of blood and death and battle, broken only here and there by moments of normalcy before twisting out of focus again.

"You done yet, Rex?" his tentmate asked, glancing up from writing his own letter.

Covering another cough with his fist, Rex shook his head. "Not yet."

"Is it to your family or your girl this time?"

He cleared his throat, desperately trying to ease the pain in his chest. "My girl."

Samantha was still his girl, wasn't she? He might not hear from her as often as he'd hoped, but he didn't fault her. The mail didn't always reach them. More than eighteen months had passed since he'd last seen her, but he'd thought of her every day. Her lovely face and his connection with God had pulled him through what had become the most difficult and gut-wrenching time of his entire life.

And yet lately he couldn't shake the feeling that he might not be worthy of either one anymore. He'd experienced things he didn't want Samantha ever knowing. Things that haunted his dreams and left him gasping for breath and sanity when he woke. Ever since Fredericksburg, though, his nightmares had changed—he was home again, but when he saw Samantha, she hadn't recognized him. She'd taken one look at him and averted her gaze.

Running a hand over his beard, he stared hard at his paper, willing the words to come. He didn't really believe Samantha wouldn't recognize him when he came home. His physical appearance would still be familiar. But the inside of him . . . Would she recognize that part anymore? Down deep he could feel himself starting to harden, to grow cold, to fester with fear. A fear that he would leave her a grieving sweetheart if he died and a fear that she would reject the man he'd become if he lived.

Rex tightened his grip on his pencil as an idea formed in his mind. He began writing, the sentences he'd been struggling to conjure up flowing without effort now. A nagging doubt presented itself—he hadn't sought God's blessing on his plan. But he easily snuffed the thought. He was doing what he must because he loved Samantha. If there was anything to pray about, it would be that she would ultimately come to accept his decision.

Michigan, One month later

Samantha drummed her fingers against the windowsill as she watched her father drive the sleigh up the snowy road toward the farm. Was the horse even moving? The animal seemed to be walking slower and slower. It had been three weeks since her last letter from Rex. Was he alive? Was he well? Nervousness and hope filled her, until her entire body was fidgeting. She couldn't wait any longer. Throwing on a shawl, she slipped out the front door, gasping softly as the cold hit her face.

"Any word, Papa?" she called out as she entered the barn.

"I believe so, yes," he said, fishing through his pockets as though searching for a letter. "Lovely day for a sleigh ride, is it not?"

She groaned. "Papa, please."

He smiled at her as he finally extracted a letter from his shirt pocket. "Ah. Here it is. I believe it's from Rex, but I can't tell without me spectacles. If you'll just go get them, daughter . . ."

With a squeal of joy, she plucked the letter from his hand. "Thank you, Papa." His laughter followed her out of the barn and back into the house.

She raced to her bedroom and sat on the bed before tearing open the letter. The tiniest disappointment pricked at her happiness when she saw that he'd only written one page. But he was busy as a soldier. She was grateful for any correspondence from him. It shortened the distance of time and space between them.

Dearest Sammie,
I hope this finds you well. You are in my thoughts constantly. Another of your letters came this week, and I have read it through several times. Please know that I love you still and I won't stop praying for you.

Something cold and panicky crept over Samantha. Why did it sound as if he were saying good-bye all over again? She gripped the letter tighter, the edge of the paper cutting into her fingers, as she read on.

I don't think we should write anymore. I'm also freeing you of your promise to wait for me. We can't know the future, Sammie. I might not make it back to you, and I won't commit you to a half-life as the girl of a fallen solider.
This war is ghastly and I thank the Lord every night that you are far removed from it. I'm not the man I once was, and you deserve better. I don't want you to write me anymore, though I'll cherish the letters you have written. This will be my final letter. Please don't send a response. I won't be writing anyone anymore except my parents.
I love you, Sammie. But this is for the best.
Yours always,
Rex

She could hardly make out his signature for the tears dripping off her cheeks onto the page. He no longer wanted to exchange letters with her or be her sweetheart. But why?

Anger began to boil within her, replacing her shock. She crumbled the letter in her hand and threw it against the far wall, where it hit the sampler she'd sewn as a girl. *To every thing there is a season,* it read in fairly even stitches.

How dare he make such a decision without consulting her? She loved him and he loved her. Surely they could have worked through whatever was devouring him from the inside out. Why did he have to charge ahead, breaking her heart in the process, and not even giving her the chance to understand?

Jumping to her feet, Samantha paced the rug, her arms pressed tight against the ache forming in her chest. She had to do something, but what? If only she could see him and talk to him face-to-face. For a moment she contemplated traveling south to find him. But she and her father had little extra money for such a trip.

Then she would write him back and beg him to explain, to reconsider. She would pour every piece of her heart onto the page, and then, he would change his mind.

But even as she thought it, she realized such a letter would do no good. Rex knew her too well. If he asked her not to write him again, she would be honor-bound to respect his wishes, and their deep friendship, by complying. Even if it tore her inside to do so.

"Oh, Rex?" she whispered as she sunk onto the floor. "What have you done?"

She had taken that step of faith by agreeing to wait for him, in spite of her fears. And he'd promised they would figure things out together, that he would show her every chance he got how lucky he felt to have her as his girl.

And yet now her dreams—their dreams—were no more, and he had blocked any effort at restoring them. How would she go on? His absence had been difficult enough to bear this last year and a half. But not to have his letters or the chance to write him back? To have cold silence replace the warmth and love and trust of their relationship? The grief sliced through her with such force that her lungs protested. She gulped in a great, sobbing breath.

After a minute or two of weeping, she reached out and picked up his letter where it had fallen. Creases marred the words and she worked to smooth them out. This was her last connection to Rex and she would keep it.

Her eyes rose to the words of the sampler. *Help me make it through this season of pain, Lord. Help me keep going. And please . . .* She blinked back fresh tears. *Bless and protect Rex.*

Though the anguish of his choice still pierced her, Samantha squared her shoulders. She would carry on. One hour, one week, one month, one year at a time. She slipped the letter into her pocket as a weight, heavy and painful, slipped onto her heart.

CHAPTER 2

Christmas Eve, 1864: Two years later

REX RAN A finger over the smooth wood of the toy carving. The tiny elephant had turned out better than he'd expected. Either this or the giraffe he'd whittled the week before would make a nice Christmas gift for his young nephew.

"Rex?" his mother called from the direction of the kitchen.

Pocketing the elephant, he exited the front room and followed the smell of boysenberry jam to the back of the house.

His mother glanced up as he entered the kitchen. "Will you take this box of jams over to the Whitefields?"

Rex glanced out the window at the snow, which had picked up since the afternoon. Hopefully his father would still be able to make it back to the farm with Rex's sister and her family in tow. It would be the first Christmas in three years that they would all be together.

But it wasn't the snow or the cold walk to their closest neighbor's that had his gut twisting with apprehension. It was the thought of seeing Samantha, in her own home.

He would never forget the shock and pain in her eyes when she'd approached him that first Sunday in church after he'd returned from the war. She'd stood to the side, waiting to speak with him, and Rex had longed for and feared the moment when she would. What would she say to him? Did she loathe him as much as he did himself?

Rex couldn't recall now what either of them had said that day. But he'd come away from the experience determined to honor the promise he'd made to himself—that someone as pure and innocent as Samantha shouldn't be saddled for life with a man like him. A man still haunted by what he'd seen and done in the war. He'd managed to keep that promise, so far, only speaking with her when they saw each other briefly at church.

"Rex?" his mother repeated, her gaze and tone full of concern. They'd been that way often the last six months.

Pushing aside his uneasiness, he moved to grab his coat from beside the back door. "I'll take it over." Perhaps her father would answer the door and Rex wouldn't have to see Samantha at all.

But that hope died when his mother said, "Mr. Whitefield is ill, so I don't know if they're venturing out this evening or not. Either way, they'll have my jam."

So much for avoiding Samantha. If her father was sick, she'd likely be the one to answer Rex's knock.

He slipped into his coat, hat and gloves and hefted the crate. His mother held the door open for him, allowing a blast of snowy air to rush into the kitchen. "Tell them Merry Christmas from us," she called after him.

Nodding to show he'd heard, he gritted his teeth against the cold—and the unpleasant task before him.

"Give me my other boot, daughter. I'm late as it is."

Samantha gripped the laces of the worn brown shoe and shook her head. "You are too sick to go, Papa."

"Nonsense." Her father's green eyes, the same color as her own, sparked with righteous fire. "So help me, Sammie... You will not keep me from my task."

"I'm not. This dreadful cold is."

As if confirming the truth, her father began coughing. He braced himself against the headboard of the bed, his shoulders quaking with the coughs and his stubborn attempt to sit up.

She placed the shoe out of reach across the room and came to kneel beside him, her hand on his knee. "Papa, you can't go out tonight. Not with your cold, and certainly not in this weather."

"It's only a few flurries," he stated flatly, motioning toward the window. But she could tell this last coughing fit had drained him.

"Yes, but it could grow heavier at any minute."

He regarded her with a sad expression. "That's my Sammie. Always a'worryin' about the future, or things getting worse."

Though she sensed the love behind his words, they still brought her a deep twinge of hurt. It wasn't as if she didn't have faith. But anyone would be susceptible to fear after losing a mother, a baby sister, a brother-in-law, and the man she'd once loved...

She attempted to shut her mind against thoughts of Rex, but it was nearly impossible. She still thought of him every day and prayed for him every night. He may have broken her heart, but she was still grateful he'd returned home alive at the end of June.

"Look who's worried about the future," she countered, standing. "Our friends and neighbors will be fine without your gifts."

Her father drove a fist into the quilt. "Confound it, Sammie. I have delivered Christmas Eve gifts for more than twenty years and never missed a year yet. Not even blizzards or a broken sleigh has stopped me."

Samantha pinched the bridge of her nose—he couldn't be reasoned with. But the doctor had strictly forbidden him from going out. "This could turn into pneumonia if you aren't careful, Hyrum," the young physician had warned. And Samantha was taking no chances. Pneumonia had taken her mother and infant sister; it wouldn't be the death of her father too.

"Maybe you can go next week," she offered.

"It must be tonight, Christmas Eve." He crossed his arms over his barrel chest and glared at her.

She threw her hands in the air. "Papa, enough. You can't go. Dr. Hobson confirmed it yesterday. And no amount of bluster will change that."

His eyes darted to the bureau, where she'd set his shoe, his plan evident in his determined expression. Samantha marched over and picked up the boot. "And just in case you attempt to try anything, I will be keeping this with me while I finish preparing dinner."

She started for the door, but he called her back, his voice full of contrition. "Sammie, wait. I heard the doctor, too, and I know you're scared for me, daughter. But I'll be fine. It's one night. Please. Some of these children won't get anything if I don't come."

Shutting her eyes, Samantha pulled in a calming breath. Perhaps she could go in his place, even if she would be alone. She or one of her sisters had always accompanied him in the past, though it had been solely her responsibility to ride with him the last five years after her fourth sister had married. The gifts they'd made were already packed in a feed sack by the front door anyway.

"I'll go," she announced, opening her eyes.

"Alone?" It was her father's turn to shake his head. "You can't, not in this cold. What if there's trouble with the sleigh or Titus injures himself while pulling it? What if you don't stay warm enough?"

Samantha gave a light chuckle. "Who's worrying now? I'll be fine."

"No, Sammie. I insist you find someone to go with you."

First insisting he goes and now insisting I don't go alone. "Papa, who am I supposed to have come with me? On Christmas Eve, no less."

"God will provide," he stated with assurance, one finger pointed at the ceiling. "I will start praying now."

"Fine. And in the meantime, I'm going to lay out our supper and get my winter things together."

She exited the bedroom and trooped down the stairs to the kitchen, willing her irritation to evaporate like mist on the pond. They both meant well. If only her father hadn't taken sick... But he would mend soon. The doctor had commended her more than once on her excellent nursing.

His compliments had pleased her. *Probably more than they should,* she thought as she set down her father's boot and began preparing his supper tray.

The young doctor was nice-looking and amiable. But she'd lost her heart in the past and wasn't sure she would ever get it back. Even though Rex was home now, he had made it clear they no longer had a relationship.

She nearly hadn't recognized him that first Sunday in church. It took her a minute or two of surreptitious staring to realize the gaunt face with haunted eyes and a trimmed beard belonged to Rex. But the revelation was quickly followed by sharp disappointment that he hadn't come to see her personally the moment he'd returned. Then came the pain, as fresh as if she'd read his letter of rejection that very morning, and the unanswered questions of *why*.

Swallowing her resentment and pride, she'd approached him as he stood talking with several others. Up close she could detect the shadows that clung to him and the absent spark from his blue eyes.

She waited a few paces away for him to finish, anxiety churning the breakfast in her stomach. Finally he turned. For one brief moment, as they silently watched each other, she thought she saw tenderness, sorrow, and raw pain in his gaze. Her pulse jerked with hope.

But the hope withered to ash when he shuttered his expression and said her name in a stiffly polite voice. "Hello, Samantha."

She managed to ask how he fared without dissolving into tears. But by the time the awkward conversation ended a few minutes later, she felt wrung out. She hadn't just lost his love the day she'd received his letter; she'd lost her dearest and oldest friend too.

They'd largely avoided each other the last six months, except for Sundays, when they exchanged courteous salutations. At first Samantha had come home from services more distressed than comforted. Gradually the pain lessened, though, until it became a manageable numbness. Now when she saw Rex, she felt only a twinge of regret for what might have been.

But her heart hadn't weathered the pain as successfully as her emotions. She sensed it had hardened even more with fear than it had in the past—making her reluctant to welcome the doctor's obvious interest in her.

She picked up her father's tray, laden with soup, bread, and tea, but a knock at the front door had her setting it back down on the table. Who would be out in the snow at suppertime?

Hurrying to the entryway, she lifted the lamp off the side table and opened the door. A man stood on the porch, stomping snow from his boots, his face obscured by his hat.

"Cold night to be out. Can I help y—" The rest of the words froze inside her throat when the man lifted his chin and she found herself gazing at Rex. It was the first time since his return that he'd come to their door.

"Evenin', Samantha." He kept his expression neutral, though a flicker of something flashed in his eyes before disappearing.

She nodded, uncertainty making her grateful she hadn't eaten more than a little bread just now. Why was he here? What did he wish to say that he couldn't in church?

"I have the jam," he said, hoisting a crate that Samantha hadn't noticed earlier. "For your father's sleigh run tonight." Mrs. Montgomery had been adding boysenberry jam to her father's Christmas Eve deliveries for years.

"Oh, yes." Samantha glanced at the lamp in her hand, debating whether to set it down and take the box or invite Rex to bring it inside.

He made the decision for her by taking a step forward. "Should I bring the jam in?"

"Um . . . yes." She stepped back to allow him entrance. "Just set the box in the parlor. Thank you."

After setting down the crate, he straightened, his glance taking her in before rising to the stairs. "How is your father? My mother said he was sick."

"He still is." A blast of frigid air forced Samantha to shut the door, though she didn't know how long she could remain there, making small talk with Rex. It was different in church. Here, in her own home, memories of the two of them filled nearly every space.

And those memories threatened to choke her now that he stood here again, in the flesh. "It's not pneumonia though," she added, in a voice much calmer than she felt.

Rex removed his hat and fingered the brim. "That's good. Will he still be going out tonight?"

"No, actually. I'm going in his place."

A look of surprise passed over his face, then he frowned. "Alone? Isn't that a bit unwise, on a cold night like this?"

Samantha's jaw went slack. He'd tossed away their friendship, with no real explanation, and now he had the audacity to come into her home and expect her to listen to his concerns? She drew herself up to full height, though she still came to just below his nose. "I'll be fine. It isn't as if I'm going somewhere far or unfamiliar."

Instead of departing or arguing further, he lifted one corner of his mouth. It was the closest thing to a smile she'd seen on his face in months. And the sight of it did something funny to her stomach. "Still as stubborn as ever," he said with an amused shake of his head.

Her fingers curled tighter around the lamp as annoyance rippled through her. What was he doing, speaking with such friendliness and familiarity? Was he toying with her heart?

Before she could ask, a shuffling at the top of the stairs pulled her attention away from him. "Rex, my boy," her father exclaimed, grinning even as his chest rose and fell with hard breaths from walking out of his bedroom.

"Papa." Samantha set the lamp down on the hall table and hurried up the stairs. "What are you doing?"

Her father shrugged. "Heard someone at the door and

thought I recognized the lad's voice. Thought to myself, *That must be Rex Montgomery.* And sure thing, it is." He leaned close to whisper to her, though not soft enough, "An answer to our prayers this night as well. Right, daughter?"

Cheeks burning with mortification, Samantha refused to glance down the stairs to where Rex still stood. He was certainly no answer to prayer, and despite his friendly teasing of a moment ago, likely wished to spend as little time with her as she did with him.

"No, Papa," she hissed. "He was just delivering his mother's jam. Now get back to bed." She gripped her father's arm, but he wouldn't move.

"You 'eard I've been sick, Rex?"

"Yes, sir." His tone rang with sincerity. "I'm sorry to hear it."

Her father waved away the apology. "I'll be right as rain in no time, what with the good Lord helping and my skilled daughter."

Samantha's face felt even hotter. She had to get her father back to his room if she hoped to end his crazed babbling. Or worse, before he insisted Rex accompany her. She would go alone, even if it meant freezing to death. There was no way she would spend the evening in a cozy sleigh with Rex.

"Glad to hear you're on the mend," Rex said.

She tried once more to nudge her father away from the stairs, but he dug his heels in. "Yes, but I can't go on my Christmas Eve run tonight." Her father's sigh sounded a bit exaggerated. "And Sammie won't hear of someone not going at all."

Stifling a groan, she pushed him gently forward. "Back to bed, Papa." He only moved a few inches.

"The girl is going to go alone," her father declared with a shake of his head.

"Not very smart." Rex's voice from right behind her made her heart jolt. She hadn't realized he'd ascended the stairs.

Her father threw her a triumphant look. "I agree with you, Rex. 'Tis not smart at all. She needs someone to go with her."

"No, I don't," Samantha huffed, throwing all her weight against her father's resistant frame. "As I told you both, I'll be fine."

"You've already discussed it with Rex?" His innocent expression set Samantha's teeth on edge. "But you can't go with her, lad?" he asked, turning to look at the younger man.

"I . . . uh . . . didn't say that, no. But . . ."

"Oh, good. Then you *can* go with her." With that seemingly settled, he finally allowed Samantha to steer him into the room. "Now you don't have to go alone, daughter."

She glanced at Rex, who looked nearly as stricken as she felt. Would he refuse? He hadn't exactly been given a choice. She considered signaling him to turn down her father's request, but she knew it would be futile. Her father would badger them both until they eventually agreed to his scheme.

As she watched Rex, a stoic mask replaced his expression of discomfort and hid his true thoughts from her. The realization filled her with sadness. At one time she could easily decipher his moods and opinions.

"I can go with her, sir." Rex's tone held only resignation. It made her want to grab him by the shoulders and shake him until he confessed what he was really feeling. Or why he'd so willingly thrown away their future together.

Her father, on the other hand, looked pleased enough to crow, but Rex's agreement only brought Samantha dread. How would she make it through an entire evening with him? What would they even say to one another?

She considered refusing or telling Rex to go by himself. Her father needed her here. But she'd already committed to making the run. Besides, she needed to prove to Rex, and to herself, that she wasn't a petulant child or a spurned maiden. She'd loved and lost, and she was moving forward with her life. Or trying to, at least. She could survive one night, one sleigh ride.

Still, as she helped her father back into bed and pulled the covers over his lap, she couldn't help pleading, *Please let me endure this night, Lord. I'm doing this for Papa and for our friends. So please, let me and my heart make it through intact.*

Chapter 3

"What am I doing, Lord?" Rex muttered as he hitched the Whitefield's new horse—or at least new to him—to the sleigh inside the warm barn.

The prayer was a faint echo of those he'd voiced countless times during his time in the war. Those silently intoned as he sat shivering in his tent, his head in his hands. Those murmured on the battlefield in the midst of death cries from his comrades, the stench of gunpowder in his nostrils, and the cold grip of fear and adrenaline around his heart. Those whispered as he lay wounded on a hard plank table, pleading to heaven that he would keep his leg.

The one time he hadn't asked such a question of Heaven was when he'd written Samantha and asked her not to write him anymore.

Rex pushed up his hat and wiped a gloved hand over his sweaty brow as he fought the painful memories. He was grateful to be alive and to still have his leg. Pushing the recollections to the back of his mind, he focused instead on double-checking the horse's harness. It was a stalling tactic. If he stayed here long enough, maybe Mr. Whitefield would give up the idea of Rex accompanying Samantha, in this too-small sleigh, for the evening.

Not that he didn't want to help deliver the gifts—he hated to see the older man's traditional Christmas Eve activity halted by illness, and Rex agreed that Samantha shouldn't go out alone. But tonight's outing would make keeping his promise to stay away from Samantha impossible.

The memory of her green eyes flashing in stubbornness filled his thoughts and drew half a smile from him. She was still as pretty as ever, her long, brownish blond hair having darkened in color during his absence. Her freckles had faded somewhat too, but they hadn't disappeared altogether—to his secret relief. He'd always liked the light brown dots scattered across her nose and cheeks.

Frowning, he shook his head. "What am I doing?" he repeated, this time to the horse. The animal flicked its ears in his direction, then away as if it also thought Rex was foolish.

How was he supposed to hold to his commitment to keep his distance if he had to keep looking into those deep green eyes of hers and listen to the words that fell from her pink lips?

The tread of footsteps yanked his attention from his inner turmoil to the open doors of the barn. Samantha wobbled inside, her arms laden with the crate of jam. "I was going to come back for that," he offered belatedly as he approached and took the box from her.

"You don't have to come, Rex." She crossed her arms and regarded him warily over her brightly colored scarf. "I can handle Titus and the sleigh on my own."

Ignoring her, he situated the jam at the foot of the sleigh's second seat. He wouldn't back out now. "Do you want me to get the toy sack?"

She huffed with irritation, a sound he hadn't heard in years. It nearly provoked another smile from him. "All right then. I'll get the bricks I warmed up." With that, she exited the barn.

Rex found two lanterns that he lit and hung on either side of the sleigh. There was a thick blanket on the tack table that he grabbed as well. Placing the quilt on the seat, he climbed in. Images of he and Samantha cozied up on the seat made him swallow hard. Tonight would surely test his resolve, at every point, to let her go and allow her to find someone less wounded in mind and spirit.

Clucking to the horse, he guided Titus outside, where the snow still fell in large flakes. The horse tossed its head, its breath forming a cloud. Beside the porch, Rex stopped the sleigh and ducked inside to grab the sack of toys. He could hear Samantha upstairs, bidding her father good-bye.

By the time Rex had the toys stowed beside the jam crate, Samantha had returned outside with two wrapped bricks and another blanket. "These ought to help," she said, "at least for a while." She set the bricks on the floor of the sleigh and sat. Spreading the two blankets over her lap, she waved for him to climb in as well. "We've got to get going if we want to make it to every house."

Seeing her bundled up and waiting for him, the snow alighting on the scarf around her head, Rex felt a pang of something. Something he hadn't allowed himself to feel since he'd written that last letter to her. But he pushed the emotion aside, a trick he'd learned as a soldier.

"Coming," he said. He slipped beneath the blankets she lifted for him and took the reins. "Where to first?" He did his best to ignore the warmth of her against his side or the way bewitching wisps of hair had escaped her scarf.

"The Hammon place," she answered.

Rex shot her a look. "That's the farthest house out."

"Yes, but that's the one Papa always starts with." She pulled the blankets up higher and folded her gloved hands on top. "He says it's better to begin with those farthest away in case the weather gets bad."

A good point, Rex wagered, but that also meant a long sleigh ride together, without interruptions for several miles. "Very well."

Digging deep inside himself for the determination to stay his course when it came to Samantha, he drove the sleigh forward.

Samantha stared at the trees whizzing past, the lanterns lighting the way down the snow-packed lane. Here and there she could see an answering light from one of the farms they passed by. She watched those lights as long as she could, as if they were beacons on the Great Lakes.

Anything to keep her mind off Rex seated close beside her on the seat. And the way the snowflakes tangled in his beard, urging her to reach up and brush them both.

Perhaps she shouldn't have insisted they attempt the same route her father always had. Now she had to suffer through uncomfortable silence alongside the man who'd chosen to end their friendship. But like their former relationship, her once-strong feelings for him were in the past.

In charge of her head and heart once more, Samantha exhaled a long breath, creating a puff of white in front of her face. "Remember that winter we tried to see who could breathe the biggest cloud of air?"

"Yes," he said. She didn't turn, but she sensed his half smile. "I believe I won."

"Only because I nearly fainted from trying. If I hadn't almost passed out..."

A deep rumbled laugh escaped his lips. "I won that one fair and square, Sammie. Unlike the time we tried to see who could stand out in that snowstorm the longest."

The murmur of her name from his lips warmed her as much as the long-forgotten memory. She couldn't help laughing herself, thinking of Rex dancing back and forth in the snow, his young face twisted into a grimace. "Why else do you think I plied you with cup after cup of hot chocolate before I suggested going outside?" Poor Rex hadn't lasted more than a few minutes before he had to abandon the dare to use the outhouse. Samantha had declared herself the victor.

"We used to give my sisters such fits," she added, smiling fully.

Rex chuckled. When he spoke again, though, his voice held sadness. "I was sorry to hear about your brother-in-law Jack."

"Thank you." A shiver swept through Samantha, but she resisted the urge to scoot closer to Rex. Instead she tugged the blankets higher. "I don't think there's a family in town that wasn't affected by the war."

He grunted agreement. "How's your sister Cecilia doing?"

"She says she's all right. Things have been less worrisome for her since she and her children moved to her in-laws' farm. Though she still wears mostly black." Samantha ached to fully erase the shadows clinging to her sister. Rex appeared to carry similar shadows, and for the first time in two years, she wondered if that had anything to do with his decision to end things between them.

She cut a glance at his face, at least what she could see beneath his hat. "Did . . . did you lose many friends in the war?" It was something she would have likely asked a long time ago, if she'd been allowed to keep writing.

His jaw appeared to tighten, and his shoulder stiffened against hers. Tension clouded the air as thickly as their breath. She opened her mouth to take back the inquiry, but Rex spoke first. "I did . . . lose many friends." He cleared his throat, his entire demeanor tortured. "Too many."

Compassion swelled inside her at his grief-stricken words, prompting her to offer him comfort. Would he allow her to give it now that they were no longer friends?

Pushing her hesitation aside, she lifted one glove-clad hand from the cocoon of blankets and placed it on Rex's coat sleeve. His gaze jumped from her hand to her face, his eyes wide and filled with apprehension. "I'm so sorry, Rex. No one should have to witness that." Perhaps talking about it would help. It seemed to with Cecilia. "Will you tell me about it?"

He tensed again and shifted his weight, breaking her hold on his arm. "No."

Sharp disappointment cut through Samantha as she slid her hand back beneath the blankets. She'd do well to remember things were vastly different than they'd once been between them.

This wasn't her childhood friend and competitor seated next to her. This was a man who no longer wanted or welcomed her friendship. Tears pricked her eyes, but she sniffed them back. Crying would only freeze her cheeks.

Silence as heavy and deep as a snowdrift settled over them, and Samantha could think of nothing else to say to ease it. Just when she thought she might choke from the strain, she glimpsed the Hammons' farm up ahead.

"Looks like we're here," she murmured.

When Rex stopped the sleigh, she hurried out, eager to navigate her way without his help. She grabbed two bottles of jam from the crate as Rex shouldered the toy sack. They moved in tandem to the front door.

As they stood there, waiting for the Hammons to answer, Samantha suddenly wished this was their last stop instead of the first. Then the entire awkward evening would nearly be over rather than just beginning.

Chapter 4

Light and warmth flooded the porch as the Hammon family crowded around the door, bringing instant relief to the discomfort icing the air between Rex and the woman he'd once loved with all of his heart. He recognized she only wanted to help him by asking about the war, but there was nothing she could do. And he wouldn't sully her mind by telling her what he'd seen and experienced.

Once he started talking, he knew he wouldn't be able to stop the tide of horror that would spill from his mouth. And he couldn't bear the thought of Samantha thinking less of him because of it. Or worse, despising him.

"Come in, come in," Mrs. Hammon called, waving the two of them inside. "We weren't sure anyone was coming, what with your father being ill. But here you are."

"We wouldn't think of not coming," Samantha said with obvious sincerity.

Mrs. Hammon's gaze flicked from her to Rex, her curiosity evident. "You've brought a new helper this year. Say 'Merry Christmas' to Mr. Montgomery, children."

Rex tipped his hat to the group as the children chorused, "Merry Christmas."

"Here is some of his mother's wonderful jam." Samantha handed the jars to Mrs. Hammon. "And now that we've delivered those . . ." She paused, a familiar spark of teasing filling her green eyes. "I suppose we'll be off . . ."

She turned toward the door, but she was smiling. The Hammon children groaned in protest. With a laugh, Samantha spun around. "Maybe we have something for you too."

Lowering the bag to the ground, Rex stepped back to allow Samantha room to pass out the gifts. The children crowded her, their gazes alight with excitement. There were carved toys like the one in his pocket and rag dolls and a fancy lace handkerchief for the oldest Hammon daughter.

Samantha smiled fully at each child as she presented the gifts. Even the lamplight couldn't compare to the radiance shining on her face. She'd always been a compassionate person; it was something Rex had greatly admired in her.

Her expression now reminded him of the night three and a half years ago, right before he'd kissed her. The trust and adoration in her gaze as she'd peered up at him had filled his chest with warmth, which had burned brighter when their lips met. He'd been so full of plans and dreams back then.

But those dreams had crumbled and died amid the ugliness of war. The same ugliness he still felt inside him. Not for the first time since his return, he wondered why she hadn't married in his absence or had herself a new beau. There would have been a shortage of young men during the last three years, but surely someone as lively and kind and beautiful as Samantha Whitefield would've been snatched up at the first opportunity.

His gaze shifted from her and the children to the man seated by the hearth, staring into the flames. Only then did

Rex realize Mr. Hammon hadn't come to the door with the rest of his family. A crutch leaned against the man's chair, and his pant leg hung empty below his left knee. Rex knew Mr. Hammon had fought in the war—he had even seen him at a distance a time or two—but he hadn't known the older man had been wounded.

He recognized the look of despondency on Mr. Hammon's face though. Rex had felt that same way more times than he could count. Nudged forward by something deep inside him, he approached the older man. "Evening, sir."

Mr. Hammon lifted his head, his eyes taking a moment to focus on Rex. "Evening, Montgomery." His voice came out flat.

Rex took a seat in the other chair by the fireplace and leaned his arms on his knees. "Feels a bit strange not being around a campfire this Christmas, listening to a bunch of smelly men sing carols."

"It is a bit strange," the older man said with a smirk. He cut a look at Rex, then away. "I heard you made it home hale and whole."

A wave of shame threatened to overwhelm Rex. Why should his prayers to keep his leg have been granted and this man's had not? "Don't know that any of us came back completely hale and whole or the same as we once were," he admitted truthfully. "I think we all left a portion of ourselves back on some battlefield down there." He cleared his throat of the lump forming there. "And maybe we don't ever get that part back."

Mr. Hammon regarded him fully, and some of the beaten quality to his demeanor dropped away. "I 'spect you're right, son." He glanced at his family across the room and Rex followed suit.

"A real nice family you've got there." Rex looked back at

the man, suddenly wanting to help a fellow solider if he could. "Can't imagine what they would've done or felt had you not come back at all." He stared down at his hands. "I went to visit a good friend's farm this summer, to see his widow and four children."

Rex saw the fire glinting off the moisture in Mr. Hammon's eyes. "I think she would've done anything—anything, sir—to have her husband back, whole or not."

They sat in stillness, both lost in their memories, interrupted only by the gleeful sounds of the Hammon children and the crackle of the fire. At last Mr. Hammon took up his cane. His eyes bore into Rex's for a moment, understanding passing between them, then he rose to his feet.

"What's all this fuss over here?" he barked good-naturedly as he shuffled toward his family.

Standing as well, Rex caught the tearful smile of Mrs. Hammon from across the room. "Thank you," she mouthed. Rex nodded in acknowledgment.

"Should we go?" he asked Samantha as he hoisted the toy sack.

She studied him, then nodded. "Yes, we probably should."

A chorus of "good-bye," "Merry Christmas," and "thank you" followed them out the door. Rex put away the sack and joined Samantha on the front seat of the sleigh. He no longer felt as if he'd made a grave mistake by coming. His interaction with Mr. Hammon had bolstered his spirits. As he guided Titus down the lane, he couldn't help feeling a bit eager at the thought of bringing more Christmas cheer to the next house.

Samantha glanced sideways at Rex, trying to puzzle out his behavior as the sleigh carried them down the road.

Thankfully the earlier tension between them had disappeared. But it was more than that. The rigid quality to Rex's shoulders and jaw had faded as well. Did it have to do with him persuading Mr. Hammon to join in the merriment? That had been a tiny Christmas miracle.

She could see that while the war had stolen a portion of Rex's old charisma for life, perhaps it wasn't all gone. That realization was further confirmed when they stopped at the Gatsons' home next. Instead of standing off to the side, Rex offered to pass out the gifts to the children.

"Looks like we have two trains in here, boys," he announced to the twins. "They must be for you."

Ben Gatson grinned as he accepted the wooden train from Rex, but Billy's expression fell with disappointment. "Got any animals in there, Mr. Montgomery?" the boy asked. "Like an elephant?"

"Now, Billy," his mother soothed. "I know you wanted an elephant, and we can still be grateful for what Rex and Samantha brought . . ."

Samantha felt a prick of remorse that they didn't have any animal carvings this year. She'd try to remember in the future that's what Billy liked.

Rex squatted next to the boy. "Do you believe God knows us, Billy? That He knows you?"

The boy scrunched up his face a moment before nodding. "I think so, 'cause that's what my ma and pa've taught me."

"I think so too, Billy. In fact, I know so. And this is why . . ." Slipping his hand into his pocket, Rex produced a small but intricately carved elephant. Happy surprise coursed through Samantha as she watched him set the toy in the boy's palm. "I made two of these and wasn't sure which one to give my nephew. But God knew which one my nephew needed and which one you needed. The giraffe will go to him and the elephant is yours."

"Golly, thanks, Mr. Montgomery." Billy threw his arms around Rex's neck. Rex looked momentarily startled, then he embraced the boy, a smile settling on his mouth.

They left the Gatsons' soon after, but with each house they stopped at over the next hour, Samantha watched more and more of the old Rex coming back to life. The part she'd known and admired for so many years. The part of him that had coaxed her more times than she could count to let go of her fears and worries and enjoy life a little.

When they piled into the sleigh after their sixth delivery, she couldn't keep her thoughts to herself any longer. "You're enjoying yourself."

Rex slapped the reins lightly against Titus, shooting her a lopsided smile—one that succeeded in twisting her stomach with hidden pleasure. "I am." He leaned toward her and added in a warm breath that tickled the tops of her cheeks, "I may have to thank your father for coercing me to come."

Her breath caught at the husky quality of his voice and the bemused look on his handsome face. Was she also glad her father had forced him to come? She wanted to deny it, but she couldn't. It had been far too long since she'd been alone with Rex or really spoken to him.

She didn't plan to tell him her thoughts just yet, though. If he knew part of her heart was softening toward him, would he swoop in and claim it once more? Did she dare let him after his decision two years ago had affected her so deeply?

"Do you still wish to see all those places Miss Rogers talked about?" she blurted out, hoping a change of subject would be a distraction from the mental tug-of-war inside her head. "To see Paris or London?"

"No." He flicked a glance at her. "I could stay right here the rest of my life and be just fine."

Samantha twisted on the seat, facing his profile. "But you

wanted so much to see the world. Did you get that during the war?"

He shrugged. "A bit, but you were right."

"*I* was right?" she echoed with a smile. "Pray tell me, what was it I got correct?"

Instead of smiling, though, his expression turned grave. "You were right about war not being the adventure I thought it would be."

She lowered her gaze to the blankets, embarrassed. "That isn't something I wish to be right about."

Except for the whoosh of the sleigh and the muted thud of Titus's hooves against the snow, there was only quiet between them. Samantha shifted on the seat, wondering how to restore the earlier lighthearted mood. Before she could think of anything, Rex straightened beside her and blew out a sigh, as if making some sort of a decision.

"War is worse than you can imagine, Sammie." His voice was low, his words tinged with severity and despair. "Men shot and dying all around you. Men dying because . . ." A shudder ran through him. "Because of you . . ."

She sat perfectly still, listening, afraid even the slightest movement would cause him to retreat into himself again.

"It's no adventure," he continued, his words louder but still filled with pain. "It's nothing but blood and stench and death and exhaustion. It's going to bed, wishing and praying it were all over, and getting up the next day to slog through the ugliness again." He ran a hand down his face. "And yet . . ."

She waited a full minute or more for him to elaborate. When he didn't, she gently prodded, "And yet?" She wanted so much to share the burden of his suffering.

Rex looked at her as if suddenly remembering she sat beside him. Visibly swallowing, he faced forward again and cleared his throat. "And yet, you search and search for those glimmers of Heaven. For those moments when you know the whole world hasn't gone mad and God still reigns."

She'd felt much the same after his letter, needing to find those glimmers of Heaven. Another minute passed before she asked, "Did you find them? Did you find those glimmers, Rex?"

"I did." His answer sounded almost reverential, and it brought her great relief. He'd had something good to cling to amid the horror he'd experienced.

"Where?" she asked.

He turned toward her, and in the lantern light, the tears in his eyes glistened. "In my prayers . . . and in my memories of you."

"Me?" But he hadn't wanted her; he'd made that very clear in his last letter. "What do you mean?"

Coughing once more, he glanced away. "Thinking about all of our dares as kids." A brief smile lifted his mouth. "Or reading your letters. Those things gave me something else to focus on."

She sucked in a breath through her cold lips. His admission filled her with joy but also regret. "I . . . I don't know what to say." Memories of the day she'd received his letter flooded her thoughts, bringing the emotions she thought she'd relinquished. "I would have written you the entire time you were gone, Rex. I would have written you every day."

"I know." His agreement was laced with intense sorrow. "I wanted you to, but . . ."

"But what?" she pressed, suddenly tired of not knowing. "What made you throw away our future?"

He tugged his hat lower. "I explained it in my letter, Sammie. War changes men. I wasn't . . . I'm not . . . the same."

Samantha fisted her hands beneath the blanket. "So your feelings for me changed?"

"No." The single word echoed across the snowy stillness before he turned to meet her gaze. "My feelings never changed."

Did that mean he hadn't stopped loving her? Could he love her still? "You never even gave me a choice, Rex. I didn't get a chance to find out more or try to work through things. You were just . . . gone."

His gloved hand found hers, his fingers curling over her own. "I'm sorry for that. But I knew how persuasive you could be, Sammie. I figured you would talk me right out of my decision."

She released a half sob, half laugh. "And you call me stubborn?"

His mouth rose. "I guess we both are."

"Did you pray about it? Is that what you felt God wanted for us?"

He released her hand at once, his shoulders lowering in defeat. "No, I didn't pray about it."

"But then—"

"It was for the best."

She shook her head, ripples of anger heating her cheeks. "The best for whom, Rex? For you?"

His expression hardened. "You don't understand. What I told you just now about the war is only a fraction of what I saw and did."

"And you think that changes how I see you?" She wanted to reach out and shake him. Didn't he know her better than that? But she quickly amended the thought. She would never fully understand what Rex had been through, and yet, she cared about him still.

"Doesn't it?" he countered, though some of the fight had left his tone. "Wouldn't you prefer someone less haunted by guilt and remorse?"

"Maybe, maybe not. But that's for me to decide." She tipped her chin upward. "Not to have someone else decide for me."

He pulled the sleigh to a stop in front of the next home, the Stuarts' place. "Samantha, don't be unnecessarily pigheaded."

"I could say the same about you," she muttered, though she wasn't sure if he heard her or not. She felt both annoyed and relieved at the interruption to their conversation. She needed time to think on what he'd shared with her. And on what she wished to do next. The thought of trusting him again, even with friendship, filled her with worry, and yet, she was tired of trying to cling to faith and fear at the same time.

Help me trust in Thee, Lord. If things are meant to be between Rex and me, help us both know.

The Stuarts didn't seem to notice anything amiss as they invited her and Rex inside and offered them seats in the parlor. Samantha perched on the settee, the oldest Stuart daughter, Regina, across from her.

While the rest of the family laughed and exclaimed over the jam and gifts, Regina sat silently in the rocker, twisting her wedding band around and around her finger. She'd married a boy from the next town over before he left for the war. But the young man had been killed two years later, leaving Regina a young widow. She didn't even have a baby to remember him by.

Though still reeling from her talk with Rex, Samantha wanted to help the other girl and lift her downtrodden spirits, but she wasn't sure how. What would fun-loving Rex do to cheer up Regina? A sudden idea had Samantha rising to her feet and moving to the piano across the room. Her family and the Stuarts were the only ones in their town who owned such an instrument. "May I play, Mrs. Stuart?"

The older woman smiled. "Of course, Samantha."

She played a few of the slower Christmas carols, to which everyone but Regina sang along. Then she switched to a livelier tune, calling over her shoulder, "Who's in the mood to dance?" Regina had always adored dancing in the past. She looked at Rex and stealthily tipped her head toward the other girl.

Without hesitation, he stood and offered his hand to Regina. "May I have the honor of this dance?"

It seemed everyone held their breath, waiting for her answer. Then the girl murmured, "Yes."

Samantha grinned and struck up the song's introduction a second time as Rex and Regina and Mr. and Mrs. Stuart took their places to dance. Some of the younger children joined in after a minute or two.

Knowing the song by heart allowed Samantha to watch those dancing. Rex met her gaze and smiled. Warmth and gratitude blossomed in her heart. They might not see eye to eye, but she was beginning to sense a return, however tentative, to their once deep and abiding friendship. And she had to admit that she was enjoying herself in his company—mostly.

When was the last time she'd been able to fully let go of her worries about her father, about life, and simply have a nice time? She had Rex—and God—to thank for that. Rex's love of life was contagious. It always had been.

Even Regina was smiling now. But when the other girl laughed at something Rex said, a shard of jealousy cut through Samantha's happiness. She didn't want anyone dancing with Rex, at least not permanently, unless it was her.

Because I still love him.

The realization made her start, and she struck a wrong chord. Cheeks burning, she lowered her head and focused on the song, ending with a flourish. But inside her heart hammered at her thoughts.

Her love for Rex hadn't dimmed with time as she'd thought. Rex had expressed similar feelings, and yet, would he keep holding with stubbornness to the idea that he'd changed too much for them to be together?

"One more," Regina requested, her face flushed with enjoyment.

Samantha couldn't deny her. "All right." She played another number for those dancing, then ended with "We Wish You a Merry Christmas." Everyone joined in the singing this time, even Regina.

There were happy tears in the other girl's eyes as she and Samantha trailed Rex to the door. "Thank you for coming," Regina whispered, hugging Samantha tightly. "And thank you for sharing him."

Samantha drew back, unsure what Regina meant. But Rex was already outside, moving toward the horse and sleigh. It was time to go.

"That was amazing, Sammie," he said as they settled onto the seat. "Getting Regina to join in by dancing."

"Thank you." She blushed at his compliment and at the remembrance of her revelation while playing the piano. "It's not so different than what you did to help Mr. Hammon and Billy Gatson."

He tipped his head as if studying her. "We make a good team."

"Best friends usually do," she replied softly, her heart beating wildly with fear. Would he deny it? Would he tell her that they weren't still friends?

"Best friends." His murmured echo and thoughtful look calmed her pulse. But only for a moment or two. When Rex's gaze shifted from her eyes to her lips, her heartbeat began thudding for an entirely different reason.

The memory of their first kiss flooded her mind and senses. It might have been more than three years ago, but she could recall it vividly. How she longed to brush those masculine lips again, to feel the graze of his beard against her chin and cheek.

She leaned an inch or two closer to show him that she welcomed his kiss. Rex matched her movement. Renewed hope leapt inside her. Just before they could narrow the last bit of space between them, a loud tapping sounded from behind.

Startled, Samantha whirled to see the three youngest Stuart children tapping on the window glass and waving. Heat filled her cheeks as she faced forward again. The magic of the moment was gone.

"Giddyup," Rex called to Titus.

This time the lack of words between them wasn't awkward or uncomfortable as it had been at other points during their ride tonight. Rex was likely sorting through his thoughts as she was hers.

Even though she felt disappointed at having their near-kiss interrupted, Samantha also felt relief and happiness that she and Rex were friends again. He hadn't argued that point. And if they were friends once more then she perhaps could convince him that she still longed to be more than that.

Is that what Regina meant? she wondered. *By thanking me for sharing him?*

There was still the matter of claiming Rex's heart. Samantha sat straighter, her shoulders pulled back with determination. They were nearly done with delivering all of the gifts, but she didn't want to voice her true feelings here, where she'd likely be interrupted again. Once they returned home, she would do her best to convince Rex—kind, thoughtful, handsome Rex—that she still loved him.

It was time to take a leap of faith with him for a second time.

CHAPTER 5

REX STRANGLED THE reins, causing Titus to toss his head in protest. Relaxing his grip, he tried to assure himself he'd done the right thing by not kissing Samantha outside the Stuarts' home. But, oh, how he'd wanted to. His attempts to keep his distance tonight had failed miserably. He'd even gone so far as to share a portion with her of what he'd experienced during the war.

And yet Samantha hadn't recoiled in horror or disgust. Instead she'd listened, as she had so many times in the past. Did that mean she didn't condemn him? He shot a glance her way and found her staring straight ahead, a resolute smile on that lovely mouth he'd nearly kissed just now. He recognized that look—she was scheming at something. But what could it be?

He thought back to her question about whether he'd prayed before issuing his edict that they stop writing each other. At the time he didn't think he needed to ask Heaven's blessing for something that made sense. He was trying to protect Samantha, albeit from himself. But had he done the right thing? Accompanying her tonight and hearing her call him her best friend again had filled a hole inside him that had been present since he'd written that fateful letter.

Rex recalled what he'd asked Billy Gatson earlier. If the boy understood that God knew him personally. Did he believe that about himself? He considered the miracle of having the elephant Billy wanted or the times of protection and comfort he'd experienced during the war.

Or, he thought, glancing to his right, *my friendship with Samantha.*

God did know him and he'd ignored that truth by acting on his own. Rex stifled a groan of regret. *I was wrong, Lord, and I'm sorry.* For the first time in two years, he could see things from Samantha's perspective and how much the effects of his choice had hurt her, even if he'd meant well. *Please forgive me.*

A quiet, nudging thought entered his mind. *You have to forgive yourself, too. For the war.*

The impression came unbidden and penetrated every space within his head and heart, including every dark, anguish-filled corner. He'd done his best to cling to his faith, even as a soldier. But perhaps the ultimate peace he sought would only come with forgiving himself.

The weight that had been pressing on his chest for three years eased at the realization. Forgiveness of himself wouldn't be immediate. But if he kept praying, kept asking God for direction, kept looking for ways to reach out to others, then maybe one day his burden would be lifted completely. Another look at Samantha reminded him that she'd helped lift some of that weight tonight, by listening to him and not turning away in revulsion.

Could they still have a future together? Rex had stopped

himself from believing that was true a long time ago. But if there was a chance ... If Samantha had no one else she fancied, then perhaps it was high time he put his own fears aside and did all he could to win her heart a second time.

A light appeared ahead, but Rex kept the sleigh moving past it. It was the new doctor's home, and there weren't any children or grandchildren living there. He'd met the newcomer at church awhile back, but he didn't think the other man was as "nice-looking" and "amiable" as he'd overheard some young women professing.

"Rex, wait." Samantha's gloved hand rested on his arm for a moment. A moment that didn't last nearly long enough, in his opinion. "I'd like to give some jam to Dr. Hobson. He's been so good about looking in on my father."

He eyed her innocent expression. Was something else motivating her desire to stop besides gratitude for the doctor's skills? "I'll turn around then." He maneuvered Titus in a slow circle and headed back the way they'd come.

At the doctor's home, he hesitated. Did Samantha wish for him to join her or not?

"I'll only be a minute," she said as she slid off the seat and selected a bottle of jam.

Rex frowned. Now what? He couldn't very well announce he'd like to go to the door too. He'd look completely foolish. "Fine." He nodded for her to go ahead. "Titus and I will wait here."

If she caught the tense edge to his voice, she didn't respond. Instead she hurried up the walk and rapped on the front door. A few seconds later, it opened to reveal the doctor standing in shirtsleeves and trousers and no shoes.

"Miss Whitefield," he exclaimed, "what a surprise." His eyes grew wider when he glanced past Samantha and saw Rex in the sleigh.

"Evenin', Doc." Rex tugged the edge of his hat, not bothering to work up a smile.

"We're out delivering Christmas gifts," Samantha said, waving at the sleigh. "I mean, my father and I are usually the ones to do it. But since he's ill..."

Rex thought she stumbled a bit too much through her explanation. Was she embarrassed to be seen with him? Or did she fear the "nice-looking" doctor would get the wrong impression about her and Rex being together?

"How is your father this evening?" the doctor asked.

There was a smile in her voice when Samantha answered, "A little better. Though he very much wished he could come himself." She passed him the jam. "This is from Mrs. Montgomery, our neighbor. She makes the best jam."

Dr. Hobson accepted the jar. "I don't know about that, Miss Whitefield. I've tasted your jam, and it is far superior to anything I've tasted before."

Rex rolled his eyes, fighting a scoffing laugh. Did Samantha like this other man's blatant flirtation? Not likely. But to his surprise, she ducked her head, as if pleased by the doctor's flattery.

"Thank you, but I'm sure you'll find Mrs. Montgomery's jam is just as good. If not better." She gave a light laugh that made Rex swallow hard. It was her nervous laughter.

"Why don't you come in?" Dr. Hobson stepped back. "Both of you."

To Rex's intense relief, Samantha shook her head. "We need to finish delivering gifts. I can't thank you enough for helping my father. You've been so kind and attentive."

The doctor grinned. "It's been my pleasure, Miss Whitefield. Truly." Lifting the jar, he waved it in the air. "Thank you for this. I will enjoy it. Merry Christmas."

"Merry Christmas to you too," Samantha called back as she walked toward the sleigh. "Good night."

Rex avoided looking at her as she sat and gathered the blankets onto her lap. Perhaps his hopes of minutes ago had been for naught. Samantha may have already opened her heart to someone else. The idea lanced him with remorse as he drove the sleigh away from the doctor's house.

"Thank you for stopping." Samantha threw him a smile, which he couldn't return. "I didn't want him to think he'd been forgotten simply because he's alone."

"Forgotten by whom?"

She regarded him with large eyes. "By us, Rex."

His next words were out before he could bite them back. "I doubt that. After all, it isn't me who makes the best jam he's ever tasted."

Rex braced himself for her argument, one that would either dash his newfound hopes or confirm them. But instead of defending herself, Samantha laughed. The merry sound rang out across the frozen landscape. "If I didn't know better, you sound jealous, Rexford Montgomery."

He cringed as much at her use of his full name as he did that she hadn't actually denied feeling anything but polite interest for the doctor. "Do you fancy him?" he forced himself to ask, even as dread pulsed through him.

"Rex . . ." He couldn't quite read the expression on her face.

He pulled back on the reins, bringing the horse and sleigh to a stop. Regardless of what she felt for the doctor, he had something that needed saying.

"What are you doing?"

"Sammie." He cleared his throat and faced her straight on. "You meant everything to me. That never changed." *I love you still,* he wanted to say, but he didn't dare give the words voice if she preferred another man. "Even so, I'm sorry I hurt you. I'm sorry for letting you go and not giving you a choice in the matter."

He thought he caught the glimmer of tears in her eyes. "I'm sorry too. I could have written, at least once more. Maybe it would have made a difference."

"Maybe," he repeated. He gazed at her pretty face, aching to cover every inch of it with kisses. But not if she liked the doctor. He coughed again. "Two more houses, right?"

She seemed to shake herself before she nodded. "Yes." Had she been thinking of the past or the future? "Do you mind?"

"No, I'd like to finish." And he meant it. He hadn't wanted to come, though somewhere along the way he'd found not only his best friend but also himself. He clucked to Titus to move on.

The next two stops were brief. Titus was tiring, and the temperature had dropped a few degrees in the last hour. Rex wanted to get Samantha and the horse out of the cold. When they reached the barn, she insisted on helping him unhitch the sleigh and care for Titus.

They worked in relative silence until the horse was ensconced in his stall, munching oats. "It must be Christmas by now," Samantha said, moving to stand at the open barn doors. Beyond them, the snow lazily circled downward.

"Merry Christmas." He came to stand beside her. Lifting her ungloved hand, he rubbed her chilled fingers with his own, reluctant for the night to end. Even if she didn't return his love, he'd cherish the time they'd spent together.

She looked up at him, her eyes like pools of dark green. "Merry Christmas, Rex."

"Thank you for letting me come."

Her laugh washed over him. "You were forced into coming, you mean. But I'm glad you did." She squeezed his hand. Rex didn't want to let go or leave. And yet, he didn't have the right to linger.

He forced himself to release her and gathered his gloves. "Good night then."

"Good night." He thought he heard a tremor of frustration in her voice. What was she regretting? That she hadn't had more time with Dr. Hobson?

He started into the snow, then turned back. "Sammie, I wish you all the best with the doctor. I really do. He's a lucky fellow."

Instead of smiling in gratitude, though, Samantha folded her arms and regarded him with annoyance. "Rex, you might just be the most stubborn man to ever walk the earth."

What had he done now? "I only want you happy."

This time she did smile as she lowered her arms to her sides. "If you want me to be happy, then come back here."

Confused, he hesitated a moment before crossing back to her side. "Did I forget something?"

"Yes," she said, pointing upward. She removed his hat and tossed it aside. "You forgot my Christmas kiss."

Rex barely had time to note the mistletoe hanging above the barn doors—mistletoe he was certain he hadn't seen there earlier—before Samantha took his coat lapels in either hand and pressed her lips to his.

The sweetness of her touch filled him with warmth until he could no longer feel the cold. Nothing existed beyond this moment. It was only him and Samantha and the promise of a future he'd foolishly thrown away.

Then remembering came with a jolt of shock. Rex stepped backward and gripped her wrists in restraint. "Samantha," he said, his breath coming in quick bursts, "you can't kiss me when you like the doctor. It's not fair, to him or to me."

Her brows tipped upward in amusement, instead of down with contrition. "I guess it's a good thing I don't like the doctor then. At least not in that way." She lowered her chin. "Although his compliments are rather nice."

Rex gaped at her, trying to make sense of her words. "You don't like the doctor?"

"Honestly, Rex." She rolled her eyes. "You didn't even let me answer your question about whether I fancied him or not."

He hadn't? His mind was slowly catching up to reality. And when it did, he grinned. "So it's the compliments that really win a girl, huh?" He gently drew her hands up and around his neck. "I can think of some nice things to say."

"Hmm." She smiled slowly up at him. "Such as?"

"You're beautiful, Sammie." He rubbed her soft cheek with the back of his hand. "And compassionate and determined and stubborn."

She chuckled. "How is stubborn a compliment?"

"Because it's one of the things I love about you. Always have."

"Always?" Her gaze glittered with unmistakable hope in the lantern light.

"Yes. I may have teased, challenged, and bested you . . ." Rex pressed a finger to her mouth to silence the retort he sensed coming and realized he liked the pliable feel of her lips. "But only because I've loved you for as long as I can remember."

Tucking her hair behind her ear, he studied her lovely face. "Have I won you over yet? Like the good doctor and his compliments?"

Tears sparkled on her lashes. "You won me and my heart a very long time ago, Rex Montgomery." Some of the moisture dripped onto her cheeks, but she was smiling. The kind of smile that made him want to sing and shout and kiss her until they both ran out of breath.

Rex touched her forehead with his. When he spoke his

voice broke with emotion, but he didn't care. Not when he was holding the woman he loved. "Then I will cherish both forever."

"You mean that? No changing your mind this time without letting me have a say?"

"No changing my mind."

He didn't wait for her to initiate the kiss this time. Mistletoe or no mistletoe. Several minutes later he eased back, cupping her face between his hands. "I love you, Sammie. And I want to marry you. This instant. But I think our families, particularly your sisters, would likely never forgive me if we woke the pastor now and had our own private ceremony tonight."

Her soft laughter filled his heart with joy. "I think you're right."

"So instead, I'd like to ask your father for permission to court you." He caressed her cheek with his thumb, already anticipating the day when they would no longer have to bid one another good night. How had he ever thought he could forge through life without her at his side? "Would that be all right? I can come by first thing tomorrow."

"It's more than all right. And it's already tomorrow, Rex." She scooped up his hat and pulled him toward the house through the swirling snow.

"Do you think he's still awake?" He glanced at the upper-story windows, where a single candle glowed.

Samantha laughed again, the sound as joyful as sleigh bells. "I know he's still awake."

"How?"

Leading him into the house, she pointed to the top of the door frame. Another sprig of mistletoe hung there.

"That wasn't . . ."

"No, it wasn't." She started toward the stairs, but Rex tugged her back toward him.

"He did go to such trouble on our behalf, especially being sick and all . . ." He winked at her. "It would be a pity then not to take advantage of his handiwork."

Samantha placed her hands against his coat, her mouth curving upward. "A pity indeed."

Happiness he hadn't felt in years filled him as he covered her hands with his own. God had granted them a Christmas miracle, a chance to mend their hearts and renew their deep and abiding love. It was a gift he would never take lightly.

"Merry Christmas, Sammie," he murmured, leaning close.

She matched his stance, her gaze tender and warm. "Merry Christmas, Rex."

Then they sealed their words with another long kiss.

Author's Note

---※---

Her Winter Suitor

From the 1870s through the Edwardian Era, more than one hundred American heiresses travelled to England. There they hoped to marry titled husbands and achieve superior social status.

The Patriarch Ball was once the most sought-after social event for New York City's wealthy class. Held at Delmonico's restaurant, the ball required an invitation from one of the social "patriarchs". While doing research for this story, I read about favors being given out, and that sparked the idea of giving out chocolates at the ball.

An Unlikely Spring Courtship

Idaho City, Idaho, established in 1862 under the name Bannock City, was once the largest city between St. Louis and San Francisco. With the discovery of gold in the area in 1862, miners flooded the Boise Basin in hopes of getting rich. In May 1865, a fire destroyed most of Idaho City. Just two years and one day later, in May 1867, another fire occurred. Thankfully this one didn't do as much damage as the first. The post office did burn down during the 1867 fire, but Lydia and Calvin are my fictional postmaster/mistress.

There was a mercantile in Idaho City at that time as well,

which was damaged in the fire of 1867. But for the purposes of the story, I kept both Tempest's mercantile and Bram's intact.

A Summer for Love

Once envisioned to be the "Atlantic City of the West," Bayocean, Oregon, was a popular seaside resort town from its grand opening in 1912 to about 1928. The sea eventually eroded away the beach and buildings until Bayocean ceased to exist.

The natatorium opened in 1914 and featured grandstands, a heated saltwater swimming pool, artificial surf, and a movie theater. The dance pavilion and the bungalows where Loralee lived were all actual buildings. The Hotel Bayocean (Annex) was also a real building and featured the automatic fire sprinklers mentioned.

I love writing stories set in the World War I era and the early 1920s, and I wanted to pair both time periods in this novella of social clashes and second chances for love, even many years later.

Romance in Autumn

During the Gilded Age, America's wealthy elite traveled to Newport, Rhode Island, where they stayed for the summer. There they built lavish mansions, like Baywood House in this novella, and attended or hosted one social event after another.

I wanted to capture some of the opulence of those Newport summers during the era of the American heiress, but also set this story during a season of the year that isn't always associated with this place and time period. So I chose autumn in Newport with its iconic New England foliage.

A Long Winter Kiss

Having lived in Michigan for a year and a half, I have an affinity for the beautiful countryside there. And I felt this location would be the perfect setting for a Christmas Eve sleigh ride.

Rex would have served in the 4th Michigan Volunteer Infantry Regiment, which went into service in June 1861 and ended service in June 1864. They fought in the Battle of Fredericksburg in December 1862. After writing a series of books set during the First World War, I gained more insight and compassion into the way war affects the soldiers who serve. I wanted to explore that element of war in this novella. I also hoped to show the Christmas miracle that occurs in Samantha's and Rex's hearts.

A *USA Today* bestselling author, Stacy Henrie graduated from Brigham Young University with a degree in public relations. Not long after, she switched from writing press releases and newsletters to writing inspirational historical romances. Born and raised in the West, where she currently resides with her family, she enjoys reading, road trips, interior decorating, chocolate, and most of all, laughing with her husband and kids. Her books include *Hope at Dawn*, a 2015 RITA Award finalist for excellence in romance. You can learn more about Stacy and her books by visiting her website, stacyhenrie.com.

www.ingramcontent.com/pod-product-compliance
Lightning Source LLC
LaVergne TN
LVHW010154070526
838199LV00062B/4360